The
View
from
Garden
City

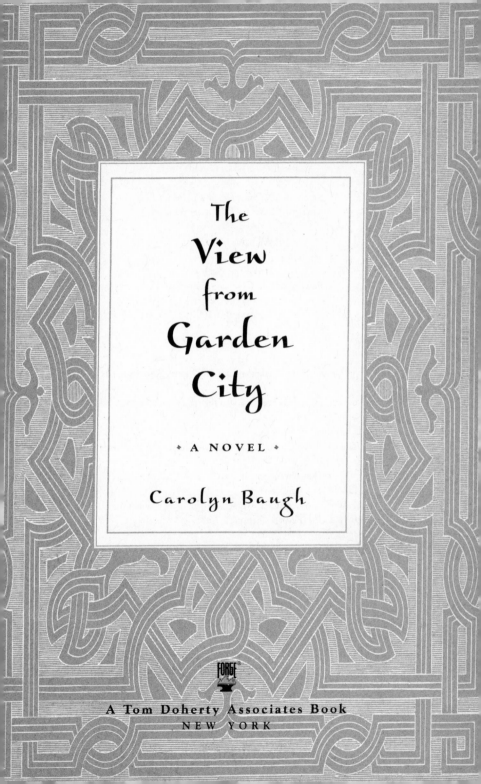

The
View
from
Garden
City

❖ A NOVEL ❖

Carolyn Baugh

A Tom Doherty Associates Book
NEW YORK

THE VIEW FROM GARDEN CITY

A Forge Book
Published by Tom Doherty Associates, LLC
175 Fifth Avenue
New York, NY 10010

www.tor-forge.com

Forge® is a registered trademark of Tom Doherty Associates, LLC.

The Library of Congress has cataloged the hardcover edition as follows:

Baugh, Carolyn
    The view from Garden City / Carolyn Baugh.—1st hardcover ed.
      p. cm.
    "A Tom Doherty Associates Book."
    ISBN 978-0-7653-1657-8
    1. Women—Fiction. 2. Women—Egypt—Social conditions—
Fiction. 3. Cairo (Egypt)—Fiction. I. Title.
    PS3602.A9354 V54 2008
    813'.6—dc22

2008019505

ISBN 978-0-7653-2183-1 (trade paperback)

First Hardcover Edition: August 2008
First Trade Paperback Edition: March 2011

Printed in the United States of America

0 9 8 7 6 5 4 3 2 1

For Nashwa

ACKNOWLEDGMENTS

It was Amira Akrabawi who first introduced me to the music of Um Kulthum; I count this among the many treasures of my memories of her. Her influence in my life, and that of her wonderful family, cannot be measured. I owe great debts to Mary Robertson (who, on a manual typewriter at Harper School, published my first story and who very much later reminded me about using *le mot juste*), as well as Cookie Sater and Val Alsop for their gentle guidance. I deeply appreciate the vision, the tempered pen, and the limitless patience of Paul Stevens.

I give thanks for my incredibly supportive and indulgent parents, who loved me enough to put me on many, many airplanes. For my tireless husband (brilliant chef, tender father, constant friend), his generous, passionate family (my professors), and the laughing little girls who link us all inexorably, there are no words—only humble gratitude and forever-love.

CONTENTS

The
View
from
Garden
City

Thwack, thwack, thwack . . .

    I pull the impassive covers fully over my head. The sound continues unabated, as though perhaps willfully seeking me out behind the fissures in the French doors. I sift slowly, detachedly, through the vocabulary of sound I have gleaned in these first Cairo weeks until I find it, that particular thwacking, in the hands of a servant girl, her red scarf knotted—harshly and without regard to line or precision—at the back of a too-thin neck whose tendons are ruddy cords, alert, tensed with effort. The carpet that she flogs dangles in disgraced submission from the sixth-floor balcony across the street. Threads of burgundy, forest green and midnight blue cough up an embarrassed fog of gray-black dust.

    The sound causes me to consider the dust in our own flat.

Reluctantly, as though expecting a reprimand, I push the blanket away from my eyes and peer about. The wide vanity table's glass overlay and the curlicued ornamentation of the heavy oak wardrobe are coated in patient layers of gray. *I should clean*, I murmur aloud. But it is an empty observation, void of any real intent. The task is too sweeping, the walls are too tall, the randomly placed frames too many, the wood and tiles of the floor suddenly endless in span and number. And I am, for now, too content to dwell in marvel at the fantastical accumulations. I wriggle out from under the covers, pulling myself out of the deep indentation in the cotton mattress where once a corpulent body—perhaps a renter like me, perhaps the original occupant—slept. My feet graze the parquet floor tentatively, tapping about for a possible slipper, losing hope immediately as they recall it has been three days since the slippers were last seen.

A flood of mote-heavy light pours in from the balcony, beckoning. I dispense quickly with the ministrations of teeth and face in my grimy green bathroom, then ease into clarity with steaming water and a spoonful of freeze-dried Nescafé. I drift back to my room and wrestle open the French doors. A swell of sound surges over me, a wave of late-morning light washes over me; I breathe deeply.

A glance confirms the reality of the girl and the tormented carpet. Perhaps my gaze is palpable, for she turns suddenly to regard me. Her scarf today is dark blue, not red, but it does not look any newer than the one I have seen each week since my arrival. Her eyes flick over my sleep-creased T-shirt and cut-off sweatpants. Her look alights on my face and our eyes hold. I have watched her unobserved before, but today she is not so swept away in the relentless rhythm of the rug beater. She pauses to observe me, curiosity swimming in wide, oval eyes that hover over bladelike cheekbones. I smile, and she seems at first taken aback. Then a wide smile surfaces from some remote store, and her face is momentarily transformed. I, chilled by the fifth-floor breezes after the cocoon of my indented bed, am warmed.

Turning back to her work, she strikes the carpet a last few times and, satisfied that it is purged of its filth, she sets her plastic weapon aside. With a tenderness that seems absurd after the violence of the previous moments, she lifts the rug from off the balcony rail and holds it aloft to keep the fringes from brushing the balcony tiles.

She has barely closed the door behind her when an identical door, one floor below, swings cautiously open. A scarved head emerges, then I watch as a woman, not young, not old, maneuvers a massive set of hips halfway through the door only to pause warily on the threshold. Her complexion is light, her eyes wide-set. Her ears, lurking unseen behind the spray of paisleys on her scarf, seem to be straining for some hint of sound. Meaty fingers clasp the long handle of a yellow broom as her thick neck cranes over the side edge of the balcony; her eyes dart about for signs of movement. Satisfied that the servant will not reappear, the woman begins attacking her own balcony with the yellow broom. The area, besieged by the dust showered upon it from above, submits to a few moments of near-obscurity as the gray cloud settles. Lips moving furiously in inaudible indignation, the woman pulls a cloth out of nowhere and slides it across the dust-coated ropes of her balcony clothesline. Every once in a while, she scratches viciously at a spot on her expansive forearm; she is irritated by the itch, and appears willing to scrape the skin off altogether rather than allow it to further hinder her chores. She disappears as suddenly as she came.

I clutch my elbows and lean against my own balcony rail. Garden City is an older neighborhood, its architecture mostly French-inspired. Graceful accents adorn broad cement buildings and squat villas long since humbled by the assaults of dust and exhaust and remorseless time. The streets of Garden City curve, twisting and twining in upon themselves like snakes unleashed in a cage formed by Qasr al-ʿAyni Street to the east, and to the west, the wide corniche that runs the length of the Nile. Trees with broad, heavy leaves make intermittent appearances along the streets, distracting the eye from the inevitable strewn trash and broken sidewalks. Ghosts of a golden age drift, spent and listless, along these streets. Old women in worn spectator pumps and persistent hairdos clutch bulging plastic shopping bags and frayed leather purses. Subdued, stooped men in ragged cardigans sit across from each other in the corner café; the chess pieces splayed out between them gather dust in the wait between turns. It is a neighborhood where the wealthy once reigned, a neighborhood of old money that seems both surprised at its own decay and bitter over ʿAbd al-Nasir's socialization programs, despite the passage of fifty years. Foreigners roam here and there, renters like me of archaic flats with startling quirks. Dark-skinned doormen, flush with the knowledge that they alone control the steady flow of Garden City's currents, lounge on rough wooden benches in gelabiyyas and carefully wound headgear.

Woven thinly among the formerly rich is a groping, grim middle class pleased with the prestigious address, despite it being only an illusory comfort against the daily grind. On the very visible peripheries are the rooftop dwellers and roaming peddlers and the vegetable sellers, who stake out sections of the sidewalks. The families of the swaggering doormen huddle tightly in tiny rooms off once-ornate foyers.

Outside my kitchen door is an interior world in which I do not attempt to tread. Fat women weighed down by astounding head-loads navigate the rickety wooden staircases that meander up and down the building's hollow core. I have seen other residents bellow out their kitchen doors, and small children materialize from rooftop shanties. A breath of a girl with a bandanna on her head and wide, bulging eyes. A barefoot boy in a Scooby-Doo T-shirt from which his scabby arms dangle like broken branches. They do errands for twenty-five-piaster tips.

'Umaymah! Run get me a kilo of milk!

Hasanayn! A box of Red Marlboros!

The trashman appears thrice weekly, toting on his back an enormous, tightly braided basket. He collects the plastic sacks my roommate and I place on the landing. He knocks on the kitchen door once each month, mutters a greeting, and takes his wages—he asks only three pounds for his services, less than a dollar. His face is tarred with filth, his hands black, the nails cracked. His gelabiyya hangs from his thin frame in grime-streaked tatters. He is always barefoot, and the calluses on his soles are lined with blackened cracks that snake up to just below the anklebone. His feet resemble a dried riverbed; the undertow tugs at me as I watch him pad away.

Our building straddles the block formed by the raging Qasr al-'Ayni Street and the milder Hasan Murad. Our bedrooms overlook Hasan Murad, but we are privy to views of Qasr al-'Ayni from the balcony off the dining room. It is here that Meg and I sit late into the night, sipping tea or whatever version of coffee we can produce; sometimes we are joined by other year-abroad students, fleeing the staid and supervised hostel.

The balcony is wide with ornate cement moldings. We peer over its edge and between the thick railings to watch Cairo churn along beneath us. Qasr al-'Ayni by night is a pathway with no visible end, alive with red taillights and yellow head-lights. The yips of indignant horns sluice across our conversations, washing away whole clauses.

When traffic noises are at a minimum, we can hear the clatter from the café that anchors the building facing ours. The sounds of backgammon pieces being slammed into place on wooden boards resound throughout the neighborhood.

There is a constant flow of people along the uneven sidewalks. Sent out for some forgotten necessity from the grocery, kids in flip-flops and sweats clutch a few bills in their hands, knuckles white and features set in responsible concentration. Arm in arm, girls in precise white scarves press against the walls of buildings in the ongoing effort not to be brushed against as small clusters of young men, pressed and slicked-back, walk rapidly, their loud, hope-heavy laughter clinging to the hot night air.

❖ ❖ ❖ ❖ ❖

I make a daily trek to the American University in Cairo. Behind sterile, whitewashed walls, as earnest air conditioners gasp, I study Arabic.

The lessons within are breathy, finite.

The uneven sidewalks I tread to get there offer me much more.

Qasr al-ʿAyni Street seethes with faces and bodies, and I walk it in a daze that despises the density while thriving on the sudden, forced intimacy of it all. A yellow-shirted man's arm brushes mine, leaving a film of sweat. The woman walking alongside me, her headscarf gathered at her chin by a purple plastic barrette, smells distinctly of onions frying in ghee. A peasant woman passes by with one child straddling one of her thin shoulders and another clutching at her hand in terror of losing it.

I sidestep the lemon lady, who cradles a great basket of tiny, green-skinned lemons on her wide lap. She grins at the earnestness with which I avoid tripping over her, and calls out something in a dialect I don't recognize. I am transfixed momentarily by the appeal of the heap of lemons, their skins still glistening with the oil of the hands that plucked them.

Sun-stained men in long robes and flip-flops thread their way along the sidewalks, avoiding clusters of uniformed, laughing schoolchildren. Men in slacks and polyester shirts dodge the drippings from laundry that sober housewives are hanging off their balcony clotheslines.

The concrete apartment buildings that claw at the sky are anchored with small shops of every imaginable function. THE SONS OF ʿABD AL-GHANI, MECHANICS. ʿADIL'S COIFFEUR. KHIDR SPICES. HASUNA FOR EASTERN SWEETS.

The first shop I pass is the dry cleaner, with row after row of plastic-swathed, crisply cleaned clothes beckoning through the large window like scrubbed children in an orphanage lineup.

The neighboring small grocery is overwhelmed by floor-to-ceiling shelves of Persil laundry detergent and Biscomisr cereal, Pampers and liter bottles of Coca-Cola. There are towers of Lux soap, Flora toilet paper and perfectly aligned jars of Nescafé. Vast tins of Al-Hanim ghee and cardboard cartons of Juhayna milk, Chipsy potato chips in every possible flavor—including ketchup and curry—and imperturbable stacks of Always packages. In the back center of the store is a long glass refrigerator swollen with cheeses and eggs. In front of the refrigerator is a huge wooden barrel filled to the brim with fat, juicy olives. The wall immediately to the right upon entering is devoted to cassette tapes. Every imaginable Arabic singer is tidily stacked, one atop the other. Eight pounds a tape, give or take.

Immediately past the grocer, in an inhumanly small shop, is the presser. He is a slim man nearly hidden behind hangered forests of shirts, pants and dresses. He operates his coal-heated iron in a desperate race with the cooling air.

The fruit vendor has huge trays of fruits angled out enticingly at the passersby. There are stacks of mangoes and guavas and whole stands of bananas. Immense pomegranates nestle against soft, fragrant peaches. Each section sports a little cardboard flag with the cost-per-kilo scrawled across it defiantly, daring the customer to question the price.

I pass the butcher's warily, clinging to the sidewalk's uncertain rim in order to skirt the menacing red carcasses that dangle from gruesome hooks. As though clinging to some thread of life, still-hairy tails swing nonchalantly.

The fruit juice stand possesses a certain siren's call after the gritty, determined air of the neighboring shops. The cassette player blasts the Gipsy Kings so loudly the mirrored walls seem on the verge of shattering. Tiled from floor to ceiling in cheerful yellow, it is adorned with mesh bags of oranges and pomegranates, clusters of bananas hanging from the ceiling, and tall stands of sugarcane leaning against the walls like recalcitrant teenagers. On the countertops, alongside battle-weary blenders, glass mugs are stacked into pyramids, awaiting the fresh, sweet juices.

And so it is that fresh juices offer a puddling oasis, a fifty-piaster invitation to restoration amid the relentless rush of Qasr al-'Ayni.

At the bean seller's, vats of pungent oil render up fried green patties to a small crowd paused on their way to work. A café spills tentative metal chairs onto the sidewalk; backgammon players sip at filmy glasses. The bakery overflows with customers who emerge with plastic sacks plumped by miniature baguettes or sesame sticks.

Thin boys on rickety bikes perch makeshift crates on their heads. Atop the crates and within are piles of steaming discs of bread. The boys grasp the crates with one hand and guide the wobbling handlebars with the other, whistling shrilly as they weave their way through traffic.

A donkey works its way along the street, keeping a fairly brisk pace despite the huge, flat cart yoked to its back. Atop the cart are massive cabbages, their pale, albino layers glinting in the sunlight. Perched above the cabbages is a boy no more than thirteen, dressed in a ragged gelabiyya and sound asleep.

Within the cool marble confines of the American University is an alternate reality. It's a citadel of pretty people, the children of Egypt's wealthiest and most powerful, who laugh loudly and plot keg parties in the desert, speaking an Arabic/English sludge that starts a sentence in one language and completes it in another. The males wear khakis or jeans, thick leather belts, and cotton button-downs with the sleeves precisely rolled halfway up their forearms. Their black hair glistens stiffly with gel. The females come exquisitely coiffed, in clingy black bell bottom pants and half-open silk blouses.

The American students among them meander across campus in jeans and faded T-shirts and dusty Tevas.

The outside world intrudes, embodied in the quiet people holding service positions.

Bent men in cheap, almost-Mao suits serve coffee to the professors. Small, lithe women in black gelabiyyas and printed bandannas scrub the marble floors on their knees. Barefooted boys carry heavy bags of mixing cement to the corner of the courtyard, where a new terrace is being paved.

Soldiers posted for security delight in giving wrong directions as they ravage with an unencumbered gaze.

❋ ❋ ❋ ❋ ❋

Our building's elevator waits in grungy dignity behind an ornate iron grating. Dark mirrors display the upper torsos of its passengers; faces distorted by the swaying of the compartment glance in near-futile dimness at teeth or hair before alighting on the desired floor. The elevator door is mostly glass, revealing the internal construction of number 10 Hasan Murad Street to the wayward voyager. Tall ceilings give sudden way to thick, dark cement interludes, which just as suddenly fall away to reveal the cracked marble tile of another floor. The fat cable attached to the compartment's top stretches as the elevator descends, and slackens with an unsettling swoosh as it ascends.

The elevator is afflicted with ineffectiveness on a weekly basis.

Often, a descending passenger will have neglected to close the door firmly upon exiting, and so the elevator lingers, faultless but impotent, on the ground floor. On the fourth floor, a would-be passenger stands squinting through the grating into the elevator shaft, then slams his hand violently against the grillwork like a wrongly imprisoned inmate. The banging and shouting ricochet in startling discord through the steeped silence of the old building: ʿAbd al-Latif! *Close the door!*

And the doorman will then either shuffle slowly from his post at the entryway and pull the ajar door closed, or holler up into the darkness of the shaft, *Out of order!*

In the latter case, the next sound is that of rapid, irritated footfalls striking the worn, weathered stairs.

I am by turns annoyed and enchanted by the elevator and its woes.

On this day, I have just given up waiting for a response to my insistent pushing of the down button and begun my descent on foot. I find a young woman struggling up the stairs with far too many packages, and I cannot brush by her as if unmoved by her panting and tottering. As she instructs, I place the packages I have taken from her in the entryway of the flat facing ours.

Her thanks and blessings are effusive. She isn't much older than me. Her hair is covered with a sedate, cream-colored scarf, fastened at her neck with a heart-shaped pin. She is plump and a little awkward in bearing. Her gracious smile does nothing to distract me from wide, grieving eyes.

Her name is Huda, and I gather from her actions that she is moving in. She is so adamant I should drink tea with her that I am unequipped to refuse. *After all*, she says, *we will be neighbors. And I know no one in all of Garden City.*

Wilting cardboard boxes, overstuffed and overtaped, are stacked about the flat, and Huda hurries to clear a space for me. She pulls a dust cover off a brand-new faux Louis Seize couch and nearly forces me bodily to sit. I am carefully pronouncing my name for her as her mother walks in.

She is mammoth, and clearly exhausted from the stairs. The brow beneath her rumpled headscarf streams with sweat. She collapses on the couch, seeming not to notice me, and accepts from Huda a glass of water. She sips, breathes, then looks at me with a smile. *You must be the American. 'Abd al-Latif told us all about you.*

I shift uncomfortably, uncertain what that implies. I cast an eye about for Huda, who is in the kitchen, rummaging through a box, looking for the tea things.

I have a son in America, she says, leaning forward, studying me, searching my face as though it were a crystal ball through which she might see him. *Do you live near New Jersey?*

I shake my head regretfully. Huda's mother leans back, disappointed. Her name is Karima, and she speaks to me in a voice that is melodic as it is forceful; she wants to know where my mother is. She is astounded that I have come alone to a strange country, and live with only a female roommate for company and protection. Huda, she tells me, is her only daughter. *We have never been apart. Not even one day*, she says. *I could not endure it.*

She studies my face, seeming to wonder if I am incredibly strong to bear such distance, or incredibly callous, or simply foreign, which can account for most things, after all.

From now on I am your mother here, she says. *Anything you need, anytime, I will take care of you.*

I gaze in surprise at her wide, open face and find that, although she does not look old, her face is riven with lines. Not wrinkles. Tears have poured over her skin and weathered it. She has slapped at her cheeks in despair, tenderizing the flesh. And she has smiled, as she smiles now at me, creasing her skin, even when her heart is squirming within her. She coos over the staggerings and stumblings of my Arabic. She pats my "yellow" hair and calls me a "moon."

Huda arrives with the tea and gives me an eager smile. I realize it is fear of this empty, dusty flat that makes her desperate for a friend. The flat is owned by her fiancé, they tell me. She is to marry, and soon, very soon, she will spend her first night as a bride under these chipped crown moldings and tarnished chandeliers. When she speaks of this inevitability, it is vividly clear that Huda is not an eager, giggling bride; clearer still that she neither loves her groom nor can she tolerate the prospect of the impending nuptials. Her fear is so contagious it slides across my skin as she clutches my hand, and I shiver.

You must come to the wedding. Bring your colleague, she says, meaning Meg. I assure her we will come, although the notion leaves me hesitant and tangibly nervous.

We have never been apart, I repeat to myself in wonder as I descend the sloping stairs to the street.

Not even one day.

✦ ✦ ✦ ✦ ✦

The hall is large, and the density on the dance floor is inhuman. The deejay has the music of Hakim cranked up so loudly that the plate-glass picture windows are trembling. The guests chant along with the lyrics: *Fire, Fire, Fire! My heart's stoked by fire!*

Karima spots us almost immediately, and rushes over in a paroxysm of hospitable gushing. Having gotten lost, we're obscenely late, but she tells us that the couple has only just arrived. Huda and her groom are installed on the massive wicker chairs that serve as the room's focal point. Gargantuan floral tableaus are positioned as backdrops to the couple, and someone has spray-painted a banner that reads HUDA AND EHAB in cheerful pink and purple script.

And there is Huda, sitting stiffly, swathed in a bright white gown that drips shiny beads and tulle. Her raven hair, exposed for the occasion, is gathered high on her head, a few sidelocks shellacked into place at curiously curled angles. Her makeup is heavy, yet no amount of rouge could give color to her pale, distracted features.

Her plump arm is a treasure map drawn in henna; clutching it is her groom. He is shorter than Huda and slumped in his chair. His stomach droops over his belt. His ears jut out at near-right angles to a head that is crowned by a slick, three-hair comb-over. Beady eyes stare unblinking from beneath too thin eyebrows, and his mouth twists in an awkward, anticipatory grin.

Karima is leading us to the newlyweds, and we understand it to be a sort of receiving line. She pushes us ahead of the line of people.

Huda smiles when she sees us, and it looks as though her mascara-encrusted eyes are in danger of brimming over. She shouts so I can hear her: *I'm so happy you came.* She kisses my cheeks extra hard. She insists that we join the dancing, and a girl that she refers to as her maternal aunt's daughter appears to guide us into the mêlée.

Meg and I start to protest, but the nameless cousin grabs our hands and forces us into movement.

I am overwhelmed. I am the most discomfited of dancers. Simultaneously, chillingly, I am certain that the wedding guests sense it to be a sad occasion, yet all are in desperate conspiracy to produce a joyful atmosphere. They dance madly. As though . . . as though if they were to stop, and cast a thoughtful eye on the bride and groom, the illusion would be dispelled. The party dresses and hairspray and starched collars and lipsticked lips would melt away, and all present would be left standing in the rags of Huda's despair.

But soon Huda herself arises from the throne and descends the two steps to the dance floor. Her husband claps his hands lamely as she dances without looking at him. The circle expands to make her its center, and Ehab shifts from foot to foot self-consciously.

But no one is looking at him.

All eyes are fixed on Huda, who, weaving herself into the now meditative rhythms of the music, is transformed.

Huda's eyes are downcast, one hand on her hip, another arcing in the air as it parallels the smooth, circular motion of her wide hips. I am surprised that such a seemingly bulky woman can move with such fluidity. The beads on her dress tremble and swing with her movements. She is untouchable for a moment, moving transcendence, a manifestation of the music's seductive nuances.

The spell is broken by a tooth-jarring ululation from Karima, and the gentler music submits to the wailings of 'Amr Diyab.

Huda looks up, and I see reality invade her gaze.

Other women in the group, aunts, friends, sisters-in-law, take up the ululations. The sound swells, and Huda, forcing a smile, pulls her mother into the circle with her.

They dance, eyes locked, for only a moment. Others join them, and the clapping intensifies with the pounding of the synthesized drums.

Meg and I join the dance, but we cannot prolong the effort for very long.

We slip away early for drinks at the Marriott. We are silent, willingly surrendering the conversation to fellow students who have met us there. We are incapable of allaying the feeling that we have just witnessed the inflicting of a perhaps fatal wound, and we, along with all present, are guilty of dancing on a blood-slicked floor. Once in a while, Meg's eyes meet mine, but we can only share wordless frowns.

We drink in Huda's honor.

❖   ❖   ❖   ❖   ❖

The morning after the wedding I awaken inexplicably early, not an easy wakening, but an unsettled stirring from a dark, brooding sleep.

I am blearily spooning freeze-dried coffee into boiled water when the violent slamming of Huda's door shakes the door to our flat in its frame. I cross to the foyer and peer out the glass inset just in time to see the flustered groom attack the elevator button, pace explosively waiting for it to spring to life, give up in a rage, and go tearing down the stairs.

The door reopens, and Huda pokes an unveiled head out into the hallway. Her cheeks are tear-streaked. She listens to Ehab's retreating footsteps, then notices me looking, manages a weak smile, and closes the door again.

I remember her face on the first day I saw her. *I know no one in all of Garden City*, she'd said.

I pad across the hall in my bare feet, and rap softly on the glass. It does not take too much cajoling to convince Huda to come drink coffee with me.

هدی

Huda

The eyes relay what we desire; in our hearts love lies buried.

—LAYLA BINT SAʿD IBN MAHDI
OF THE BANU ʿAMIR
(the beloved of Qays ibn al-Mulawwah,
the Madman of Layla, or *Majnun Layla*)
c. eighth century C.E.
(from *The Book of Songs*, volume II,
Abu al-Faraj al-Isfahani, d. 967 C.E.)

تُبَلِّغُنا العيونُ بما أردنا   وفي القلبين ثَمَّ هوّى دَفِينُ

Sharif was nothing to look at.

He was far too thin and too tall for his frame. His wire-rimmed glasses were always crooked, the lenses so filthy that he was constantly pulling them off in order to see better. Tight curls crowned his head, and in order to subdue them, he cut his own hair. Tiny barbs of hair stuck out every which way, and he was given to patting at his head in order to smooth them down. Dark half-moons underscored black, restless eyes.

She watched him ambling across the campus and toward their bench.

He stood shyly before the trio of girls. "Good afternoon," he said.

"Good afternoon," they replied in chorus. Huda saw

Larinne and Nuha exchanging glances, but she pretended not to notice.

Sharif looked to Huda expectantly.

"I have your notes right here," she said, pulling the sheaf of papers out of her notebook.

He smiled gratefully. "Bless you," he said. "Did he cover a lot of material?"

Huda shook her head. "Not so much, but it's all going to be on the test. And there are some difficult equations midway through."

Sharif nodded. "I don't know how to thank you," he said, his black eyes smiling even if his lips did not.

She blushed despite herself. "No thanks are necessary," she mumbled.

He excused himself then, saying he was late for work. She watched as he walked away clutching the stack of papers she had photocopied from her own notebook.

Larinne waved a hand in front of her line of vision. "Hello?"

Huda looked at her. "What?"

The two girls laughed, imitating her. "*What?*"

"What are you daydreaming about?" Nuha demanded.

Huda sighed. "Nothing."

Larinne pressed the backs of her long fingers against Huda's forehead. "*Nothing* is right. Are you crazy or just sick? They don't get any poorer than that one."

"I hear he has six sisters," said Nuha.

Larinne was nodding. "And his father is dead."

Huda was silent, realizing that she didn't like having him discussed by her friends. She pulled her lips into a casual smile. "He's nice, that's all."

Larinne grinned. "You had better hope that's all, because it will never happen. He has to work two jobs just to take care of his family. By the time he gets all his sisters married off and can start saving for himself, he'll be sixty."

Huda shrugged. "I have nothing against older men."

"Darling, *you'll* be *dead* by then," said Nuha, tightening the pin at her chin and standing up. "How long has he been taking your notes, anyway?"

"About three weeks," said Huda, also rising from the bench. "He doesn't have time to actually sit through the lecture."

Nuha winked at Larinne. "Sharif never asked me to write notes for him," she said.

"*I* have better handwriting," said Huda, ending the conversation, even though her friends continued smirking as they gathered their notebooks.

The last lectures of the day were letting out, and the campus of Cairo University was thick with students. The three threaded their way through the crowds, out of the main entrance to the Faculty of Commerce, and onto 'Abd al-Salam 'Arif Street.

Larinne vanished into the crammed minibus that would deliver her to Hada'iq al-Quba, and Huda and Nuha were left to walk arm in arm down to Dokki Street toward home.

They greeted the Dokki Street beggar woman who occupied the busy corner. Her shabby gelabiyya was stained and torn, and she leaned heavily on a grimy little girl. The child would run between her grandmother and the cars paused at the stoplight. She would motion at the crippled old lady, whose left leg ended in a rag-swathed stump that dangled just below her uneven hem. Drivers would hand the girl a half-pound note, or wave her on to the next car. The pair had been at this corner only a few weeks; Huda had seen them, a fixture at the Gelaa Bridge, only two months ago.

They had given the beggar money at the beginning of her Dokki Street sojourn. Now the stooped woman would always give them blessings for free, shaking her gnarled hands at them as they passed. *May God make you beautiful brides! May He give you long lives!*

"Do you love him?" Nuha asked when they'd passed the beggars.

Huda laughed. "Can we talk about something else, please?"

Nuha nodded, and fell silent a moment before saying, "Okay. A suitor is coming tonight."

Huda stared at her friend, wide-eyed. "You didn't tell me before."

"I was hoping I could forget it."

"Is it someone you know?"

Nuha shifted her satchel from one shoulder to the other, then took Huda's arm again. "No. An engineer," she said. "A friend of my cousin Anwar's."

"And the apartment?" asked Huda.

"In Maadi," Nuha answered.

Huda considered this. "Maadi's good," she said.

Nuha shook her head. "Not the good part of Maadi."

"Oh," said Huda. They walked on, letting the rush of traffic fill their silence.

Nuha said at last, "I hear he's handsome."

Huda smiled at her, taking in her smooth olive skin and warm chestnut eyes. The lavender headscarf did nothing to conceal Nuha's quiet radiance. "He'd be lucky to have you," she said, squeezing her friend's arm. "What are you going to wear?"

They talked awhile of skirts and blouses and shades of

lipstick, until they came to the corner where Nuha departed for home.

"What time?" asked Huda.

"Eight o'clock."

"You'll call me and let me know?"

"You call me," Nuha said. "If I'm stuck talking to him and I want an excuse to leave the room, you'll be it."

Huda continued her walk past the underpass florist and across the teeming Dokki Square, past the grocer and the row of jewelry shops. She hesitated a moment before a window jammed with gold bangles and slinking chains of varying thickness. She stared a moment at the *shebka* that caught her eye—a large red velvet box displaying a necklace of thick gold braid studded with pearls, dangling pearl earrings, a matching bracelet, and a large pearl ring. In the center of the box sat the thin gold band.

"So when are you coming back with the groom?" Hatim Wassouf, the jeweler, appeared, leaning on the peeling door frame, wiping his hands on a smooth cloth. A bushy mustache topped a wide smile.

Huda jumped, startled and mortified with embarrassment.

"I was . . ."

Hatim arched his eyebrows. "Yes?"

"The bracelets, I . . . My mother's birthday . . ."

Hatim laughed loudly as Huda hurriedly continued her path toward home. "We'll be waiting!" he called after her. "Just bring over the lucky man. We'll find you a *shebka* to meet his budget, big or small! A *shebka* to make a mother proud!"

Huda shrunk in on herself, cheeks blazing. She felt that all eyes on the street were riveted on her. She passed through the open-air market on Sulayman Gohar Street, and practically ran the remaining few paces to her house.

Her chest was heaving as she closed the door behind her. The apartment was dark, caught suspended between afternoon and evening, and she knew her father must be sleeping in the shuttered living room. A pool of light spilled out of the kitchen onto the curling linoleum of the hallway. She found her mother standing over the small stove, browning rice in clarified butter as a chicken simmered in the deep pot.

Karima looked up and, still holding the wooden spoon, accepted Huda's kisses.

"What's the news from the university?"

Huda opened the refrigerator and leaned in, searching for the rice pudding she'd made last night. "Nuha has a suitor coming tonight."

Karima turned to look at her daughter. "Someone she knows?"

Huda shook her head, sinking onto the foam-leaking vinyl-covered chair at the kitchen table.

Karima nodded and turned back to her cooking. As though reminded, she said suddenly, "Your aunt Amar knows a young man at work. She says he's a great catch."

"Mama—"

"I said to her, when Huda's friends start getting engaged, she'll be ready. But they all just want to play now. Playing at university."

Huda said nothing.

"I was already married at your age, you know," Karima said, adding the rest of the rice to the browned portion and dumping a few cups of water on top of that.

"I know, Mama."

Karima lowered the gas flame beneath the rice pot and covered it. She came to sit opposite Huda, wiping her face with the rolled-up sleeve of her thin cotton gelabiyya.

Huda looked at her mother, swallowed hard, then said, "There's a boy I like at school."

Karima narrowed her eyes. "What kind of boy?"

Huda shrugged. "A good boy."

"From a respectable family?"

"Very."

"You've talked with him?"

"He copies from my lecture notes."

Karima narrowed her eyes. "You've met him away from school?"

Huda glared at her mother. "Of course not."

Karima sighed in relief, and Huda looked away, furious at the suggestion.

"Has he talked to you of marriage?" Karima asked finally.

"No. And he won't."

Her mother watched her carefully, sipping at her water glass. "Why?"

"Because he doesn't have a millime."

Karima harrumphed. "*That* story?"

"He works two jobs to support his mother and sisters. His father's dead."

Karima regarded her daughter steadily. "Exactly what do you want me to do, Huda?"

"I want you not to talk about suitors for a while."

Her mother rubbed her hands across her eyes. "Until when? When you're old and wrinkled?"

Huda placed a spoonful of the pudding in her mouth, thinking. "Until I know his intentions," she said at last. "That's fair, isn't it?"

Karima sighed again, staring unseeingly at the seeping cracks that skated along the length and width of the weary kitchen walls. "For now," she answered.

Nuha's voice was choked with rage as she whispered into the telephone, "He's handsome, all right. A beautiful *fat* man."

Huda pressed the receiver closer to her ear. "Tell me."

"Fat. Fat. Fat like someone who eats whole jars of *samna*. Even Mama was surprised."

"But is he nice?"

Nuha practically spat into the phone, "Fat people have to be nice."

Huda sucked in her stomach reflexively. "Maybe he's fat from loneliness. He'll lose weight once he wins your heart."

"No, I already told Mama *no*."

"She won't mind?"

Nuha was silent a moment, considering. "She really liked his qualifications. His family has money, even if he's just starting out. And his car is brand-new. It's parked downstairs. A Hyundai. Red."

Huda pictured Nuha riding in a red Hyundai next to an oozingly fat man.

"What's next?" she asked.

"We'll wait and see who shows up the next time. It has to get better, right?"

The next morning, Huda sat before her vanity table, staring at herself. Her face was round; her lips were full and precisely shaped and sat under a nose that took up more space on her face than she would have liked. She had just finished taming her eyebrows into two high arches. They floated now over cocoa-colored eyes that, properly lined, could catch someone's attention.

She rubbed her hand thoughtfully across her cheeks and chin, then fluffed at her hair. Her hair was long and coarse, but she had curled it with the curling iron so that it framed her face in gentle waves. She tilted her head slightly, left then right.

She stood surveying her wide curves, resolving again to go with Larinne to the gym. Adjusting her vertical-striped blouse—it made her appear thinner—she decided she looked full-figured and sensuous rather than all-out plump.

Her mother paused at Huda's door on her way out to work. "Dressing up for school today?" she asked.

Huda smiled at her mother, caught.

"Marriage is a matter of Fate, you know," Karima said.

Huda nodded. "I know. I'm trying to encourage Fate."

Nuha was waiting, as she waited each morning, a few steps beyond Radwan's Shawerma Shop. She noticed the extra measures immediately.

"The eye makeup looks good," she observed, reaching a hand to adjust a lock of Huda's hair. "The hair looks beautiful. I always wondered why you wear it braided instead of loose like this. It frames your face nicely."

"I hate my hair," said Huda, starting toward school.

"Every female hates her hair," said Nuha.

If Sharif noticed the difference, he did not give any indication. Nor did he give Huda extra attention on the next day, or the next.

"He's shy," said Nuha.

"He's broke," insisted Larinne.

"He doesn't know you like him. If he knew, he'd have the courage to speak up."

Huda laughed. "So now I'm supposed to go and tell him how I feel? That's too much."

But something of a plan was hatched. Sharif had gotten into the habit of approaching Huda when the other two were present. One day, as soon as he appeared, Larinne and Nuha suddenly remembered a vital and pressing meeting with their section leader.

Sharif stood awkwardly in front of the bench, his eyes following the girls' retreating figures.

Nervousness nearly silenced Huda completely, but she fought for the words.

"Would you like to sit?" she asked finally.

He stared at the ground for a moment, then his head bobbed up and down. He sat as far from her on the bench as possible without being on the ground.

Huda shifted uncomfortably, imagining the eyes of passersby drawing conclusions from such a scene.

"How is your work?" she began, her voice uncertain.

"Which one?"

She shrugged, smiling. "Both?"

He nodded briefly, staunchly. "Work is all right. *Al-hamdu lillah.*" He did not say anything at all for a while, then began, "Huda, I—"

"Yes?" She looked at him directly for the first time that morning.

He blinked and looked away. "I don't know how to thank you for the notes. I wouldn't be able to pass without them."

She smiled, and took to staring at the fingernails of her tightly clasped hands.

Silence engulfed them, and Huda was about to stand and make her excuses before they became the object of gossip.

Sharif noticed that she had begun fidgeting. "Huda, I need you to know that I—"

She froze, the fingernails of her left hand digging deeply into her right.

"I would ask for your hand in a second, if only I had something to offer you." The words came out in a soft rush, and he exhaled audibly after completing the sentence. His eyes were still focused on the patch of cement in front of his shoes.

"I would accept." She gazed at him, willing him to look at her.

He turned his face to hers, and their eyes met. His eyes were black pearls, and she felt something within herself slacken, a ridge of tension swept away by a warm wave.

But too soon Huda saw a frown work its way from his mind onto his skin, knitting itself above his uneven eyebrows.

He tore his eyes from hers. "But I don't even bother hoping for this. I have nothing. I just needed you to know it. I just—I just wanted you to know."

She nodded slowly, and watched helplessly as he stood up, gathering his notebooks and the pen that had fallen to the ground. She was desperate to say something, anything to keep him from walking away.

His gait was quick and crooked as he made for the crowded street.

Her mother was in tears when Huda entered the flat; the sobs had echoed out into the hallway as she turned her key in the lock. She rushed to her mother's chair and knelt beside it, looking to her father for an explanation.

Baba sat smoking a long Cleopatra cigarette, despite the doctor's specific orders. At last he said softly, stiffly, still staring at the telephone, "Wagdy isn't coming for Ramadan."

Huda kissed her mother's wet cheeks. "Mama, you knew he wasn't coming. How can he come? If he comes he can't go back; he'll never get the right papers again now that he's broken the first visa. And then what will he do?"

Her mother practically shouted at her, "You mean he's going to just stay there forever?"

Huda swallowed, fighting her own tears. "And what if he does? At least he'll have a future there. . . ."

Karima's sobs increased. Huda tried to wipe her mother's tears with her fingertips, but Karima caught her hands in hers, fiercely, as though furious at her. Her grip remained strong, but her features softened as tears continued to slide along the fullness of her face.

"I miss my son," she whispered hoarsely.

Huda nodded, biting her lips hard to keep from crying. "So do I."

The two fell silent, clutching each other. The only sounds in the room became Karima's subsiding sobs, and the soft crackle of the diminishing cigarette.

Huda walked into her room slowly and opened the creaking wardrobe door. The blouse hung separately from her others, and she fingered the rayon gingerly. It was a pale peach color, with gold buttons in the shape of roses.

Huda pressed the cloth to her face, trying to detect a trace of Wagdy's scent. He had sent other things from America, tied up in plastic bags and delivered by friends of his who'd come to see their families. Perfumes for Mama. Thick leather slippers with warm padding for Baba's woeful feet. A pair of Clarks Shoes for Omar, the eldest, and durable white socks that could withstand the long, upright hours at the grocery. He had sent Huda makeup and cassette tapes and T-shirts.

But this blouse was the most beautiful gift yet. The tags still dangled from the left sleeve's seam.

She could not wear it.

She could only touch it, imagining his hands as they'd folded it into the bag.

Ever since Huda could remember, it was Mama Selwa's habit to come for the weekend, leaving her son 'Adil's home and the three grandchildren she cared for while her daughter-in-law taught school. Huda's cousins were much younger than she and her brothers were, for Uncle 'Adil was ten years Karima's junior. On weekends, Huda and Mama Selwa shared Huda's large bed, just as they had when Huda was little.

When nightmares had yanked frightened tears from Huda's small eyes, Mama Selwa used to rub her back and whisper, *There's nothing to worry about. Just go into the bathroom, open the faucet, and tell the dream to the water. As it goes down the drain, it will take the nightmare with it, and nothing bad will ever come true.*

Sometimes, even when she was not there, Mama Selwa's soft snores and midnight murmurs would lace themselves into Huda's dreams. Huda would awaken and stare confusedly about her in the dark, imagining her grandmother's nearness.

Friday was when Mama Selwa would preside over the family gathering for late-afternoon lunch.

On this day, Karima was still at market when Huda set aside her notebooks, stretched, and navigated the parlor's shifting tiles to cross into the kitchen.

Mama Selwa sat at the kitchen table, peeling cloves of garlic for mashing into the okra stew's spice mixture. Huda studied her for a long time before her grandmother looked up.

"Are you going to help me or are you just going to stand there like a monkey?"

Huda laughed and crossed to the table.

"Your mother invents work for me every time I come," she said. "I should just stay at your uncle's, where I belong. What is it you do all day, anyway, that you don't help her enough?"

"Studies," answered Huda automatically, breaking a clove away from the bunch. "Pray for my success."

Mama Selwa cast a dubious glance over the rim of her glasses. "Studies. Have you heard she's looking for your groom?"

Huda frowned, flaring her nostrils, and crushing the clove against the table's surface to loosen its peel.

"You're not interested?"

Huda shrugged.

"You're interested, but in one boy in particular?"

Huda could not meet her grandmother's eyes.

With her paring knife, Mama Selwa tapped the space of tabletop that lay in Huda's line of vision. "It doesn't matter, you know," she said.

Huda looked up, her eyes a question.

"He doesn't matter. You matter. You've got everything you need right in here." She gestured to Huda's chest.

Huda blinked, watching Mama Selwa's face for any further clues.

She offered none, but lowered her voice conspiratorially. "You'll see. You're not waiting for anything from anyone," she said. "It will be all right. Despite him."

Huda rose, hesitance weaving itself into the uncurling of her body as she stood.

"I have to study," she murmured, wiping her fingertips on a damp rag.

"With success," responded Mama Selwa, her wide jade eyes swimming with meanings that Huda could not divine.

Lunch that day was just as it had always been. Karima spread newspapers across the surface of the dining room table, hiding the masking tape that sealed the splintered surface. She piled its center with the warm, circular loaves of cracked wheat bread. Dish by dish, the table crowded in on itself with golden fried rice, tidy stacks of stuffed cabbage leaves, and a deep bowl of the okra stew. Two chickens lay spread-eagled in their baking pans, framing a casserole of zucchini in béchamel sauce.

As Karima distributed massive portions to each expectant plate, Omar recounted the latest gossip of all of the grocery's customers, those who were marrying, working, giving birth, and arguing publicly. 'Alia coaxed and cajoled her eldest, five-year-old Rami, begging him to eat something in addition to the rice.

Mama Selwa regaled them all with stories of her daughter-in-law's latest crimes. Mama Selwa was constantly fielding telephone calls from her son's mistresses, although once in a while she left his wife to answer, relishing her blushing furies as punishment for her sharp tongue.

As Mama Selwa's laughter brought on their own, tears streaked her cheeks. Huda observed the scene in sated silence, loving the sound of her family's laughter, wishing that she could bottle the sound and sip it like sweet *sahlab* each time she thirsted.

One evening, Nuha refused to take Huda's call.

Huda stared at the receiver for a long time after placing it on the base. She sat on the edge of the bed, paralyzed, imagining the scene at Nuha's house. There had been a steady stream of suitors, at least one a week for the past three months. Nuha had complained and groaned, sometimes not even bothering to lower her voice as she gave Huda assessments while the young man stewed in the parlor.

But never once had she not come to the phone.

Huda waited for almost an hour, busying herself with

outlining a chapter on auditing. When the phone finally rang, she pounced on it.

"Well?"

Nuha's laughter billowed through the line. "This one isn't so bad."

"What does he do?"

"Journalist."

"Apartment?"

"Faysal."

"Car?"

"Not yet. But he said his brother is going to sell him his Peugeot when he gets his new car. He's older, so he's had longer to save. He offered a *shebka* of five thousand and either two rooms of furniture for the flat or a *mahr* of ten thousand."

Huda digested this, then asked, "How old?"

"Thirty."

"Ten years!"

Nuha laughed again. "That's nothing. Larinne just had her mother accompany her to dinner with a man who is thirty-five. And she's serious about him—she thinks he'll come to make a formal proposal next week."

Huda shook her head. "What did you talk about?"

"*Politics.*"

"What do you know about *politics?*"

"I can learn," Nuha answered, indignant. Then, changing her tone, she said, "He's so handsome, Huda. He has the kindest eyes and the sweetest smile."

"How did it end?"

"I told Mama to tell him he can telephone me anytime."

Huda laughed. "Progress. You told her to hit the rest of them with shoes."

"This one isn't like the rest of them."

Huda smiled, envisioning her friend's beaming face. "I'm glad. May God work it out for the best."

When Nuha's engagement was announced three weeks later, Karima began to lose patience.

Huda avoided her gaze all evening, but Karima cornered her as they washed dishes.

"How long are you going to wait for the pauper?" she demanded.

"As long as I need to," said Huda, placing a dripping plate on the rusting wire rack over the sink.

"Did he even express an interest?"

"Yes."

"And?"

Huda rubbed the bar of soap against the rag, then resumed scrubbing the baking pan. "He knows he can't ask for my hand yet, Mama. His life is hard enough. He doesn't deserve to have Baba throw him out for the crime of not having an apartment to marry into or a millime to call his own."

Karima was silent, stacking dried plates in the cabinet. When she could restrain her tongue no longer, she said, "So how is it that you imagine he'll ever be able to take care of you?"

"I can work, can't I? I am going to university, after all."

Karima scoffed. "I haven't noticed university degrees doing anyone any good these days."

"Sharif is a good boy. And he wants me. That's the important thing. No one told him about me, no one said what a nice family I have, or how well-mannered I am and what a good mother I'll make. He wants me for me. And that's why I want him."

"Did he promise you anything?"

"He wouldn't ask me to wait for him."

Her mother was exasperated. "So what is your solution to all this?"

After a squeaking turn of the handle, the faucet fell silent. Huda faced her mother, her eyes brimming, her hands sopping. "I don't know what to do. If I had something to sell, I'd sell it and give it to him. If I had a home, I'd write his name on the deed."

Karima sighed. "Tell him to do what he can. But tell him to do it soon."

Huda started for her room, but her mother held up a hand.

"I won't let you throw away your life. You're not getting any younger, do you understand?"

There was no reply to that. Huda walked through the semi-darkness of the flat to her bedroom, wishing for once that the door closed all the way. She huddled on the floor beneath the window, grasping her knees, relying on the sounds of the restless souq to obscure her sobbing.

Her puffy eyelids were the first things Nuha saw.

"What happened?"

They fell in step together. "You tell me where you went last night with your fiancé," Huda said.

"No. Later. What's wrong? Tell me now."

Huda sighed. "Sharif. Mama has lost patience already."

Nuha curled her arm into Huda's, choosing her words carefully. "Maybe she's not that wrong."

Huda looked up. "What do you mean?"

"Maybe . . . maybe he just isn't right for you. How can he ever afford to set up a house, to care for a wife and children? Do you really want to live your whole life worrying if you'll make it through the week?"

"It can't just be hopeless, just because of money. It just . . . it just can't work that way."

Nuha shook her head sympathetically. "If I had some, I'd give it to you both. But I don't even know what money looks like. That's life, you know? There has to be a reason. And maybe your mother will find someone nice for you. A good man. A good catch."

They passed the beggar woman and her granddaughter in silence. The old woman was seated on the sidewalk, her bent back propped up against the wrought iron fence. The scant child was draped across her grandmother's lap, her rib cage swelling and deflating as she snored. The beggar called after them toothlessly, *May you soon be beautiful brides! May God grant you long lives!*

Huda moaned softly. "I have to talk to him. Maybe if he knew how much I want him to come propose . . ."

"Do you think he's waiting for encouragement?" asked Nuha. "Don't you think if there were any way, he would have done something at the start of the semester?"

She considered this pensively, but she could not prevent herself from lying in wait for him after business administration.

"Sharif," she called, as he was descending the marble steps of the lecture hall. "One minute."

"I'll catch up," he called to his three friends. "Huda. How are you?"

His eyes locked with hers, and the words she'd prepared crumbled in her mouth. He had seemed so weary just moments before, so heavy of limb and gray of face. But when he saw her, a light pulsated deep in the pupils of his eyes, and a smile found its way to his lips. They stood thus for an interminable moment, Huda watching the effect she had on him, and Sharif basking in her cocoa-colored eyes.

A passing shoulder knocked him slightly off balance, and remembering where he was, he pulled his gaze away reluctantly.

"How are you?" he repeated, pushing his glasses up on his nose.

"I—" She paused. "How is your mother? Your sisters, are they well?"

He nodded. *"Al-hamdu lillah."*

She swallowed hard, crossing her arms so that he couldn't see the shaking of her hands. "I—I don't know what to say, I . . ." She faltered, then decided just to launch into it. "Well, do you remember what you said about wanting to marry me?"

He flushed and toed the cement with his already worn shoe.

She continued hurriedly, "Please, I don't . . . I'm not trying to put you in a bad position. It's just . . . Well, my mother is starting to pressure me, and I've told her all about you, and if you thought there was any way, any way at all that you could speak with Baba . . ."

She saw the tendons of his neck stiffen as he raised his eyes to meet hers.

Her voice faded as she looked at him. "Any way at all . . ."

Regret simmered in his eyes. "I'm sorry. I . . . I wish I had something to offer. But . . . I have nothing. I have nothing to give you."

"I don't want much," she offered weakly.

"You know what I mean, Huda." His eyes took in the great dome of the campus, and the mighty high-rises beyond it that lined Giza Street. "I go for days eating only *foule*. I don't even remember what meat tastes like. Do you understand? I've fixed these shoes seven times. Every piaster I make goes straight to the house, my sisters, clothes, food . . . Some days I don't have half a pound for the bus and I walk all the way from Shubra to school. I only stay in school so I'll be qualified for that *someday* when one of the businessmen whose cars I service will offer me a nice office job. But even then. You know how long it takes to save up enough."

He looked at her, and she saw in his eyes a hopelessness that was slate-gray and cold. She shrank from it but found the voice to say, "I would work too."

"Where?"

"A bank. I'm interning this summer. It could lead to an appointment after graduation."

"How is that? Do you know someone with connections?" His voice was jagged with bitterness. "And even if you got lucky— two hundred pounds a month doesn't even buy bananas. How long would it take us together to save enough for a flat?"

"I would wait," she said, meaning it.

He smiled his lopsided smile, then, pulling his glasses off his face, he gazed at her with a look that was so intimate she felt naked. "I know," he answered softly. Then he shook his head, quickly, as though to clear away a fog within. "But what's your crime that you should waste your youth on me?"

"How about that I have a feeling I could make you happy?"

He reached as if to take her hand, then caught himself and let his hand fall to his side. "You already have," he said, as he turned and walked away.

Sharif. She wanted to call his name aloud, so loudly as to drown out even the clanging from the bell tower.

But all she could do was stand paralyzed, and stare at the hand that he had wanted to touch.

She mentally constructed his touch, wrapping his strong, dark fingers around hers.

When she heard the doorbell that evening, she took refuge in her room, her sanctuary that overlooked Sulayman Gohar Square's swarming market. The parlor interrogations would be drowned out by the cry of the onion seller lauding his produce, the haggling of women and indignant vendors, and the shouts of a fierce street-soccer match.

The vanity mirror mocked her as she leaned on her elbows, studying her face.

Already, a creeping sadness began to infiltrate her eyes, seeping across her dark irises like spilled ink.

She rose from the tiny stool, turning this way and that, tugging her already long blouse down even farther in an attempt to disguise the bulge of her behind. Her ankle-length black skirt had picked up the usual lint and she brushed at it idly, caring and not caring.

She shook her head, hating the taste of fear in her mouth. She smoothed her hands over her blouse, across her hips. *Fat. Too fat. He'll think, "If she's this fat now, what will she be like after we're married? Like her mother, that's what."*

As if on cue, Karima burst in, flushed and aflutter, a fine film of sweat shining on her forehead. "Quickly, quickly. I've prepared the tray. Now you take him the coffee, just as we discussed. Did you take down your hair? Hadn't I put it up in a barrette for you? Oh, well, there's no time for that now. He says his apartment is in Maadi. It would be *perfect*. Hurry, darling, your groom is waiting!" And with that Karima propelled her toward the kitchen.

The tray was indeed waiting; the cardamom cast silken raiments of scent over the dilapidated kitchen. So, he was a coffee drinker, then. The delicate demitasse with the tiny matching saucer occupied the center of the silver-plated tray Mama used only for special occasions. A glass of Nescafé in hot milk sat next to it, and she divined that this was for the suitor's mother, Aunt Amar's coworker. She regarded the beverage warily, feeling in its heat the heat of the woman's appraising gaze.

Baba, on the other hand, drank sugary tea. She touched his steaming glass with her fingertip, imagining his detached silence as Mama had gone from gossiping with the mother to flattering and questioning the young man.

She knew he had spent the whole time sliding his prayer beads swiftly between his fingers, his lips moving absently through the simple prayers. *Subhan Allah. Al-hamdu lillah. Allahu Akbar.*

She sighed and picked up the tray, carrying it carefully into the sitting room. She did not look up, only watched the shuddering surfaces of the beverages, silently commanding them not to slop over. She set the tray on the coffee table and carefully handed over the drinks. As she served the suitor his coffee, she was flirting with the idea of dumping it in his lap; she suppressed the desire, hating her own cowardice.

She backed slowly into the chair next to the high couch that Baba occupied, his swollen feet mashed into his dress shoes for the occasion, the laces limp and untied.

Only after sitting did she raise her eyes to look her suitor in the face.

He greeted her politely, and she summoned a weak smile in reply. His face was pockmarked with the eternal scars of picked pimples. His eyes were small and set widely apart, giving off the illusion that he was walleyed. His hair was thick and wiry, and she noticed with mild disgust that he had to shave his neck all the way to his collar. To keep all that hair at bay, she thought. To keep it from overtaking his face and suffocating him.

His mother, slim and gray-faced, asked her about the university. As though expecting criticism, she related how her son had graduated from an accounting institute, a two-year degree, and he worked seasonally as a tax reviewer for a government contracting company. The rest of the time he looked for other work, and drove his cousin's taxi at night. He had an apartment, still only exposed brick inside, but his alone, thanks to some foresight by his father, who'd bought when the edge of Maadi was still desert and the apartments were cheap.

The suitor himself chimed in at this point, explaining how he could use the taxi almost any time, so it was as if he had his own car, too.

She listened as he spoke, hating his thin voice. It was like a plastic bag stretched so hard that it was about to rip apart. She hated how his eyes periodically swept over her, swiftly, as though no one would notice. Evaluating her.

So I'm too fat, she thought, defending herself against those walleyes. *But at least I have good skin. At least I got into college.*

She cast a glance at her father, and caught him looking at her. His stern, disinterested look did not fluctuate, but he winked at her—so quickly she almost didn't catch it.

All her muscles and nerves seemed to detangle then, and she felt her breathing go back to normal. It was going to be all right. Baba was on her side.

She rejected this one firmly, immediately after he left. She was surprised to see her mother crying. "He's such a good catch, that one. So what if he didn't go to university? No one went to university in my day. Did we die from it? No. Your aunt Amar wouldn't have sent him to us if he weren't from a good family. With good manners. And the apartment—are you forgetting the apartment? Could we hope for a better section of town than Maadi?"

For so long now, Karima's tears had been preserved for the subject of Wagdy. *Wagdy hasn't called, Wagdy called and he's taken up with an American girl, Wagdy doesn't love me enough to come home, Wagdy won't be coming for a visit this Eid, maybe next Eid, maybe next year. Maybe.*

Huda had never been a subject of pain for Karima. Huda had always been her comfort. She looked to Baba to say something, but he only patted her tenderly on the head, gathered up his cane and hobbled off to his ongoing backgammon game at Lutfy's Café. Her mother's tears brought on her own, and she fled to her room.

She lay for hours in her bed, clutching her pillow, listening to the street creaking and shifting beneath her closed shutters. The realization that things would get no better settled over her like the red dust of the *khamasin* over the restive city.

As she walked arm in arm with Nuha after the last test of the year, she noticed that the beggar woman and her granddaughter were nowhere in sight.

Nuha said, "The police finally sent them off to beg somewhere else."

Huda nodded sadly, feeling the sidewalk to be empty despite the constant stream of people.

Listlessly, she would once in a while evidence a little interest in a candidate. However, the obligatory period wherein her family would ask neighbors and coworkers to recommend or discredit him always brought up some flaw or other. One of them was famous for accepting bribes at work. Another had been engaged six times. Another turned out to be forty-two—too old even by Karima's lax standards. One was a known alcoholic, another had a problem with hashish. Another's apartment was in a horrible, run-down building in Safit al-Laban, a part of town that, in mentality and living standards, might as well have been a village in the depths of Upper Egypt.

The whole summer passed thus, and Huda welcomed the start of school in the fall.

But Sharif did not ask for her notes anymore. He greeted her from afar, never approaching the bench where she sat murmuring with Larinne and Nuha.

Huda would watch his thin, gangly form as it wended its way through the campus grounds.

If he felt her persistent gaze, he never acknowledged it by looking back.

When the second semester of the senior year began, he was not present among the ranks of students. Larinne admitted that she'd heard he was just too busy with work to attend. Huda knew he had failed three of five subjects the previous semester, and would have to repeat them.

All three girls graduated comfortably but unremarkably from the Faculty of Commerce. Although Huda couldn't get appointed anywhere, the Ahly Bank—where she had done her summer internship—welcomed her as a sort of perpetual intern. She was paid an eighth of what an employee made, although she did triple the work.

But Huda loved it. She loved the bank. She loved the smell of it and the way her shoes clicked against the smooth marble of the floors. She loved the soft hum of the central air-conditioning. She loved the responsibilities and the tasks. She loved it when she was the only one who could solve a problem on the computer, or when the supervisor said, *Thank you, Huda. I don't know what we'd do without you, Huda.*

The bank was where she felt reliable and competent. Precise. And finally, perfect. Her work was perfect. Nothing in her life had ever before breathed even a breath of perfection. And even if it was trivial, and even if she was grossly under-paid, Huda, for once, was proud of herself.

She sat with Larinne at Nuha's wedding.

Karima had refused to come because, she admitted, she had secretly chosen Nuha for Wagdy, and seeing her would be too painful. By this time, Wagdy had told them of his marriage to a yellow-haired girl. He did not spend a year's salary on a *shebka*, only produced, in increments, enough for a small diamond ring. She paid for half of a rented apartment. They slept on a mattress on the floor, and ate off a table purchased from a place that sold items other people had thrown away. They shared the loan on a used Mazda.

He was happy, he said.

He would send pictures, he said, with the next friend who traveled home.

Moreover, he promised, he would be able to come home, maybe within a year, depending on the paperwork and God's facilitations.

This point alone dried Karima's bereft tears, and allowed her to recover from the pain of a new, unknown daughter and a still-distant son.

And so it was that Huda went without her mother to her best friend's wedding. She and Larinne wept when they saw how beautiful the bride looked in her flowing white gown. Nuha was stunning. It had been just over a year since her engagement, and in that time she had grown to love her groom as much as their phone conversations and monthly outings could allow. Her cheeks glowed. Her exposed hair fell in a cas-cade of ringlets studded with pearl barrettes. Every part of her seemed adorned with the heavy jewelry of her *shebka*—a unique gold and ruby combination that looked even more expensive than it was.

Larinne, whose intended was an aging engineer with a brand-new Fiat 128, leaned over and embraced Huda. "I hope the same for you soon."

Huda could only nod, missing her friend with a hollow ache as she watched Nuha dancing with her husband. She knew Nuha was happy, and she could tell from the man's gentle features that he loved Nuha, and would keep her happy.

And so the process works, doesn't it? she insisted to herself. *A happy ending is possible.*

But Huda was nothing like Nuha. Nuha's presence was sweet and light like the breeze off a butterfly's wings. Nor was she anything like Larinne, whose biting wit had startled her suitors, then entranced them.

Night after night, Huda's meticulously painted fingernails would float to her face, tracing the plain, solid features as she lay in the dark. This was not the face that men desired or fought for.

I am not that girl.

What do I have?

What do I have that is worth the trouble? If I were a man, I wouldn't want to marry me.

Yet she did have something. For Karima had tended her like a master gardener tends a seedling. And when Huda might have sprouted vines in many directions, sun-seeking vines that could have budded with a scattering of exotic, hitherto nameless flowers, Karima had sculpted carefully. She had hacked and trimmed until Huda stood perfectly straight and tidily pruned.

Yes, she had something.

She could settle.

She could gather up her skirts and put down her roots. She

could be a shelter amid the torrid rush of souls that was the city. She could sweeten the air around her; she could nourish. She could be a quiet place, a resting place. A leaning place.

A home maker.

The more swept up her daughter was in the world of work, the more frantic Karima became. How could Huda go and come, sleep and awaken with that insufferable nonchalance? As though day by day, moment by moment she wasn't getting older and older and older still. And the stream of potential bridegrooms had slowed from a trickle to a mocking faucet drip. Yet Karima's wardrobes and chests were bursting with Huda's trousseau. They were stocked with china and crystal and dish towels and frying pans she'd been hoarding for twenty-two years. Lingerie and robes and blouses and underwear, far more than she would ever need. Towels, bath mats, bedspreads, doilies, and small appliances. Each time she'd pass by them, the wardrobes would hiss at her their urgency: *Quick! Be quick! You're running out of time!*

She'd look at her only daughter in despair. "Why do you chase them all away?" she'd moan, forgetting the failings of those Huda had tentatively agreed to.

Everyone in the family had been put on alert. Karima had informed everyone, tearfully, that her dearest wish was to see Huda married. Oh, Lord! Her dearest wish, her greatest burden. Her shame . . . *She* had married at seventeen. Her daughter was *twenty-two*. It had never happened in the history of the family. People were already writing her off.

Huda came home from work one late afternoon to find her father alone in the apartment; Karima was visiting Mama Selwa in Faysal.

She could barely believe that she had her father all to herself. It seemed lately that Karima was almost always hovering around, seizing any moment of silence to bring up prospects or pass on gossip about this bride or that, her arrangements, her dress, her apartment location. Baba would flee for the café at every opportunity. Huda, having nowhere to go besides work, could only seek refuge in her room above the souq.

Happily, she set about making mint tea for two, so eager to sit with him that she spilled a bit onto the tiny tray as she walked from the kitchen to the living room.

She lingered for a moment in the doorway, memorizing the scene. Baba lay stretched out on his side on the high couch, his elbow propped on a long oval pillow. The graying lace curtains filtered apricot sunlight over the huge *klim,* so old now that the design itself had worn off in places. The tall walls proclaimed her ancestry with elaborately framed black-and-white pictures, hung with wire from the flaking crown molding. A few knickknacks and framed Qur'anic verses perched atop the console television. It was Karima's fondest possession, her constant, patient companion; the wire hangers stabbed into its back clawed the air like the skewed legs of a dying ant. It stood dark and numb now, submitting for once to silence. Instead, Baba had turned on the battered record player, and Um Kulthum now sang her passions in a voice that ignited the apartment's heavy summer air with longing. Baba took advantage of Karima's absence to smoke a Cleopatra cigarette unmolested, a faraway look on his face. Huda sank into the chair by his elbow, leaning her head against the oval pillow, and he took to patting her hair in rhythm with the music. He was humming softly, something that Huda had not heard him do in a long, long time.

"Baba . . . do you love Mama?"

"Oh, daughter. Don't ruin the song!" he moaned.

She laughed, then leaned back to look at him. "No, I mean it. Please. I have to know. Do you love her?"

He nodded slowly, exhaling a pale cloud of smoke, accepting from her the glass of tea. "Of course I love her," he said guardedly.

Huda motioned to the spinning vinyl record. "Like Um Kulthum says? Is she 'the light that began the morning of your life'?"

He looked at her wryly. "What are you driving at?"

She sipped at her tea, blowing a tiny mint leaf across the steaming surface so as not to swallow it. "I don't understand. Even all the new songs on the radio are about mad and undying love. But nobody marries the one he loves. So who's getting all that love? Where are all those happy people?"

"Ah . . . That's why we love the songs so much," he answered, lighting another cigarette. "The idea of love. The ideal love. What's worse, I ask you, to always have the dream of love, or to marry the one you love, and then one day you wake up next to him and realize that you hate the stink of his breath, you despise the way he chews with his mouth open, how he farts all night under the blanket, how he never looks you in the eye anymore when you talk . . . how he's bored with you, and longing for another? . . . Wouldn't that be more of a heartbreak?"

She shook her head at him, trying not to laugh.

He sighed deeply. "I loved your mother intensely once. I would watch her pass by my store every day; I knew her schedule exactly, what time she would go to work in the morning, when she would come home in the afternoon. I waited for her to pass, just so I could watch the way her hair fell across her shoulders as she walked. Or to see the way her calf muscles moved in the stretch of leg that showed between hem and shoe. When I saw her smile, I thought I would go mad. I lived for a very long time in dreams of love."

Huda stared at him. She had never heard Baba speak so. He sat up then, leaning forward to set his tea on the slightly listing table.

"Life chips away at dreams little by little, Huda. That's why among God's mercies is music like Um Kulthum's. To remind us that the heart can stretch to amazing depths, and that life is still beautiful despite the daily ugliness."

She looked away, her face saturated by sadness.

Baba stretched a hand to pat her hair. "Listen to me, Huda. Marriage is a matter of Fate. You can rail against it, cry and moan, but in the end you marry whom you're supposed to. You can decide to love someone. You make it work because it has to, overlooking the bad and living on the good. You work, you have your children, you do right by them. You laugh when you can. You savor peace when it comes. And eventually you die and in heaven, if you've been good, you're allowed to love the way your heart demands." He nodded toward the record. "The way Suma says we should."

The needle had reached the record's tiny inner circle just as they heard Karima's lumbering step on the stairs.

Huda stood and leaned over her father, kissing his hair, breathing in the scent of him.

He looked up at her tenderly. "Don't worry," he said. "The right man will come along. *Despite* your mother."

She nodded, managing a smile. She quickly gathered the tea glasses, heading for the kitchen as her mother's key turned in the lock.

And then came the dry spell, wherein there were no leads, no calls, nothing whatsoever for an entire, excruciating month.

Karima was like a madwoman, even calling the mothers of her older sons' friends to put them on the alert. She had Omar's wife alert her sisters and mother, who all alerted their husbands, who informed their friends of the marriage opportunity from this good and available girl.

Karima told the neighbors she met in the street, she told casual acquaintances and total strangers. She told the competing grocer 'Am 'Irfan to spread the news, as well as the fishmonger Basyuni, Hatim Wassouf the jeweler, and the two mildly retarded brothers who sold sewing supplies.

Every step that Huda took in her neighborhood was mined with people who knew that she was virtually unweddable.

Finally, one late afternoon, when the lunch dishes had just been put away, a telephone call came from Aunt Amar. Huda, drying her hands on a dish towel, did not hear even her mother's half of the conversation.

But Karima cradled the receiver a changed woman. Relief flooded over her features like dawn breaking over a corpse-strewn battleground.

This ongoing humiliation was due to no flaw in Huda, no failure on Karima's part. None of them was to blame.

"Someone's cast an evil spell on you," she announced, panting and flustered.

Huda brushed her off, making for the refuge of her bedroom, but Karima followed her down the hall.

Finding herself pursued, Huda declared, "You have to be joking."

"I gave Amar your green blouse. She took it to a *shaykh* she goes to now and then out in the countryside. From the blouse he could divine that you've been cursed. Amar's coming now with the amulet he made you."

"The amulet," Huda echoed, her lips twitching in disbelief.

"You'll wear it . . . and you'll see. Amar has personal experi-ence with this *shaykh*. A good friend of hers wore one of his amulets and was married in no time. He's touched, they say."

Huda narrowed her eyes. "Touched?"

"Oh, speaking in strange languages, chanting. He would have whole days where he would make animal sounds, just ter-rifying the whole village."

"And then?"

"And then he recovered, *subhan Allah*, and ever since he has been undoing evil works for people from all over Egypt. They say one of his eyes sees the Unseen."

"Is he an Azhar *shaykh*?"

"No, no. They only call him *shaykh* because he has the gift. He works in a mill."

Huda shook her head, frowning. "Who would want to curse me, anyway?"

"That doesn't matter," Karima replied quickly. "Amar said the *shaykh* says never to ask, simply to trust in God and work to undo the curse."

"This is absolutely ridiculous," fumed Huda.

Karima poked her. "There's no need to be uppity. A girl in your position needs to exhaust her every option."

Huda bit back the question, *And what is my position?*

She knew.

She knew.

And when Aunt Amar came, she extended her hand to accept from her the tiny pouch on the rough leather cord. Her mother's sister spoke in hushed, conspiratorial tones:

You mustn't look inside it. Its contents are secret. When one lunar month has ended, you must take what is inside the pouch and put it in a pan. Go into the bathroom and pour water over yourself so that it rolls off of your body and into the pan. The water must be from seven different faucets, and you must say the Fatiha *in your head as you pour the water over yourself. The water that collects in the pan will dissolve the paper on which the amulet's inscription is written. Divide the water from the pan into three different portions. One portion you must throw into the Nile, or any flowing body of water. One portion you throw into the street. One portion you throw down the drain. Each time you dispose of a portion you must recite the* Fatiha.

Huda stared wide-eyed at her aunt, whom she'd previously considered a fully rational woman.

Do as I say, and with God's permission you'll marry soon after. You'll see.

Five potential grooms made inquiries the following month.

One of them was a colleague of Huda's from the bank, a skinny, simpering young man with a lisp. She could not bring herself even to give him her telephone number, lying to him that she had already reached an agreement with someone.

Another was a young engineer from the neighborhood, whose mother had telephoned Karima with the request to pay a call. Karima despised the woman, though, having heard all manner of gossip about her and Fouad the jeweler. Hoping that none of the neighbors would contradict the lie, she informed her with regret that Huda—ever headstrong!—had insisted on a hiatus from suitors.

One man came highly recommended by Huda's paternal uncle's wife's sister. A meeting was arranged, but in the end, he wasn't overly charmed by Huda herself upon meeting her.

There was a young accountant who was about to accept a position in Saudi Arabia, a double transition that no one could envision Huda enduring, least of all Huda.

And finally, there was the brave Ehab. Despite Huda having

refused him once before, he decided to test her weary waters again—at the safe distance allowed by maternal inquiries.

Karima was ecstatic. Being intimate friends with Ehab's mother, she had supported him as a candidate the first time around: *The family you know is better than the family you don't know.* Ehab's was a good family, a respectable family, with just enough money to qualify him as an acceptable candidate. And what's more, what simply could not be overlooked, his mother had been beneficiary of his maiden aunt's assets.

Ehab now possessed a large apartment in Garden City, of all places.

"Could we hope for a better part of town than Garden City?" Karima asked no one in particular.

Ehab. Huda had mocked him in their youth for his protruding overbite and jutting ears. Was this, then, to be the man? This balding accountant would hold a husband's authority over her? She would entrust her life and welfare to this rat-eyed man with the high, nervous laugh? Her children would bear that thin little name?

Garden City.

"Close," Karima murmured, her voice coaxing. "You would still be close."

Sitting at her vanity table, she could no longer look at herself in the mirror. Surely a prettier face would garner a finer catch than Ehab. She laid her cheek against the cold glass of the tabletop, watching as teardrops splashed and pooled on its surface. Could it be that she deserved no better than this man?

She heard her parents arguing, their voices tangling with the din of the television.

Her father's voice was indistinct, her mother's clear as she screeched, "You'd be content having her sit by your side till

you die, leaving her with no husband, no house, no children!
You're selfish!"

This was followed by the sound of the front door thudding
into place and her father's cane tapping in the stairwell.

Delaying her surrender was merely prolonging the agony.
She wanted peace. To sit with her family and laugh again, the
way they always had before. What was she waiting for, anyway?
A rescue? The 'Antar of childhood legends to come snatch her
up, sword swinging?

Hers was not a remarkable story. Of her friends, only Nuha
could claim happiness with her spouse. Of the rest, each
traded stories no better or worse than Huda's. The only real
difference was that Ehab was . . . physically distasteful. Was
she so surface a person that she would discard a perfectly nice
man on the basis of looks alone? As her mother said, *Looks?*
What are looks? What, you think our family is so beautiful?

And after all, she had been refused on that basis herself.
She presented this question to herself as she followed the
shaykh's directives for dissolving the amulet. She stood in the
deep porcelain tub, slowly pouring the warm water over herself. She watched as the water sheeted over her chest and nip-
ples, the soft stretch of her belly, and the wide, warm thighs to
drip loudly into the metal pan that held the paper. The ink
inscription blurred then ran together, obscuring the secrets
once etched there. The thin paper squirmed momentarily at
the bottom of the pan, then floated to the top, surrendering to
the water's warmth, melting away to nothingness. Huda squatted to empty the first third of its contents as the *shaykh* had
instructed. She breathed deeply, encountering, as she crouched,
her own damp scent. She watched the inky water escape into
the murky underworld of the drain; exiting, it seemed to her,
without regret.

The night that she came to her decision, she sat for what seemed like hours at her window, the room behind her darkened, her elbows cushioned by her favorite pillow as she leaned on the hard windowsill. Sulayman Gohar Square shifted and swayed to its accustomed rhythms. She watched and listened to the familiar sounds of the souq, wondering what it would be like to peer thus from another windowsill at an unfamiliar neighborhood.

Um Basim, as was her habit, was venting her aggressions on the slim farmer who in early summer occupied the eastern edge of the souq with his anemic mule and his cart full of Ismailiya strawberries. Um Basim, her fat feet jammed into cheap vinyl pumps, her homemade blouse laboring to contain her generous bosom, had a weakness for the tiny bloodred berries and a passion for dispute. Over and over she would insist that the beleaguered vendor tampered with the ancient iron scales that perched on the cart's edge during business hours. Night after night she would take the bag full of strawberries to at least two other vendors in the souq for comparison weighing, her red-veined cheeks streaming with the sweat of her efforts. Her truculent screeching could be heard even with the windows tightly shuttered.

Huda sat shaking her head, watching the embattled strawberry seller, wondering if Um Basim's business was worth the belittling and the nasty accusations. The farmer finally accepted from Um Basim the three-pound notes, kissed them, and tucked them away in the folds of his tattered gelabiyya. He regarded her thoughtfully as she hobbled away on shoes too flimsy to support her daunting frame. She could be heard muttering to herself all the way to her flat at the far end of Sherbini Street, overlooking the Sixth of October Bridge.

Abu Badr the fruit seller waited until she was out of earshot before calling out to the diminutive farmer, "She puts up a pretty good fight for someone who shits strawberries, eh?"

The souq exploded in laughter.

A cloud of dust and the sound of prepubescent voices raised in anger arose from a street soccer scuffle. 'Amr and Tarek from the building across the street swore on their mother's life that neither was responsible for the glaring foul against the bloody-shinned Kamal Husayn. Huda watched, loving ten-year-old 'Amr's innate ability to lie with flair. 'Abd al-Samad the army captain, who'd lost his arm and his patience in '73, flung open his peeling, lopsided shutters and drenched the small group in a waterfall of invectives. He ended his tirade with a fierce, *Go home and help your mothers!* The boys began their game anew, their fight forgotten, united by a common enemy.

'Aziz, the emaciated boy who worked for Tahir the butcher, watched them. He leaned wistfully on the long handle of the squeegee he was using to push the soap and water over the white tiles of the corner shop. Huda observed his muscles contracting and twisting as he imagined his own responses to each pass of the half-deflated ball. His reveries continued until the voluminous Tahir, cleaver in hand, shouted at him to resume his duties.

At the far end of the souq, 'Am 'Irfan the grocer had come out of his narrow shop to sit on a folding chair next to Abu Badr's fruit stand. His belly-jiggling laugh resounded up and down Sherbini Street. Huda leaned her hand against her cheek, watching as the old man pulled the glasses off his nose and let them rest on his gigantic potbelly as he wiped the tears from his eyes. She wondered what it was Abu Badr could have said to inspire such mirth, but resigned herself to never knowing.

Both men fell silent as Nariman 'Abd al-Bari crossed the open square and passed by them, hugging a stack of books to her chest. Huda, too, watched her walk as if transfixed. What was it about her? Her beauty was simple, understated, tempered. Her skirt was long enough not to be daring, her blouse loose enough not to accentuate her lavish curves. Her hair was uncovered but not sprayed or teased in any way. She wore it almost carelessly in a thick plait that bounced from shoulder blade to shoulder blade like a hypnotist's charm.

The effect she had on the vendors of Sulayman Gohar Square was devastating. As had occurred daily since she could remember, Huda witnessed the moment of silence as Nariman passed. When she had disappeared into her building, a collective exhalation swept through the souq. Huda watched no less than seven married men exchange knowing looks of longing before each one went on about his business.

She, too, then, was destined to be the woman a man came home to, not she whom he desired.

She would never know true love, would only listen to its echoes in love songs.

She rose from her position at the window, clutching her pillow as she latched the shutters into place. Slowly, she walked to the doorway of the living room, watching as her parents stared at the television, her father visibly daydreaming, her mother completely transfixed by the actions of the soap opera's heroine.

"I will marry Ehab," she said simply.

But neither of them heard her, and so she walked all the way into the room and took the remote out of her mother's hand. She punched the "off" button and faced them.

"I will marry Ehab," she repeated, her mouth having gone suddenly dry.

Her mother launched into a stream of ululations, hefting herself out of the chair to kiss her daughter on both cheeks, tears of relieved joy pouring out of her eyes.

Al-hamdu lillah, al-hamdu lillah, al-hamdu lillah, she cried over and over, as she went to call the future in-laws.

Her father held his position on the couch, gazing at her, then motioned for her to come and sit down next to him. He said nothing, only encircled her with his arm and kissed her left temple, stroking her hair with his fingers. He pretended he didn't see her tears.

The engagement was brief.

From time to time, Ehab would appear at the door to take her out. His mother waited in the backseat of his limping Lada, leaving the front seat for her significantly larger counterpart.

The two mothers would chaperone together so as not to be bored. They would sit and discuss curtains and carpets and the price of major appliances for the soon-to-be-newlyweds' apartment, while Huda and her fiancé would sit in silence eating ice cream.

Listening as their mothers laughed.

If she had understood the compromise, she would never have agreed.

It was Wagdy who paid for her share of the furniture. One thousand two hundred fifty hours over a blazing stove—his hands chafed by licking flames, his joints throbbing, his hair and skin and clothes reeking of grease and garlic—paid for:

The bedroom suite.

The dining room suite.

The living room and dining room rugs.

The curtains.

The couch and matching coffee and end tables.

It was impossible to expect him to pay for a ticket home in addition to this gift, her brother Omar explained, ashamed that he had not mustered the necessary monies. His two little boys leapt and tumbled over him as he spoke softly to Huda. She would have to tell Mama, he was saying.

But Huda had stopped listening.

Wagdy's arrival had been the only imagined pleasure in the whole vast charade.

Now there was not even that.

She stood for what seemed like hours before the bathroom sink, whispering to the water as it swirled into the drain.

An insidious angst settled over the Dokki apartment, seeping into the skimming cracks and flaking cornices.

Not only was Wagdy not coming home for the wedding, Huda was leaving. She was leaving Karima all alone with a dying man in a crumbling home.

Now, with each day advancing on the agreed-upon date, Karima could be found mopping at her eyes. Angry, Baba demanded to know if this was some new realization, or if she had simply forgotten reality throughout the long parade of suitors.

But Huda understood. Paused outside of Karima's bedroom, she listened to the sounds of the souq mingling with the suppressed sobs. Karima had known all along that she could not admit this pain until after the groom had been secured.

If she had acknowledged it any earlier, she would never have been able to let her daughter go.

When the door to the Garden City flat closed behind them, and Huda was left alone with Ehab for the first time, she was unequipped to pretend.

No matter how tightly she closed her eyes, she could not dispel his sweating image; the way the damp hair at the nape of his neck leaked perspiration onto his collar, or the creeping stains beneath his armpits.

So that when he leaned over to kiss her, she shrank from his searching lips.

Another man might have forced himself on her.

But the look on her face was enough to quash even the ability, if not the intention.

He withdrew from her in silence, refusing to respond even when she guiltily offered him tea from the crystal glasses Karima had purchased twenty-three years before.

❧ ❧ ❧ ❧ ❧

Huda leans on an elbow, a manicured nail tracing the logo on the coffee mug. Guilt has snaked into each sentence she utters; her voice is riddled with it. *It isn't Ehab's fault, after all,* she murmurs. *He isn't a bad man. He just isn't . . . the man.*

I light a cigarette to distract the consuming silence. Huda stares at the smoke's hollow ballet as it climbs toward the ceiling. She speaks in a near-whisper.

Last night . . . we call it the Night of Entry, when a girl becomes a woman. It is, you know, a point of honor for men to have done their . . . duty on this night. He is already having to endure the questions of his family and mine. It will be the topic of the day across the family phone lines.

This is why he was so angry this morning, so ashamed. This is why he left.

It isn't his fault.

She stares at me, an ancient weariness devouring her eyes. *I suppose it is mine. . . .*

* * * * *

A netherworld of exotic treasure lies braided tightly in among the city's Medusan snakes. The Khan al-Khalili bazaar is itself Aladdin's lamp—the grubby exterior belies the magical contents; a bit of tender coaxing, and the secrets are revealed. Treasure! A thousand trinkets and adornments, all totally superfluous and startlingly tempting.

To reach the ethereal contents of the bazaar it is necessary to wade through a heaving sea of humanity. Claustrophobic, crammed, dizzied with its own congestion, al-Azhar Square is a dripping human watercolor, its colors swirling in and through each other. The imposing administration building of al-Azhar—the great and ancient center for Islamic learning— occupies the square's western border. Facing this structure are the towering spires and mighty arches of al-Husayn Mosque. Between these two impressive edifices is the southern face of the bazaar, lined with restaurants and coffee shops, which presents the courtyard's final border.

Clerics drift in and out of al-Azhar, projecting an air of learned transcendence over the mêlée. Pilgrims and locals mill about al-Husayn, taking off shoes, putting on shoes, entering and exiting in an endless flood. Tourists with fanny packs and water bottles, eyes glued to camera shutters, endeavor to endure the crush of people. Malaysian women, students of al-Azhar, walk about in little flocks, billowing white *khimars* enveloping their petite forms.

Six- or seven-year-old shoeshine boys, fatigued eyes lost in filthy faces, lug their boxes and brushes, circulating throughout the crowds.

Thursday nights always guarantee at least three or four

wedding parties posing for pictures in the square with the great mosque as a background.

Evenings are when strains of music waft out above the crowds: Al-Fishawi, the bazaar's corner café, is attended by a grizzled old man strumming an oud, singing alone a plaintive love song, or joined by raucous clapping and the loud, grateful laughter of overworked men.

Meg and I go to Al-Fishawi's often. We sit down at the rickety aluminum tables, order our Turkish coffees, and listen hard and long. Night falls subtly over such a press of souls, sidling up ever so slyly, such that we are surprised to find the lights of al-Husayn Mosque shining above us. The oud player lifts his deft fingers from the strings, his song in momentary submission to the muezzin's sunset summons.

Some days we head exclusively for the silver shops. Mirrored walls give off the illusion that the treasures within are endless. Bangles and bracelets, rings and key chains, necklaces, pillboxes, candy dishes, trays, tea services, colossal prayer beads inscribed with as many of the Beautiful Names of God as each giant bead can accommodate. . . .

Other days we try on gorgeous *gelabas*, of heavy taffeta with beautiful, hand-placketed braiding. The garments sneer at our plainness as we peer into the murky mirrors, shoving our hair atop our heads, turning left and right. The beauty of these gelabas demands that the body within be a wraithlike Shahrazade dripping palace jewels, not these unadorned creatures whose frayed blue jeans cuffs pout beneath the hems.

There are brass shops, with enormous tiered platters engraved with birds or swirling Arabic script, or legions of Pharoahs issuing edicts. Gigantic planters, coffee tables, pitchers, and decorative knives rise in daunting layers from floor to too-low ceiling.

Inhabiting the woodshops, giant mother-of-pearl inlaid headboards, intricate screens, and massive mirrors overwhelm the eye. Tall-backed chairs and couches appear at once cripplingly uncomfortable yet somehow seductive.

The gold shops offer a thousand charms to dangle temptingly from the chest. Hieroglyphic cartouches reduce a name to entrancing timeless symbols. Arabic charms, in complex and delicate calligraphy, quote portions of the Qur'an. Great lapis lazuli eyes of Horus grant protection from the Evil Eye the ancient Egyptian way.

The thin alleyways curl in and around each other. *Shisha* smoke hangs like a gauzy veil over the whole area, smelling richly of burnt molasses or apple tobacco.

There is nothing for it but to get lost, then. To wander in, trusting that one will wander out eventually, with the where-exactly of it not mattering. Enriched, even if not laden with all of Ali Baba's plunder.

✦ ✦ ✦ ✦ ✦

We are stuck on the Sixth of October Bridge. The taxi is smaller than usual, one of those Russian jobbies still puttering away after four-odd decades of hard use. 'Abd al-Halim Hafiz pines away from a cassette deck that lacks its faceplate. The heat of the air is a thick, sliceable hot. I shift, impatient, choking on exhaust.

I notice the driver studying me in the rearview mirror.

He is well over fifty, with a shock of bushy gray hair and either a new beard still in that nasty in-between stage or a seriously neglected shaving regimen. His body overwhelms the seat he occupies. His legs look as though they'd been shoved against their will down between the dash and the seat's front edge. Oozing side slabs rebel against the thin seams of his polyester shirt, and seem to get in the way of his arm when he shifts gears. His meaty hands render the small steering wheel toylike in comparison.

But he is grinning at me with a startling grin.

American? he asks.

Yes, I say.

He nods thoughtfully. *You know Bruce Willis?*

I hesitate. *The actor?*

Now he's an actor. I knew him when he was shining shoes.

I give him a wary smile.

We go way back, he and I, the driver says.

I laugh, dismissing him.

Oh yes, he insists. *He was my neighbor in Boulaq. We used to play street soccer together, but God was generous with him and now he's famous over there in Amreeka.*

He watches me laughing in the mirror. *You don't believe me? When you get back there, you go to Hollywood and say, "Bruce,*

Bruce: Medhet Salih sends his regards." And don't you know, the doors will swing right open for you!

It is about then that he breaks into an amazing belly laugh that literally shakes the immobile cab. The sheen of Cairo frustration that had gathered across my brow is wiped gently away.

* * * * *

Huda often seems to listen for the sound of the elevator's iron door. She intercepts me in the hall as I am getting home from school, and pulls me inside for afternoon tea.

The ritual is a long and sweet one. I sip oversugared Lipton tea from a thin crystal glass. Somehow, she always seems to have desserts on hand, *basboussa* or petits fours, *konaffa* with cream or rich layered cakes. I am consistently surprised by her dauntless desire to spoil me, wondering what it is I provide in return.

At first, it seems that our relationship is merely a matter of my getting to practice my Arabic and her getting a minor distraction until Ehab's return from work. Later, after many, many cups of tea, and the sound of Huda's soft laughter baptizing the still-preening furniture and drapes . . . tugged from the mazes of my groping sentences, I find that I have a friend.

On the first afternoon, only a few weeks or so after the wedding, I see that she is in a stupor of boredom. A restructuring at the bank where she'd interned has deprived her of her work. She complains of her futile job search, thwarted constantly by her lack of connections. She peppers me with questions about school and fellow students, famished for conversation.

Her hair is braided in a tight French braid. She notices me looking at it, and pats it self-consciously. It's been too long since she's gone to the coiffeur, she murmurs. She complains of frizz.

I ask her why a woman who covers her hair still goes to the coiffeur.

She widens her eyes, but I see her tell herself that I'm a foreigner and know no better. *I don't stop doing my hair just because I wear* higab, she says. *I'm still a woman.*

But because of Ehab, you can't be a woman in front of other men?

Ehab? she repeats, frowning her confusion.

He won't, you know, let you show your hair in public. . . .

She laughs incredulously. *You think I wear it because he makes me?* She put it on after she and Ehab became engaged, she says. She thought if she could show God that she is really a good girl with pure intentions, He'd make the marriage easier for her.

I ask her if she's happy with God's end of the deal.

She looks at her hands. *At least I know I've done the right thing, met all my obligations. Sometimes the thing we love is bad for us, and the thing we hate is good for us. It takes us a long time to figure it out.*

Are you talking about Ehab or the higab?

She laughs. *Ehab, of course. The* higab *is easy.*

Huda sips at her tea, chuckling.

What? I say.

You thought I wear higab *because Ehab ordered it.* She shakes her head, smiling. *I wouldn't wear diamonds, if he told me to.*

She asks about my family. We have in common two older brothers. She doesn't understand when I tell her I only see them on holidays or for family weddings.

Aren't you in the same country?

I shrug. *Different states.*

Why did they leave the place where they were born?

I consider this for a long while. Why does any of us? *So that they could stand on their own two feet. Be independent.*

She is frowning deeply. *It must be hard for your mother, with all of you scattered. . . .*

I laugh. *It would be harder for her to have all of us living at home.*

Huda raises her eyebrows.

I regale her with a few stories of the teenaged years of my

clan. I leave her wide-eyed and tsking. She leans forward, laying a hand on my shoulder.

Don't you know that whatever grief you cause your mother will appear in the behavior of your own children . . . but worse?

I study her features. She is very serious. I tell her that my mother's version of that curse was always, "I hope you have children just like you." To which I would always answer, "I'm *never* having children."

Huda is shocked. She murmurs something prayerful that I don't quite catch. *You must never wish such a terrible thing upon yourself.*

Thinking, I tap my cigarette against the heavy crystal ashtray. *My mom made a lot of sacrifices for us. Sacrifices we mostly didn't deserve. I don't believe I have it in me to do the same for anyone.*

Huda looks at me thoughtfully, her features gentle, her gaze almost patronizing. *I think you'll surprise yourself one day.*

The warm silence between us is broken only by the clang of the elevator door, signaling Ehab's return.

* * * * *

There are days when a diaphanous haze of smog hangs like a waiting ghoul overhead, seeming to slink along, hovering just above my shoulders when I walk. I am not alone in this haunting. On these gray and grayer days, it seems that every passerby suffers a seething disquiet. The smell of the air is metallic and burnt, as though the city herself is teetering at the mouth of a massive incinerator, the contents of which are dubious at best.

Ambling along solemn sidewalks, shopping for necessities, tending to the tasks of perpetual routine, Cairenes utter forced pleasantries as they mask a bridling impatience to return home.

On such days, it is with a rich relief that I enter the foyer of number 10 Hasan Murad Street. There is an exhalation particular to the foyer: a sigh ripe with the promise of home yet content enough with the nearness present in the building's gaping entryway. It is a sigh that purges the soul of the chafing of the outside world, the unfamiliar, clearing room for all that is known and comfortable to drift back in.

On this particular day, I have just pressed the elevator button when I am joined in the foyer by a woman laden with groceries and an overstuffed leather satchel. She is short, several inches shorter than I am, and I am by no means tall. Her hair is littered with gray and cropped to just above her small ears. Intense eyes glisten from their housing in a face of softly proportioned features. Her every movement, even the waiting stance before the coquettish elevator, is charged with a crackling, suppressed energy.

A broad smile reveals nicotine-ravaged teeth. *You live here?*

I nod, infected immediately by the welcoming smile.

How long since you punched the button? she asks, motioning with her chin at the silent elevator shaft.

Too long, I reply.

She gives a knowing nod, then bellows at a decibel I would never have expected to emanate from within her slight frame: *'Am 'Abd al-Latif!*

The metal door to the *bowwab*'s room swings open with a recalcitrant creak, and out pops the head of 'Abd al-Latif's slim, pale wife. *He went on an errand; he'll be right back.* The head disappears; the door scrapes definitively closed.

The woman nods again. *Of course he did. He's probably in there watching a soap opera,* she mutters, stepping toward the staircase. *Come on then; thus humans are humbled by machines.*

Her latent, pulsing energy floods out of her during the ascent in the form of a chatty, rapid-fire interrogation. I reel slightly, unused to speaking more than I listen. All that I have been able to divine of her in the largely one-sided conversation is that her name is Afkar and she is a professor of litera-ture at Cairo University.

Dr. Afkar's efforts, combined with the climb, have left her slightly winded. I offer to carry a shopping bag or two, but she laughs at me, a husky, smoker's laugh that underscores a fierce pride in caring for herself.

She deviates from our circular climb at the fourth floor, and I extend my hand, so warmed by her acquaintance that I find myself dreading the chill silence of the stairwell. But Dr. Afkar looks at me as though stunned. *You can't possibly be con-sidering going home!*

I pause, never having considered an alternative.

Don't you smell it?

I frown, questioning her.

She opens the palm of her hand, in a motion suggesting I should pull free the outermost sack. I open it curiously, then meet Dr. Afkar's dancing gaze. She gestures at the small, folded bag within the plastic sack. *I've just come from 'Abd al-Ma'bud's. Surely you wouldn't turn down a cup of freshly ground Turkish coffee? Not even an American could be so ill-advised.*

The scent is sultry and beckoning, the commingling of cardamom and cacao like the swirling of scents on two entwined and sated bodies.

It is at the hands of Dr. Afkar, and while seated on her faded sofa, that I discover the precise cup of Turkish coffee. *Precise*, in coffee contexts, means not too much sugar, not too little. Rather, it is the perfect harmonization of sweet and bitter. It strikes me that this harmony, this spanning of tension and resolve, cardamom-laced and compressed in delicate demitasse, renders the *precise* cup of Turkish coffee a truly great facilitator of conversation.

Dr. Afkar chain-smokes, never lighting a cigarette until having offered me one. I smoke, but I cannot keep pace with the swift flow of filter to mouth to ashtray, sip, exhale, sip, smoke, extinguish, extract a slim white replacement, coax from a reluctant lighter a short burst of flame, repeat.... When paused in thought, she runs short, rounded fingers through her thick hair. She laughs sharply, asks piercing questions, and listens with relish. Like a skilled, efficient surgeon, she has plunged sterile tweezers into my innards and plucked out my wide-eyed essence.

We talk earnestly and thoroughly, and I suddenly find myself telling her about Huda. She speaks as though to reassure me. *In traditional families like your friend Huda's, marriage is wholly an issue of socioeconomics.*

Socioeconomics, I repeat.

She is nodding. *In scouting out a prospective family, elements such as reputation and social standing, the potential bridegroom's job, his prospects, and his ability to provide take priority. The man* himself, the substance of him, the marrow of him, the "who" of him . . . this is often relegated to the irrelevant. After all, if the family is good, it can usually be assumed that the man is good. Prudent generations have imparted on us the wisdom that love is surprisingly finite, and it surely does little in the way of buying one's daily bread.

She observes my skepticism with a sharp stare. *Think of it this way: a scrappy sort of social Darwinism. Emotions aside, it's all in a woman's best interest. The best gene pool for her future cubs.*

I sigh sadly. *But this man . . . surely she doesn't deserve such a man,* I say, imagining it all again.

She leans forward on her elbows, sepia eyes flashing. *I will tell you one thing. He is an ugly man? This means nothing. Maybe he will treat her well and she will come to see him as a prince. I was married to a man so beautiful that women would stop in their tracks to watch him pass by. Women would openly flirt with him when we walked down the street together. But from the way he treated me, wallahi, I felt that I awoke each morning next to the devil himself!*

It is only then that I realize her tiny hands are void of rings.

أفكار

Afkar

Another was asked, "Who are your people?"
He replied, "I am of a people who, when they love, they die."

—IBN QUTAYBAH,
d. 889 c.e.,
The Book of Poetry and Poets

وقيل لآخر: مِمن أنت؟

فقال: مِن قوم إذا أحبوا ماتوا. . .

The commotion on al-Gadawi Alley had seemed normal at first, but suddenly voices were raised and men were shouting. Afkar's mother, who had been drawn to the front balcony, started screaming and slapping her cheeks.

"Your father, your father is beating up that neighbor boy," she cried.

Afkar ran to the balcony, and her heart convulsed, shuddered, then shrank in her chest. Her fingers clutched at the balcony rail for support as she swayed, disbelieving what she saw.

Salah lay crumpled on the sidewalk, his hands shielding his face as her father kicked him brutally in the stomach, in the thighs, in the back. Various voices from among the onlookers intimated to him that restraint might be welcome at any time. But no one attempted to hold him back. Only her father's voice was constant, though the timbre rendered it unrecognizable, as he issued a torrent of insults.

Son of a whore.

Son of sixty dogs.

Faggot.

Salah could only moan, writhing in the dust and discarded food containers littering the sidewalk.

"Get up, you bastard, and fight like a man. You think you're a man? Do you?"

And he unleashed another round of kicks.

"Talk to my daughter, you son of a filthy whore? Lay a hand on my daughter? I will raise your family's dead, just to kill them all again, do you hear me?"

It was on hearing these words that Afkar fled the balcony for her room and the protection of her sister. She had never dreamed her father capable of violence. He had never struck any of them; he barely ever raised his voice.

Who had seen them?

Oh, they had grown careless. Desire had made them careless. She should have known better than to dare to hold his hand in the street. But still . . . they had been on the other side of Roda Island, drinking cold Coca-Colas from the tiny kiosk by the 'Abbas Bridge. Far enough from the neighborhood that they should have been safe.

But her father's friends were many, and Cairo was a sea of eyes.

She burrowed into Maha's embrace, waiting.

Her father's shoes thudded against the stairs as he ascended, two steps at a time. The door swung open and he demanded of the house in general, "Where is that daughter of a dog?"

And then he was pulling her away from her sister by her long, soft hair, and slapping her face over and over. "How dare you?" he shouted. "Have you no regard for your reputation, for the reputation of this family? Are you out of your mind?"

Afkar sobbed and wailed, ducking his hand, clutching at his ankles. "Baba. I love him, Baba. . . ." She repeated this over and over, as though in rhythm with his blows.

When he saw the blood dripping from her lip, he pushed her away and fell exhausted onto the bed the two sisters shared. He stared at his favorite daughter, the light of his eyes, in disbelieving sadness. He had never hit her. He had never in his life even considered hitting her.

He walked miserably out of the room, leaving her to be comforted by her mother and sister. But the sound of her sobbing inundated every room of the small apartment. He listened angrily at first, then curiously, wondering what had suddenly transformed his adoring little girl into a young woman so wracked with passion that she would profess her love even when being beaten.

They say it's harder to raise girls than boys. The parents' reward is greater because raising a virtuous girl is more difficult than any other task.

Did I fail?

He knew he had not. She was a good girl, a smart girl, who could quote Khansa' just as easily as she could embroider, who could write verse on any subject from custard apples to backgammon, whose laugh was like mist off the Alexandrian surf.

But when the grocer, the *grocer*, had whispered to him the news that had already circulated around the neighborhood, that Afkar 'Abd al-Raziq had been seen clutching the arm of Salah Hamid, all the way over on Roda Island . . .

The vision had evaporated from his eyes, and all he saw between blinks was pitch black. He thought for a moment that the shock of it had blinded him. And then he'd dropped the bag that Abu Hasan had just finished preparing for him, the olives and eggs and soft white cheese thudding to the floor of the shop as he rushed out in search of that boy. That boy.

That boy whose balcony butted up against that of his daughters' room.

He had warned them. Warned them to keep the shutters permanently closed.

But Afkar . . .

She was strong-willed, that one. Always having to try things out for herself before she took anyone's word for anything.

Afkar.

Afkar would sit late into the night, holding her book before her, staring at the same paragraph, waiting for Salah to crack open the shutters of his room and edge out onto the balcony, his eyes shining in the dimness, an eager smile stretched across his lips.

"Good evening."

"Good evening," she would reply, the breath catching in her throat.

Their brief conversations would take place in whispers. To her, their voices carried throughout the neighborhood like exploding firecrackers, so terrified was she of discovery. To talk thus with a boy was far beyond any normal crime like bringing home a poor mark in math or fighting with her sister. But . . . Salah was not just any boy.

His were the blazing coal eyes that she saw before sleep overtook her, and as soon as morning light invaded her dreaming. His olive skin, his dark, wavy hair, the tiny dimple in his chin. The mole on his right cheek. Just like Omar Sharif— before he got it removed to act in the West.

She tried to remember at what point she'd realized she was in love. Salah had lived his whole life in the adjacent apart- ment building, teasing her and her sister as they walked to school. Throwing various projectiles at them. Yanking their dangling braids. Taunting. Abusing. She had come home cry- ing after encounters with him throughout her primary and middle school years.

He was several years her senior, and had taken a govern- ment appointment right after high school. She had not seen him since then, really. He rose later in the day than he had risen as a student, came home later, ran with a different crowd. He was part of the adult world now, and could not be troubled even to tease a young schoolgirl.

So it came as a surprise to her, the day when she was on her knees scrubbing the tiled floor of the balcony, that she looked up to find him standing on his own balcony, staring at her with a gaze so smoldering that she felt her skin would burst into flame.

She was stunned.

He had never looked at her before with anything but con- tempt. And now he was devouring her with his eyes. She self- consciously pulled the bodice of her gelabiyya higher over her chest, and before she could restrain it, found that her hand had reached to smooth back the wisps of ebony hair escaping her long, thick braid.

That gesture was all it took. Salah pursued her then with the single-mindedness of a man possessed. He would position the record player such that the croonings of 'Abd al-Halim Hafiz would pierce the balcony shutters. She knew that the lyrics were aimed specifically at her, and she would press her forehead against the shutters as she murmured the refrains.

It seemed to her that only the Arab poets whose collections bent the shelves of her father's bookcases had loved thus. Qays for Lubna, Jamil for Buthayna, Kuthayyir for 'Azza . . . they haunted her as she sat throughout the night, her pen gliding soundlessly across sheet after sheet of notebook paper, her fingernails tapping out meters as she bent and tugged her longing into measured hemistiches.

Afkar became obsessed with how best to position herself night and day by the balcony doors, so that if by chance he should appear she would be waiting.

The first time that he proposed they meet she was sick with terror. Her mother had warned her about what happened to the kind of girl who would talk to a strange boy in the street. It would ruin her reputation permanently. At its core, every neighborhood could be reduced to hundreds of pairs of eyes, watching, waiting breathlessly for any morsel of gossip. *She looked the wrong way at a man*, or *She was seen clasping the hand of a man*, or, most unforgivable of all: *She rode in a car with a man*. In her gentle voice, Afkar's mother explained that such a girl would never attain a respectable husband. Such a girl was responsible for the gossip about her, for she had put herself in a questionable position. No matter what, she must be above reproach.

And having thus spoken, her mother would give each of her two daughters a loving pat on the cheek. *A girl is a jewel to be protected at all times.*

Where, then, could they go that was distant enough to eliminate the danger . . . and yet close enough that they could manage the trip?

That is when they began meeting on the far side of Roda

Island, near the 'Abbas Bridge, renamed Giza since the Revolution but still known to most as 'Abbas. The corniche there was wide and quiet, nothing like the one that ran the length of Garden City and into downtown, all the way past the Broadcast Center and beyond. Here they could walk along, gaze out at the eternally flowing river, and talk. It was a thirty-minute walk from the heart of Bab al-Khalq, or a brief minibus ride if there was enough allowance money for it.

The problem for Afkar was that her excuses to be out of the house were few, and so she had often to feign illness and meet him in the hours when she would normally be in school. As soon as her mother left for work at the bleak law office on Tala't Harb Street, Afkar would dress quickly, indulging her already flushed cheeks in the lightest dusting of rouge. Then she would ease down the stairs in her bare feet so that Um Ahmad, the neighbor one flight down, wouldn't hear her footfalls and peer out from the peephole.

She would walk the route she normally took to go to the grocer's or the dressmaker's, then duck quickly into an alley just past Ahmad Maher Square. Through Bab al-Luq and into Tahrir Square, along Qasr al-'Ayni Street until it ended in the Salah Salim thoroughfare that led in one direction toward the Citadel and in the other toward the Nile and Roda Island.

The Nile.

Now that she loved, she saw in its swift, dark waters the face of her beloved, and heard in its rhythms his whispered promises.

It was she who arrived first, that first time they had agreed to meet. She stood nervously on the sidewalk, watching the traffic inch over the bridge. Lumbering ferries spurted black exhaust as they carried passengers to opposite riverbanks. White felucca sails shuddered in the cooling breeze.

She glanced repeatedly at her wristwatch, feeling at any moment that she would bolt and run for home. Meeting a boy, lying to her parents, slinking out of the house like a thief: she could not believe what she had allowed herself to do.

Salah was the one, the one for whom she'd been born. She knew it. He knew it, for it was he who told her so in words as fervent in their ardor as any spun by the greatest Arab poets—if lacking, after all, in their eloquence.

And then she heard his voice behind her, and every nerve in her body crackled to life.

"Good morning," he said.

She turned, breathless, and found him more beautiful up close than she had dreamed. And she had dreamed of this meeting all day every day and throughout the endless nights since they had agreed to it.

Here they were at last.

Close.

Up close, his eyes shone like polished cherrywood. He looked at her as though he were starved for her, and in that moment she would have done anything for him, anything at all, as long as he promised never to pull his eyes away, never to turn that gaze on anyone else.

They spoke that day of many things. Undying love. The distant future. She would get a secretary's job like her mother just as soon as she got her diploma, and she would save and save, never buying new dresses or even so much as a scoop of ice cream from Groppi's downtown.

Salah's government salary would be adjusted soon enough to keep pace with the rising costs of the new Infitah policy's market economy. In a few more years he would have enough saved to buy an apartment.

Then he could go to her father full of confidence. He would

be able to ask for her hand with the certainty that there was no better man than he for the beautiful daughter of the Arabic teacher 'Abd al-Raziq Al-Basyuni.

But until then, they would meet when they could by the 'Abbas Bridge.

They would exchange longing glances through half-closed shutters.

They passed what notes they could, tossing them over the rails of the nearly adjoined balconies. Afkar wrote to him in perfect literary Arabic, ignoring the mistakes he made in his rush to reply.

Salah paid dearly for the note that missed its mark. It floated nonchalantly down into the tiny alleyway below. Carelessly. As though that tiny slip of paper—in the wrong hands—couldn't ruin their lives. He'd run like a madman, bursting out of his room and through the living room, out the front door. He galloped down the stairs in a headlong charge and out onto the street, then skidded around the back to the alley where 'Abd Allah, the oldest and savviest of the washerwoman Fakiha's seven children, had seen the note fall and pounced on it.

Salah bought his silence that day with two whole pounds. His monthly salary was only twelve, so such a bribe was a fortune. He vowed that after he'd married Afkar he would return to this alley and beat 'Abd Allah until he blinded him or got his money back. Or perhaps both.

But only after he and Afkar were safely married.

The day came sooner than either had expected. For 'Abd al-Raziq was known throughout the neighborhood as an honorable man with a respectable family, as well as a peace-loving man. Although he actually fantasized about it, he had no basis upon which to kill the young Salah. And after all, the two families had been neighbors for a lifetime.

'Abd al-Raziq was only forty-four, but his thick, wavy hair was already mostly gray. He was a tall man with broad shoulders. His wide coal eyes had dimmed after years of reading in low light, and now were imprisoned behind wire-rimmed glasses that made him look even older. He taught Arabic at the Abu Bakr al-Siddiq High School for Boys. It was a government school in a particularly impoverished portion of the al-Khalifa district. His students adored him, because it never occurred to him to slam his pointer stick down across their daydreaming knuckles. Nor did he insult and degrade them as did the majority of their other teachers. The parents of his students adored him because he did not omit vital information from the classroom lessons and then insist that the boys have him for private lessons to cover what was missing. Such tutorials were the only way that teachers could supplement their negligible government salaries. But 'Abd al-Raziq thought it criminal to force the boys into lessons their families couldn't afford, when most of them came to school in patched shoes and threadbare uniforms.

There were those boys who, despite his sincerest efforts, could not comprehend even a hemistich of *Majnun Layla*, much less navigate the grammatical pitfalls of the hollow verbs. These enlisted his aid as a private tutor, paying only two pounds a month for the privilege of his weekly evening house calls.

And although he was enduringly exhausted, he was a man who was blessed with contentment. His mother had chosen his wife, and she had chosen well. Zahra was strong and still beautiful, gentle and slow to criticize. Her greatest pleasure was to sit with her needlework on the high couch while he strummed the love songs of 'Abd al-Wahhab on his oud, or as he read to her from poems composed eleven centuries before, when love stood as elemental as fire or earth.

While every other family in the neighborhood had long since begged, borrowed, or sold off meager assets to attain a television set, 'Abd al-Raziq refused, insisting that there was enough racket in the streets without inviting it into the home.

And so it was that his daughters grew up able to recite ancient poetry as they drifted into sleep, and steeped in the sounds of the oud and their father's low voice, singing love songs to their mother until late, late at night.

When 'Abd al-Raziq appeared at the home of Hamid Subhy with a solution to the scandal, the door swung open to him immediately.

"They'll get married," he said, furious that Salah and his father had not come knocking on his door with the suggestion.

Hamid nodded, having expected just as much. He did play devil's advocate, heeding the objections of his wife. Um Salah never refrained from denigrating those neighbor girls with their open shutters. . . .

"Salah is only newly appointed at the ministry; he is not yet a man. And Afkar is still only a girl," said Hamid, offering tea and being refused.

'Abd al-Raziq frowned menacingly, as menacingly as he could muster. He'd grown tired of playing the part of injured father. "They're old enough to be walking about town garnering gossip. They're old enough to be married. *You* were married at that age."

Hamid couldn't argue with this point. "But I'm sorry to say that Salah has no apartment to offer, and only a meager starting salary."

"They can live here," Afkar's father replied, making a gesture that encompassed the peeling walls and worn carpets, the cheap wooden furniture and the flickering fluorescent lights. He felt a part of him recoil. He wanted to withdraw the words as soon as he'd said them. His daughter . . . he could still smell her hair as she nestled into his lap, her finger tracing the lines as he read to her.

He would have married her to a prince, and even this with whimpering reluctance.

Hamid interrupted his reverie. He was asking about their requests for the *mahr* and the *shebka*. 'Abd al-Raziq regarded him sadly. Hamid was a good man. It wasn't his fault that his son was . . . a boy. They, too, had been boys not so long ago. Hamid had failed only in that he hadn't taught his son the benefits of patience. Yes, he was a good man, but he was also a poor man.

'Abd al-Raziq weighed his options carefully. The boy was not providing an apartment or new furniture. Surely it was reasonable to demand that he pay a respectable bride price.

'Abd al-Raziq started high. "A thousand pounds for the *mahr*."

Hamid paled. It might as well have been a million pounds sterling. His job at the Ministry of Agriculture barely paid him thirty pounds a month. With a lot of maneuvering and the tempered indulgence of Abu Hasan the grocer, he managed to feed Um Salah and the three children.

A thousand pounds. He looked at the floor, clearing his throat nervously. "I—that's beyond my means, my friend," he finally said softly.

'Abd al-Raziq knew that he could just as easily have been in this situation. He certainly had no savings and nothing of value. He ached for Afkar as he bargained with her future father-in-law.

Well, damn her, too. Didn't I give her everything she needed?

He realized at last that he was jealous. Jealous that she was so willing to give away the affection she had always reserved just for him, and to one so . . . He shook his head. How could this boy possibly value her? 'Abd al-Raziq had poured himself into this girl. His wife loved him. But Afkar . . . Afkar had always worshiped him. *"Mama, if you don't mind, please,"* giggled her six-year-old voice, *"I would like to marry Baba. . . ."*

She had always listened to him read with more than the respectful tolerance of her mother and sister. She demanded explanations for the difficult words, she memorized quickly and efficiently, she grinned with a contagious delight at the same passages that he found genius. He closed his eyes tightly, shutting out Hamid's face and the bald neon bulb of the sitting room; he could feel Afkar's ten-year-old fingers interwoven with his own as they walked down the street. *"When I grow up, Baba, I'm going to be a teacher just like you."*

This boy is the one she wants. Could I refuse? Could I break her heart?

'Abd al-Raziq listened distractedly as Hamid bargained the sum down to four hundred pounds, with a *shebka* of at least two hundred. He compromised as regret gnawed at his churning stomach. At least he wanted to secure his daughter's future by demanding a high *muakhr*. She should have the guarantee of a healthy sum of her own money in case Salah chose to divorce her later on. The idea of divorce caused 'Abd al-Raziq to shudder, but the young man's behavior to this point had done little to encourage him. In any case, the *muakhr* was only a promissory note of sorts and would not strain his neighbor Hamid's budget.

After having bargained so hard on the up-front expenses, Hamid could not disagree with the requested *muakhr* of three thousand. He would just make sure that the boy stayed married, so that the dizzying sum could never become an issue.

As he watched 'Abd al-Raziq sighing, Hamid was wondering how he would convince Um Salah to sell off a portion of her gold jewelry. But after all, that's why he'd given it to her in the first place. It certainly didn't enhance her watery, bovine eyes or permanently pursed lips. No, gold was his only investment, and draping it on his wife had been the only way to preserve it. If nothing else, the clinking row of slim bangles that crept up her arm alerted him to her presence before she entered a room.

When the two men finally came to an agreement, they clasped hands and recited the *Fatiha* together to seal their intent.

"*Mabrouk*," Hamid said to him, patting him on the back.

"*Mabrouk*," 'Abd al-Raziq mumbled. Then he grasped Hamid's arm, looking him squarely in the eye. "I could have killed him, you know."

Hamid nodded, taken aback.

"I will kill him if he causes her pain."

Hamid forced a smile, working to reassure himself as much as 'Abd al-Raziq. "Afkar is a good girl. Salah is a good boy. Marriage is a matter of Fate, and this is theirs. It will all work out for the best."

Afkar's joy filled the small flat with light. She fell to her knees beside her father's chair and took to kissing his hands, laughing, kissing both his cheeks.

He placed his palm against the cheek he had struck only last night. "I want you to listen to me for a moment, Afkar."

She curled her legs beneath her and gave her father her full attention.

"Marriage is not easy. And the situation you're going into is far worse than most brides. This . . ." He sighed sadly, looking away. "This is why I wanted to choose your groom. So I could be sure that you would get all the things that you deserve."

"But Baba—"

He raised his hand, stopping her. "Don't interrupt me. I know you're going to say that Salah is all you need. I am telling you it's not true. Until Salah can make enough money to get an apartment, you are going to live under the rule of his mother. The house you are entering is hers, not yours. The *mahr* and *muakhr* I agreed upon for you are far less than a girl of your upbringing and beauty deserves. I cannot deny that I hate this marriage, and I don't feel that any good can come of it. But it is the only option you gave me when you agreed to trade your honor and your reputation for a schoolgirl crush. It's a mistake that I think you'll pay for the rest of your life." He sighed again, patting her head gently. "I hope I'm wrong."

She leaned her head against his knee. "You're wrong, Baba. I know you're wrong. We can make the best of it, Salah and me." She tilted her head back to look at him. "We'll be strong together. You'll see. You'll have beautiful grandchildren you can sit on your lap and read stories to."

He shook his head, wanting to catch the hope in her eyes and preserve it so he could give it to her later on in small doses. "The First Lady has some ideas about family planning that you would be wise to explore."

Afkar blushed. The new initiative had caused a national furor. Jehan Sadat's free birth control pill project was all the women were talking about.

"Now go on and see what your mother's doing. She's in charge from here on out." With that he went back to his book, and Afkar dashed into her mother's room.

Her mother and sister were waiting for her. They all leaned their heads together in an exultant embrace. And whereas each had been crying last night, Afkar's grief infecting them all, her happiness overtook them now.

"I need a dress. The most beautiful dress in all of Egypt!"

The date was set for after the college entrance examinations. It was to be a small family wedding, and it would take place in the home of 'Abd al-Raziq. But for Afkar it might as well have been at the Mena House itself. Wa'il the dressmaker had created a wedding dress that was an exact replica of the film star Mervat Amin's. No matter how intensively they manipulated the figures, 'Abd al-Raziq's budget could not stretch to include the finishing touches, so Afkar and her sister would sit for hours stitching tiny beads into the bodice and pondering aloud what life would be like after the monumental occasion came to pass.

Maha, for her part, was overjoyed. Her sister would be living but one building away. She had been Afkar's confidante from the beginning, and she had lived in terror for the past year, certain that the lovers would be discovered and uncertain as to what would ensue. She had feared disasters boundless and unnamable.

And now . . . everything would be all right. She would look up from her stitching to regard her sister bent, intent, yet clearly lost in daydreams. Maha would smile contentedly.

Afkar was to marry Salah. What could be better?

It was 'Abd al-Raziq who insisted she sit for the test. It was his last dictate before releasing her into Salah's authority, and no manner of protest from Afkar could sway his decision. She had barely studied at all the last six months, first because she was weighted with the burden of an impossible love, and then because she was swept up in wedding preparations and the stitching of exactly one thousand tiny shining beads.

When the results came back and she had performed well enough to gain admittance to the faculty of her choice, she implored her father not to tell. Who would benefit, anyway, when she didn't intend to enroll at all? There would be time when Salah had been promoted for her to go back and see about college. It was time now for real life.

Her mother's employer had very kindly arranged for Afkar to obtain a secretarial position in the office of a colleague. She would be assisting a lawyer appointed as legal advisor to one of the newly formed corporations just stretching their limbs under Infitah. Her pay was fifteen pounds a month—more than Salah was making but less than they needed to contribute to the household and still put something aside for their future. *In sha allah*, it would be enough.

'Abd al-Raziq stared at her, swallowing his frustration. Considering their situation it was probably best. A university education for his daughter was really more his own dreams begging for realization through her. *Idiot. Only an idiot would have gotten caught in broad daylight.* He laughed at himself then, realizing he wasn't as angry about the relationship as he was about their blundering indiscretion.

He shook his head. *Damn that boy. Son of sixty dogs.*

Um Salah was forced to do some major rearranging of her sixty-meter flat. Her initial priority was to remove her remaining sons from the bedroom that claimed the guilty balcony, preventing further mishaps with 'Abd al-Raziq's other loose daughter.

Thus it came about that Salah's parents moved into the bedroom that formerly housed all three boys, and the smaller of the two bedrooms was designated for the newlyweds. The dining room was converted into a bedroom for the two younger brothers, Kamal and Rida.

The ornate dining room table had been sold to pay for the *shebka* after Um Salah refused to sell any more of her gold jewelry. She had surrendered quite enough for the *mahr,* she said, claiming if her gold were touched—and she knew its exact total weight to the gram—she would walk the neighborhood, home by home, telling whoever opened each door about a particular virility problem afflicting Hamid for the past two years. In a rage, Hamid had gone across the street to Zaghlul's Café and returned with three friends who helped him disassemble the massive table and carry it piece by piece down the street to Haj Mahmud's furniture shop. All of this occurred to the remonstrations and melodramatics of his wife, but beyond such verbosity her hands were tied. She had told him to figure out another way to get the money. And the table was among the few things that Hamid had provided—other than his tiny apartment—when the two had entered into perpetually disgruntled matrimony.

Um Salah invited Afkar and her mother to look over the room only once. Afkar mentally measured each wall to determine what of her things would fit the already cramped space. In the end, all she could do was stake out a portion of the wardrobe—enough for an eighth of her trousseau. She would bring the towels she'd embroidered, and the bedspread her mother had made for her.

It was enough, she insisted.

It was all she needed.

And the night finally came, and the door was closed behind them, and they were alone together for the first time ever.

They sheltered under a gossamer canopy—a crack-ridden ceiling and fatigued, fusty walls—and discovered each other in long, exploratory kisses and fierce, clinging embraces.

"Did you ever dream it?" she whispered to him in the dark, tracing her fingertips across the soft incline beneath his ribs.

They lay nose to nose; her hair spilled a black satin pillow beneath his head. He tasted her breath, pulling it into his own lungs. "This is far better than I'd dreamed," he admitted.

"I want nothing more in the world than this," she murmured.

When finally they slept, it was curled together, a tangle of warm limbs, a spent tumble of flowering vines.

When her parents knocked on the door the next morning, Salah answered first. They had left Maha at home, for they came expecting the worst. But Salah had already blushingly surrendered to his mother, who discreetly passed it along to her new in-laws, the towel that he himself had used to wipe the blood from between her soft thighs, hating that he had hurt her, but loving the feeling that she was wholly his at last.

'Abd al-Raziq could not hide his relief. To the last he had doubted the veracity of their innocence. He knew the entire neighborhood shared his suspicions, and he wanted to fling open the shutters and wave that towel out of the window for all to see. In any event, he could now look his neighbors directly in the eye. *But was it worth it . . . ?* He had submitted to this line of thought only a few times throughout the process. And always he answered himself with the conclusion that there had been no other way. No matter how innocent she might have been, the whispers would have haunted Afkar for the rest of her life. What bridegroom would have accepted such a girl, a doubted girl? No, this had been the only way to salvage his daughter's honor. And his.

And despite the circumstances, his daughter was alight with a joy he had never felt or encountered, but merely read about in the ancient poems of true love and its requisite madness.

Perhaps the boy would surprise them all.

Um Salah, having been so called since the birth of her eldest son, had almost forgotten her own name.

Her husband, who needed the constant reminder of that son to tolerate her presence, refused to call her anything else, even in what passed for intimacy between them.

She knew her own shortcomings. Her husband, though useless, was far more attractive than she. Her temper was known as historic, her scorn for Hamid bottomless, her vocabulary limited to carping.

What she had done of merit in her thirty-six years was to bear three boys who resembled their father.

Her love for Salah was mighty in force and depth.

Her jealousy knew no bounds.

Afkar had suspected as much. Her mother had warned her about Um Salah, providing her with a whole repertoire of the proper responses to denigration, humiliation, and psychological torture. Zahra had used them to deal with her own mother-in-law, a delicate and tender lady, whose subtle, devastating insults were famous among her sons' wives.

So Afkar was prepared for the relentless campaign against her that started as soon as she had settled in.

They developed a routine.

"Is that all the better you can wash his shirts?" Um Salah would demand.

"Show me how to do better, *Hamati*."

"Is that the way you make a béchamel sauce?"

"Teach me your method, *Hamati*."

"How can you use so much garlic? Are you trying to kill us all with that smell? Throw it out immediately and start all over again."

"I'm sorry—it won't happen again, *Hamati*."

"Are you going out dressed like that?"

"What do you suggest, *Hamati*?"

"Your room is filthy. Were you raised in a barn?"

"I'll try to do better, *Hamati*."

And although she returned exhausted each night from 'Ayn Shams, a forty-five-minute commute in an inhumanly packed bus, having worked a ten-hour day, Afkar endured her ever-bitter mother-in-law. She would find the presence of mind to smile sweetly at the endless jibes, and go about help-ing to prepare the evening meal in amiable silence.

And when they would at last close the door on his mother and the outside world, Salah would kiss away all the pain. They would laugh together about the tantrum of the day, and he would promise to get them an apartment on the Nile, in one of those tall new buildings that didn't even require shut-ters, so high was it above the prying eyes of neighbors and mothers-in-law.

Aflame with resentment, Um Salah paced nightly outside their locked door, clutching her bangles to silence them, lis-tening to the lovers' laughter and their peace-filled sighs.

Some in the neighborhood would later claim to have seen her at Shaykh Gibril's, begging him for a spell for her son that he might remember a bit of allegiance to his long-suffering mother. Or, better yet, a curse to put on that shameless girl who'd trapped her son into marriage.

It would not have been the first time. It was in fact a habit of Um Salah to visit the aged *shaykh* requesting vengeance on whichever neighbor she had had a falling-out with. The worst instance occurred when Farhat, the grocer's wife, refused to extend her further credit after Um Salah was seen buying a gold bangle the previous day. Um Salah went into such a disconsolate rage that she had to be bodily removed from the small store.

She had not even returned home. She headed straight for Shaykh Gibril, marching up the three flights of stairs to his apartment in such a bangle-clattering, foot-pounding fury that the building seemed to shake, and the neighbors below him opened their doors in curious wonder as she ascended.

It was a mere two weeks later that Farhat became so ill with influenza that the *hakim* insisted she be admitted to Qasr al-'Ayni hospital. It took truly grave illnesses for the *hakim* to acknowledge defeat, and Farhat lingered for several weeks in that grim, gray hospital before the doctors there returned her to her family.

Nothing was ever said between the two women about what had happened. Farhat simply tended to disappear when Um Salah would enter the store. And Abu Hasan never refused the family credit again.

In any event, whether or not Shaykh Gibril had agreed to craft an amulet, it was not long thereafter that the newlyweds suffered their first of many setbacks. Having completed his first two years as an employee, Salah should have automatically received a pay increase and promotion. However, he received neither. What's more, he got a poor proficiency report from his supervisor.

"He's trying to prove he's private sector material by demanding accountability for mistakes and inefficiencies. He thinks

the more he criticizes, the more he'll seem hard and discern-
ing. And the more cost cutting he does in the department, the
more capitalistic he'll seem. He's just maneuvering for when
the corporate recruiters look him over."

"But what can we do?" asked Afkar, rubbing his shoulders
as they whispered in the darkness of their room.

He sighed. "Just hope it's better next year," he replied.

She was quiet a moment, pressing against a knot just under
the ridge of his shoulder blade. "What if you were to start
looking for work in the private sector?"

He laughed. "You know what Baba says. The whole thing
could come crashing down at any time. Sadat's just a peasant;
he doesn't really understand world economics. Infitah is designed
to appease the International Monetary Fund, so they can jus-
tify aid by opening the country to their interests. If I leave the
ministry now, I'll lose all my social security. You have to think
of the big picture, Afkar. The private sector's fine for you,
because you don't have to support a family. But my job is what
will take care of us in the long term."

Prices kept rising. Initially, the government would announce
price increases. But the demonstrations had gotten so intense,
and the anger in the streets so palpable, that such tactics were
abandoned. Even as so many prospered, an ever-larger chunk
was left floundering with salaries that could not meet the dramatic increases in the cost of living.

"At least," Salah's father took to saying whenever he felt
depressed, "they've brought back 'CaCola." The happiest
memories of his youth had involved groups of laughing friends
and the fizzy beverage with the red-and-white bottle cap. And
although he had worshiped 'Abd al-Nasir with every fiber of
his being, whatever statement had been made by severing that
economic tie was lost on Hamid Subhy.

To which his wife would snap, "Now if only you could afford to drink it."

Afkar had received two raises, and on the day that the attorney promised her a third, she returned home with a furrowed brow.

She didn't mention her news. The family was gathered in the living room, sipping tea after dinner, watching as Kissinger walked across the television screen muttering to Begin.

Salah was sitting next to her on the couch. He looked tired. His lips were pursed together in a hard line.

"Did you have a good day today?" she asked.

He did not look at her. "No," he said simply.

She laid her hand on his arm. "There are so many jobs out there. I know you could do almost anything, if you'd only submit your résumé. . . ."

He yanked his arm from her grasp and slammed his palm against her cheek.

"How dare you nag me! Isn't my salary good enough for you?"

Afkar reeled, clutching the arm of the couch for support, more surprised than hurt. She composed herself quickly, refusing to show pain in front of his mother. She stood and walked to the room, closing the door behind her. She went to the mildly fractured mirror that hung on the wall, the bottom half of which was wide enough to encompass a whole face, if the looker was willing to hunker down a bit.

She stared for a long while at her reflection, rubbing the injured cheek, curiously regarding the woman who returned her gaze. Her eyes seemed dim and empty, her complexion was a disconcerting shade of gray. Afkar tilted her head at herself, fighting tears of self-pity. She didn't understand how Salah could have done such a thing, or why . . . or why he had yet to come after her to apologize. They had fought before, but he had never spumed such fury as she saw tonight. And they had never argued in front of any member of his family. Surely there was something else . . .

He came to her, but not until much later. She was hidden deep beneath the covers, her face buried in a soft pillow to muffle the sound of her sobbing.

He hesitated a moment. He had never made her cry anything but tears of longing. It shook him. "Afkar," he started, laying a hand on her shoulder. She promptly pulled away, edging farther onto her side of the bed. "Afkar. Sometimes . . . you just have to understand the pressure I'm under. With you making more money than me, and getting promoted, when the job I do is far more complicated, but no one appreciates me . . . And with us stuck living here, when we should have our own place . . . Sometimes, I just don't feel like a man. And with you nagging me all the time to get a better job, it's as if the hard work I do all day isn't even enough anymore."

He pulled out a cigarette, his newly acquired pastime, and struck a match, illuminating the outline of her body under the heavy winter blanket.

"You understand, don't you? *Ma'lesh, habibti.* I was wrong. Just . . . ease off a little. Sometimes I feel like I can't breathe."

She turned over slowly to face him. Her eyes were regretful beneath their swollen lids.

"I never thought of it that way," she said softly.

He offered her a cigarette and she took it uncertainly. He lit it for her and then went to crack the shutters, ushering a shaft of cool air into the room. "All of this and I have to watch my colleagues laughing and joking, going out and having fun. I feel as though all I have are worries."

She frowned.

He rushed to amend his words. "Well, and you, of course. But you're so busy with work and the housework. . . ."

Afkar inhaled timidly on the cigarette, expelling the smoke in a hail of coughing.

He laughed, sitting her up to slap her on the back. "Take it easy now. You have to get used to it." Ever so lightly, he kissed the cheek he'd slapped, then gathered her into his lap, pulling her head against his shoulder. They sat thus for a while in silence, smoking, until he took from her the cigarette and stubbed it out in an empty glass on the bedside table. He kissed her hair, and was just about to pull the gown from her shoulders when she stopped him.

"You don't have to make love to me to win me over. If you want to go out with your friends, go. Every boy should have a gang to run around with. I can't deprive you of that."

She had been half teasing, but the expected banter did not ensue. This was the part where he was supposed to alleviate her fears, and deny that he would want to go out with his friends when he could be lying beside her, fingers interlaced, staring up at the cracked ceiling, dreaming aloud of children and summer vacations and apartments overlooking the Nile.

But he pushed her away angrily. "*Boy?*" He leapt from the bed, buttoning his shirt as he spoke, his face dark and twisted. "I'm man enough to teach you a few lessons in respect."

He made for the door.

"Where are you going?" she asked, an arctic disbelief flooding through her yet again.

"Out," he said, pulling the door closed behind him.

In the dimness, her swimming eyes wandered the room, seeking answers in the mute walls and inert furniture. Her gaze came to rest on the bedside table, and she contemplated for a moment extracting the pen and notebook that lay in the drawer. But the poets had deceived her; to practice their craft, then, struck her as a cruel futility.

Her eyes made out the pack of Dunhills on the bedside table. As the moments after his departure writhed and multiplied, breeding in a dark pool of emptiness, she reached for the pack. Sniffling softly, she extracted and, after some thought, lit a precisely rolled cigarette.

Um Salah immediately took advantage of the fissure in their lives to reinsert herself into Salah's routine. She would hear the doors shutting behind him, and she would rush to the balcony to gauge his direction. She would doze lightly, then arise and prepare for him a light meal, some soft white cheese and wheat bread, some *foule* with eggs, a steaming glass of sugary black tea with milk.

She stood on the balcony, wrapped in her shawl against the cool air, and waited until she saw him ambling along the dark alley.

Then she scurried into the tiny kitchen and loaded everything onto a tray. When he would stumble in slightly before dawn, she would be waiting, the food and tea spread out for him on the coffee table. Their voices low, they talked of family gossip and neighborhood scandals, news of the Ministry and the prices of this and that.

Um Salah fussed over him, pretending that the reason for his bloodshot eyes was an impending cold, and that his slurring speech was from exhaustion brought on by overwork.

They would part from each other just as the sun was pulling most of Bab al-Khalq's residents into waking.

In the end, the most painful thing for Afkar wasn't living with a tyrannical mother-in-law, or suffering the buses and the grind of the endless workdays, nor was it surrendering her rightful place in the Faculty of Literatures in favor of typing and correcting legal briefs, filing motions, billing clients and facilitating the successful professional lives of men far less intelligent than she.

Her pain came from finding that the feelings she and Salah had shared, once enshrined in ink and song and restless gaze, could be so easily untethered and wind-flung. When she leafed through her old notebooks, she found that the words of her poems had been hollowed. They stood scattered across the yellowing pages like brittle skeletons.

Her loneliness was soft, damp earth; by night she burrowed into it ever deeper.

The lawyer for whom she worked had prospered over the past four years, taking on several large corporate clients, and even expanding and taking two partners to share the burden. Another secretary was needed for the formidable caseload that had arisen from the lawyers' continued successes. The firm had even taken new offices in Mohandeseen, making Afkar's commute far less exhausting. Her salary was now fifty-five pounds a month.

Afkar never spoke of her raises and bonuses. She simply tucked away the extra money into the specially stitched lining of an old green cardigan she never wore. Until her latest raise, she had always made a percentage contribution to the household expenses, living up to her agreement with Hamid to the piaster.

Now, however, with both Hamid and Salah's salaries frozen, and prices steadily rising, she took to picking up extras on her way home. She started coming home with a few kilos of mangoes, a tall bag of roasted watermelon seeds, Lebanese apples, or a small tray of *basboussa* from the famed pastry kitchen of Al-Samadi.

All of this was received happily by Kamal, Rida, and Hamid, grudgingly by Um Salah, and silently by Salah.

Then came the day when she decided to indulge them in a few kilos of fresh lamb from the newest, most expensive butcher in Giza, Subki. Salah was late coming home from work, and he arrived to find them spreading a feast across the coffee table—their unofficial dining room table since the wedding. He sank onto a floor pillow, staring suspiciously at the *fatta*, the kebabs, and the plates piled high with rice.

"What are we celebrating?" he asked when they had all gathered.

Hamid said, "We're testing the quality of Subki, thanks to your lovely wife."

He looked at Afkar, who smiled sheepishly, then at the trays of meat before him. "Bon appétit," he sneered, shoving his plate aside and standing.

His father frowned, calling after him, "Where are you going, son? Come back here and eat."

"From now on I'll eat only the food I can afford on my salary. I'll eat in the street with people more on my level."

The door slammed loudly behind him.

For once Afkar could not hide her tears from her in-laws. She buried her face in her hands. Hamid reached across the table to pat her bent head.

"*Ma'lesh*, daughter," he said gently. "Men in Salah's position can't support their families. It's not Salah's fault. These things are hard on a man."

She did not look up, but she could imagine Um Salah's self-satisfied smirk.

She never admitted to her parents that she was unhappy. She knew that such a divulgence would only pain them, especially her father. She so wanted to prove his initial misgivings wrong.

Afkar became an expert at the masking smile, the breezy reply, the manufactured laugh. Only Maha, who knew her better than anyone, could tell that she was faltering.

But Maha herself had married by this time, and was not free as she once had been for long sessions of sisterly confessions.

They still gathered every Friday for dinner, but now Afkar was constantly inventing excuses for Salah's absence. She told them that he was looking into new job opportunities, or that he was driving his friend's taxi for some extra money. Once she said he'd gone to Alexandria for work, but her mother bumped into him on her way to buy milk. He barely even greeted her.

Zahra related this occurrence to 'Abd al-Raziq with concern. He listened without looking up from his book, blinking angrily, watching the words swim across the page in a blur.

There were no secrets on al-Gadawi Alley. He knew that Salah was seen leaving his father's apartment late in the evenings. He knew also that he returned only just before the dawn call to prayer. He knew that his son-in-law smoked hashish in al-Bataniya with a group of young men who shared solidarity in their situations: squelched potential and thwarted ambition. There was no place for them in the country, no niche for them in a world that was scrambling to define itself. They had no illusions about founding meaningful futures with what money they made. Sanctuary lay in clouds of pungent smoke that obscured them from themselves.

'Abd al-Raziq decided to invite Salah for a glass of tea at

Zaghlul's Café. He told him in no uncertain terms that his daughter deserved better than a shiftless hashish smoker. He reminded the young man of Afkar's many sacrifices on his behalf, and told him that any money he spent on hashish would be better saved for an apartment. The better to really start their life together. Moreover, was he insane to go into al-Bataniya after dark? He could be killed. The entire area had become a haven for drug dealers and criminals. A handsome young man like him could be kidnapped or even murdered.

After listening politely to every suggestion his father-in-law offered, Salah returned home and beat Afkar so savagely that she urinated blood for three days. He was careful, however, not to lay a hand on her face. *You complain about me to your father? You would dare complain about me to your father? Do it again and I'll kill you, I swear it.*

Afkar was forced to double her efforts to project the image of a happily married woman.

There wasn't much to do at the ministry. Most days, Salah would sit at his desk reading the paper, mulling over the section wherein people would write in anonymously with their problems asking for advice. He would compare his tribulations with theirs, more often than not calling it a draw.

He made a few halfhearted attempts at searching for a different job, but with the lumbering bureaucracy suddenly forced to compete with the private sector, waves and waves of government employees were looking for work. Those with college degrees were given preference over those without. Those with experience were taken over the still-junior employees. Those with poor performance reports were taken hardly ever.

Salah's outings with his friends increased to four nights a week, and money began disappearing from the old green cardigan. Afkar would count out the bills four or five times, willing them to complete the amount she knew by heart. She remained silent for a few months, fearing the confrontation, then could bear it no longer.

He staggered into the room at four in the morning. She was waiting, smoking, angry.

She spoke softly, refusing to allow the rest of the flat to listen in on their troubles.

"You've been taking from our savings. The money we're relying on to build our future. How could you do such a thing?"

He squinted at her through bloodshot eyes, and she realized suddenly that he was not altogether lucid.

"Are you buying hashish with our money? Our children's money?" she whispered, clasping his arm.

He shoved her away. "What do you care? It's not like you've given me any children." The sound of his contempt for her seemed to echo out onto al-Gadawi Alley and resound throughout the neighborhood.

She stared at him, astonished. "We both agreed we would wait until we had our own place, until we were standing on our own feet."

But he had already fallen onto the bed half clothed, and his reply was a derisive snore.

Afkar considered this conversation in the few idle moments of her days, wondering to what extent she was responsible for Salah's feelings of inadequacy. Perhaps if he had a child, he would forego the gatherings of friends and hashish for a home life. Even if it was, still, the home of his parents. He would regain his focus, his desire to rail against the odds.

She doubted it.

But she had run out of ideas and approaches. She threw

away those precious pills of Jehan's and embarked on a tepid campaign of seduction.

It worked.

Two months later, on the day before her twenty-third birthday, she confirmed her suspicions at the doctor's office.

She walked home all the way from Dokki, her palm pressed to her belly. The day was cool; a cleansing breeze swept off the Nile and skated across the tangled city. As life began to whisper in her womb, a once-familiar hope cantered through her veins. Suddenly, here was proof of their fated connection. Surely Salah would feel it, too. He would reassess, give thanks, fall in love with her anew.

She mounted the stairs with a light step, entering the apartment with a smile reminiscent of those that never used to leave her lips.

It was early evening and Salah was napping in preparation for a long night out.

She shook him gently, murmuring his name and kissing the deep V that appeared between his eyebrows when he frowned in his sleep.

He stirred and looked up at her drowsily, then pulled her down to him and began kissing her.

She complied, then pulled away. "Perhaps we should abstain for a while," she said smiling.

He blinked, uncomprehending.

"*Mabrouk*," she said. "What do you think we should name him?"

He sat up suddenly, staring at her. "What do you mean?" he demanded.

Light surged behind her features. "I'm pregnant."

"Pregnant? Pregnant by whom?" The words were a whip's lash.

"By *whom?*" she echoed, stunned.

"No wife of *mine* would be pregnant. My wife agreed that we wouldn't have children until we had our own place." He grabbed her wrist and twisted it violently. "Or did you forget that?"

"But you said—"

"I said what?"

She fell silent, realizing that he probably had no memory of that night.

"I guess we had a misunderstanding," she said softly.

"You guess? Well, you guess right." He spat out the words. "Where are we supposed to put a kid in this place? How are we going to afford it?"

"Well, it'll be a lot easier if you stop spending all our money on drugs," she retorted.

"What?" His arm swung back, threatening. "How dare you speak to me that way? I can do whatever I want with that money. That's my reward for throwing my life away on you."

"Go on and hit me," she shouted at him for the first time ever. Her voice sounded strange to her. "Hit me!" she shouted again. She threw open the door to the room. "Do it in front of everyone. Show them the man you are!"

Her boldness was simply too much for him, and he tackled her with an animal grunt.

She went down hard, the back of her head striking the bed frame. The room spun for a moment, then settled back to normal. "Divorce me," she said.

He leaned over her, placing his hand under her chin and pushing it back hard. "Say that again. I thought you said, 'Divorce me.'"

"Do it," she said. "Please. I don't want anything from you. Just let me go."

He laughed a thin, hollow laugh. "But I want something from you. I want you to feel as trapped as I have for the last six years."

She was crying now, despite herself.

He continued, "And now you want to trap me further with a baby, isn't that right? Wasn't that the plan?" He kicked her, then, in the stomach. "It won't work!" he shouted.

She screamed in agony, pulling her knees to her chest, but he pulled her up by the hair and shoved her hard out of the room. She stumbled, falling against the coffee table, and he kicked her once again in her abdomen, harder.

It was only then that Hamid and Rida pulled him back, shouting at him to leave her alone, but he screamed at her shrilly, "You'll never leave here alive!"

Hamid persisted in trying to silence him, but Salah went on raving. "She put a curse on me. That's how I fell in love with someone like her. It was a curse!"

Afkar closed her eyes, then opened them to stare at Um Salah, recognizing that refrain as hers alone. She tried to rise, but a lancing pain prevented her from straightening up. She started crawling instead toward Salah's parents' room. Kamal rushed to try to help her, but she rebuffed him with a glance.

She had never entered that room before, the room that had once been Salah's. She pushed open the door and found it dark and musty, the walls water-stained and cracked. She made her way slowly over to the balcony shutters and pushed them open, letting the last vestiges of daylight enter in a cool saffron rush. She clasped the balcony rail, hauling herself painfully to a stooped position, her head just high enough to see over it.

She gazed for an interminable moment at her old room. She laughed softly, imagining her girl self peering across from a crack in the shutters.

She laughed herself into a crescendoing hysteria that had shutters swinging open all up and down the alley. Um Salah, alert to the questioning gazes of the neighborhood, screeched at her to enter and shut the balcony doors before she made a spectacle of them all.

Afkar only laughed louder. With all her remaining strength, she swung herself over the balcony rail and down onto the pavement four floors below.

Along with the broken ribs and hip, she lost her entire uterus. By the time 'Abd al-Raziq had secured her in Qasr al-'Ayni hospital and returned to kill Salah, as he had promised he would if ever Afkar were pained, the boy had turned the lining of the old green cardigan inside out and retreated to the hashish warrens of al-Bataniya, never to be seen again.

Because Salah hadn't bothered to divorce her before disappearing, she remained married to him for four full years until the court agreed to grant her a divorce on the basis of abandonment. 'Abd al-Raziq did not shrink from collecting the exorbitant three-thousand-pound alimony from his neighbor, even though he knew Hamid had been forced to sell off all of his wife's gold and had gone into debt he could not repay.

Um Salah was a broken woman. No clinking of bangles accompanied her heavy step. The child whose existence had named her had vanished without a trace. She was left to stand each night on the tiny balcony, wrapped deep in her woolen shawl, peering out onto al-Gadawi Alley, awaiting his return.

❖ ❖ ❖ ❖ ❖

Her living room is, by this time, choked with smoke, and we have gone through several demitasses of 'Abd al-Ma'bud's Turkish coffee.

I shake a little, from wonder, from caffeine.

My father, she says, grinning at me with stained yellow teeth, *did not leave my bedside for even one moment after that.* "Daughter *of a dog,"* he'd say, in as gruff a voice as he could muster, after por- *ing over my notebooks full of verse,* "didn't you ever notice that the *ancient Arabs loved best from afar?"*

The rest of the time he strummed his oud, or read to me from the collections of al-Mutanabbi or Ibn Zaydun or the Maqamat of al Hamadhani—to get me better prepared for when I went to univer- sity, he would say.

When I could walk again, and returned home, I found they'd bricked over the balcony off my room. When the muakhr finally came, I took my three thousand pounds and used them for the deposit on this flat. My parents came to live with me until they died. She rises to open a window, releasing some of the smoke. She leans thoughtfully against the ledge, then murmurs, *I write only in free verse these days. . . ."*

I inhale, feeling the breath forge deeply into me. I watch as the dangling pillar of ash from her cigarette tumbles onto the ledge, some of it spilling over the edge.

She killed herself off to gain her freedom. A hollow abdomen exchanged for a whole body; a withered heart for a mind released to circumambulate the world of words.

❖   ❖   ❖   ❖   ❖

The Bold and the Beautiful is the number-one program in Cairo. I had never heard of it before coming, and I discover it to be one of the USA's very own daytime soap operas. Here, at least for a while, it commands a prime-time spot. My professors sputter over this. Their secretaries debate plot twists.

Walking down the street at 7:00 p.m., I hear Caroline and Ridge battling it out from open windows. I stop to pick up some apples to snack on during my evening walk, and I find Maher the fruit vendor staring at a portable television. He is transfixed, eyes glued to the subtitles, and he barely notices my presence. His television is small and the picture comes across in tremulous black and white. It is propped on a wooden table near the open doorway, its antennae stretching thirstily skyward. The cord snakes along between crates of aromatic guavas and mounds of slick red apples before disappearing behind the grapefruit.

I pause to watch a moment. It is clear where the censors have been chopping. Kisses are almost infinitesimally short.

Maher shakes his head at me as he shoves my fruit into the brown paper bag. *That Ridge is no good*, he says.

I nod as if I know what he's talking about.

But Caroline . . . He pronounces it Ca-roo-leen; a dreamy smile slides across his features. I glance at her over his shoulder. Her thick blond hair frames her face in soft waves. Her skin is flawless alabaster. Her career-woman garb is a micro-miniskirt, a boxy silk jacket and knife-blade heels that make her stockingless calves look like hard, underripe peaches.

His eyes graze my sweatshirt and jeans, and the stringy pony-tail that keeps my hair from infesting my face. His chastisement is brief and unspoken. *Are you certain you're an American?* he wants to say.

I smile at him, apologetically perhaps, and he goes back to the program. I walk my favorite path along the subtly curving streets of Garden City until I reach its western edge, the corniche. I cross the busy street to the wide sidewalk that borders the river.

There is a bench on the corniche I have come to call mine. It looks out over the cool, composed water, the Meridien hotel on the left, the great midriver fountain just ahead, the Qasr al-Nil Bridge to the right. The Gezira Sheraton rises from the facing bank, and behind it the Tower of Cairo and the Opera House.

I sink onto my bench and pull out my journal. The corniche behind me is alive with promenaders. A couple passes; the young woman's thick, wavy hair is adorned with blond streaks, and her too-thin face is an artist's palette of eye shadows and rouges. Her high-cut skirt clings to her every curve, and I find myself recalling the mannequins from the Zamalek and Mohandeseen stores I am too scruffy even to enter. Her beau wears jeans and a black T-shirt that shouts *Calvin Klein*. It is clear they have been arguing, for her red lips are arranged in a daunting pout, and his actions all seem geared to assuage.

Another couple passes going the opposite direction. Her denim skirt reaches almost to the ground, topped by a light cotton blouse and paisley-printed headscarf. His faded button-down is of muted plaid; his hair glistens slightly from oil or gel. Their fingers are tightly interwoven and they walk slowly, deliberately, as if perhaps their time together will end with the ending of the potholed pavement, and they mean to draw it out as long as possible. They talk softly, swiftly to each other, their faces intent, etched with the pent-up passions of time apart.

A family walks by. The man, heavily bearded, in a long white gelabiyya, has a small boy perched atop his shoulders. His wife, draped in a royal blue *khimar*, clutches the hand of a tiny girl in a frilly white dress and twin ponytails. The boy is whining for ice cream, pulling at his father's hair. The mother hisses reprimands as the father pats at his tender scalp.

In the middle of the river, tall-masted feluccas cradle whispering winds in their patched white sails. Small fishing boats pass before me, wooden oars splashing. Some are brightly painted with the names of their owners or with phrases and symbols to ward off the Evil Eye.

I bite into my apple, and notice a rowboat with faded paint and the name BESMA stenciled on it. A sinewy little boy works one oar; his slight sister commands the other. Their mother, clad in a once brightly printed gelabiyya and a graying bandanna, leans out to gather in a fishing net. The little girl looks up at me, and our eyes hold. I smile, and her face lights.

Sometimes I remember to write.

Most of the time I sit, fused into the scene, not wanting to break the spell. Writing damns me to observing rather than being. And my sweetest times in Cairo are when I can simply be, and let her flow over and under and thoroughly through me.

❈ ❈ ❈ ❈ ❈

When Huda opens the door, I can see that something is up. I stare at her expectantly.

She raises her eyebrows at me, challenging me wordlessly to guess.

I start to shrug, then stop. *Oh, my God. You're pregnant!*

She nods vigorously, her face cracking into a wide smile. I can't help but throw my arms around her.

When I ask about her due date, she tells me June.

June! You've been pregnant—I count on my fingers—*three months without telling me!*

Ma'lesh. We don't tell anyone until at least the second trimester.

Evil eye?

She laughs aloud. *Of course.*

I tell her she has nothing to fear from me, but she pinches me. *You'll have beautiful children one day, and you'll remember that I told you I knew it would be so.*

She still insists on making me tea, and I revisit the past three months, and all the moments when Huda had looked pale or tired. I feel inclined to ask her if she's all right with her situation. *Didn't you plan on getting a job?*

She shakes her head at me. *The banks will still be standing by the time I'm done nursing. Anyway, is there any more important job? The world is so full of hateful people . . . and now I get the chance to raise a nice one.*

Huda's contribution to the cosmic balance. I grin at her. *Your child will be a wonderful person.*

In sha allah, she whispers.

Do you want a boy or a girl?

She shrugs. *I want a healthy child.*

Ehab?

She rolls her eyes, and we say together, *Boy*.

We laugh loudly, and I study her face, still surprised that my friend carries a whole new life within her. *June. You must have the baby before I go.*

Her eyes sparkle. *You must not go until I have the baby.*

I couldn't possibly, I say, reaching out to give her tummy the gentlest of pats.

✦ ✦ ✦ ✦ ✦

The subway is a subterranean world of order. Peaceful, efficient and sweetly cool on the hottest day, the subway shines with an alien cleanliness; there are fines for littering and eagle-eyed policemen who enforce them conscientiously.

It is a woman's right to cut to the front of lines hundreds of men long to get her subway ticket. Every time I do it, I feel a combination of guilt and power. The women's car of the subway poses a problem, though. At first, I regard it as a "coloreds only" sort of thing, and refuse to ride in it on principle.

Then one day, as I stalwartly await a midtrain car, an older woman with limpid eyes and twin chins shoos me onto the women's car before I can really protest.

You see? she asks, when the doors swoosh closed behind us. *You see?* she says again, as though she has revealed to me a delicious secret.

I see that the car is jammed with scarved heads and pony-tailed little girls in school uniforms and overlarge backpacks. There are boys, too, but only as old as the ones seen in a women's bathroom before they notice any difference.

I am about to insist that I am strong enough to go it alone in the normal cars, that I can bear the stares, and the gossamer violations of accidental bumpings and brushings as the metro barrels through the city's belly. I would tell my well-intentioned shepherdess that I can stake out a place for myself in that grim, male world . . . but suddenly, the two little girls before me start giggling. They at turns hide their faces in the gauzy cloth of their mother's *khimar* and look up at me and giggle some more.

I pat my face, making sure it's free of crusts and residues. Their mother is chiding them softly and giving me a chagrined grin. I wait patiently for resolution as I cling to the pole and sway with the motion of the rocking car.

Finally one of the little girls looks up at me, flushed, and pronounces in precise rote English, *What's your name?!*

Then she collapses again in a swell of high-pitched laughter.

I answer her, and ask hers, and then her sister's, and then her mother's . . . and suddenly there's a whole class of conversational English raging along as the subway shudders through tunnels.

Women laugh in the women-only car.

Aboveground, it seems the laughs are different. Walking along the street, sitting in a restaurant or ice cream shop, most women laugh softly, subdued, voiceless laughs that do not garner male attention and therefore cannot be misconstrued as flirtations.

It is on the subway that I hear a woman laugh deeply, and watch as laughing tears leak out of her eyes to be mopped up with the tail of her scarf.

Sometimes, I am reluctant to emerge from that warmth and onto the cool, littered streets, yellowed by late-afternoon sunlight.

✦ ✦ ✦ ✦ ✦

Ehab's Fiat 128 is sandwiched brutally between two substantially larger cars. The battered bumper of an old Renault is so embedded against Ehab's that the two cars resemble unwieldy, conjoined twins. He stares forlornly, then asks Huda and me to wait on the sidewalk while he frees the Fiat.

I regard her as she watches him struggling. The silences between them are not so strained after all; the air about Huda is one of graceful acquiescence, like a gazelle that is little by little teaching itself to graze the grasses found in captivity.

The trip to Dokki is not a long one at this hour of the evening. We cut through Garden City, making the wide, forced loop around the American embassy and skirting the mighty Semiramis Hotel to gain the Qasr al-Nil Bridge. The waters of the Nile are black and silent. The colored lights of cruising restaurants and tall billboards spill across the shuddering face of the water, a floating confetti of neon. The Coca-Cola sign electrifies the night in startling red, as a vibrant spectrum of signs vie for the eye.

We pass the Opera and inch along in the valley formed between Tahrir Street's towering high-rises, past Cinema Tahrir with its explosion of lights and its judicious offerings—one Hollywood film, one Egyptian. Moviegoers overrun the steps of the theater and flow out into the street awaiting the next showing. Slim girls in tank dresses defy the late-November chill. Their bony shoulders are weighted down with overlarge purses. They press fuchsia fingernails against one ear and cell phones against another. College-age boys stand in clusters, cleaned and cologned, surveying their prey, teasing each other until baiting punches lead to raised voices and half-serious chases. Mascaraed eyes stare thoughtfully, observing, then open and close excitedly as groups of magenta-glossed lips huddle together, processing such theatrics, seeking out deeper meanings.

It is just beyond the cinema that the car turns right, and a more soft-spoken Dokki appears. The buildings are but four stories at most; a few dilapidated villas hunker in between. Huda's street is a dead end, with cars aligned like dominoes along each side. To conduct the Fiat through the slim passageway between them is to risk losing a sideview mirror, and upon leaving, to be forced into a six-point turn with cars on both sides. Ehab parks at the periphery of the outdoor market, and we thread our way among the stacks of Iranian apples and Delta grapes and Aswan oranges and onto Sherbini Street at last.

We are greeted by a wizened man pushing an old movie theater popcorn popper. Huda pauses, calling him by name, and buys three bags of popcorn. When he speaks, his mouth is revealed as a great gap; two gray teeth hang precariously on either side. He calls Huda "daughter," and kisses the pound note she hands him before tucking it away in the folds of his stained brown gelabiyya.

Huda hands me a bag of popcorn. *That's 'Am Saber,* she says. *His wife died in childbirth, and he raised four girls by pushing that popcorn cart all across this town. He married them off, but refuses to live with any of them and be a burden. He only has to support himself now.*

I chew the popcorn thoughtfully; it melts on my tongue, salty, buttery, light as air.

Don't eat it now, she chides. *You'll ruin your appetite, and my mother is about to stuff you.*

I obediently refasten the twist tie at the bag's neck, following Huda and Ehab along a thin passageway to the building's entrance. As soon as our feet strike the stairway, the first-floor door swings open and Huda's mother appears, wiping her hands on a dish towel.

We find ourselves in a deluge of reprimands about how late we are. She pulls us inside, pressing resounding kisses against our cheeks each in turn. She wrenches Ehab's cheek with a pinch, then pats his balding head, and shoos us all into the living room, where we find Huda's grandmother and father.

Her father lies reclining on a high couch, his swollen feet elevated slightly. He raises himself on thin elbows to smile a wide greeting.

Huda's grandmother, Mama Selwa, sits accepting Huda's kisses before she casts emerald eyes on me. *The American friend?* she asks.

Huda introduces us. From all of Huda's stories about Mama Selwa, to be finally introduced to her feels vaguely redundant.

The old woman motions me nearer, and pulls my wrist until my ear is level with her mouth. *You look like a good girl,* she whispers.

Thank you, I whisper back, my eyes drifting to Huda, who shrugs.

The grandmother's breath is hot on my ear: *Do you have any American cigarettes?*

I laugh out loud as Mama Selwa shushes me. *Bas!* she hisses. *Our secret, you understand?*

I nod, ever amenable, and she releases my wrist even as she raises her eyebrows evocatively.

Huda's brother and sister-in-law arrive, with two noisy little boys in tow. Huda's brother Omar is surreally handsome, with smooth skin and large olive eyes. His laugh is loud and deep, and the women in the room appear hypnotized by him; they listen to his stories of the goings-on at the family grocery with rapt hunger.

We sit in the living room, sheltered under a ceiling that towers at fifteen feet or so. I take in the apartment curiously, realizing that although it is bigger than my own, it is almost unbearably crowded with worn-out furniture and peculiar artifacts. A collection of crippled stuffed animals crowds across the patched pink slipcovers of the formal couch. Dusty silk flowers droop in bright vases, wilting despite their lifeless buds.

When we are called into the dining room, the surfaces of the buffets are lined with a box record player, chipped statuary, marble ashtrays and a doll—yellow hair and ivory skin equally graying—whose eyelids hover half closed as she leans. She is propped up by an aged telephone, the spiral cord of which ends abruptly in a spray of exposed wire. Some capricious hand has left a spattering of Incredible Hulk stickers, most picked at then abandoned, across all the room's relics, uniting all in a disgraced ignominy.

As we sit around the expanse of tabletop, my eyes stray to the headlines of the newspapers that are spread to catch the crumbs and drips. Seated at my right, Karima keeps up a steady chant: *Don't read, eat.*

I grin at her. *What's your sign?* I ask, tapping the horoscope section with my spoon.

The water bearer, she answers immediately, craning to see.

"*You will encounter a new love in the near future,*" I read.

The table erupts in laughter.

They only write such things to keep up the spirits of the youngsters, says Huda's father. He tilts his head at his wife, considering. *But then again . . .*

Karima tsks, putting another slab of meat on my already-overwhelmed plate. *Don't you worry about it. If I meet a new love, you'll be the first to know,* she says to him.

And so goes an evening's conversation, voices resounding

off fatigued walls, eyes alive with the need to laugh, awaiting and pouncing upon the slightest breath of humor in every sentence. I fight to keep pace with their conversations, asking Huda to rephrase and repeat until things make sense. She is patient, precise in her explanations, and intent on letting me see the wit in things. They all wait until I get it, then laugh all over again when I do.

Omar's eldest son is six. His black eyes sparkle as he leans in to whisper Sa'idi jokes to me. The Sa'id is the area known as Upper Egypt, or the south of Egypt around Luxor and Aswan. Cairenes consider it a repository of rednecks. The jokes are many and simplistic enough for my intermediate Arabic.

The doctor says to the Sa'idi, "I'm sorry, but your father has died from a brain tumor"; the Sa'idi responds, "That's terrible! But where did he get the brain?"

Once a Sa'idi fell in the irrigation ditch and the parasites went off screaming to the doctor.

The boy, Rami, can barely contain himself when I laugh loudly. Everyone else laughs at his body-convulsing laughter.

I pore over my friendship with Huda, seeking what it was I could have done for her to prompt her to pull me into this tender circle. She makes certain Ehab's plate is full before she cuts into her own meal. He in turn resists her attempts to give him the best pieces, slipping them onto her plate when she looks away.

She smiles at me as she chews delicately.

As I kiss Mama Selwa good-bye, I press the box of cigarettes surreptitiously into her warm palm, feeling a friendly complicity in her rebellion against the orders of doctors-who-know-nothing.

She pats my cheek, then tucks a tendril of my hair behind my ear. *I knew you were a good girl.*

✦ ✦ ✦ ✦ ✦

Meg calls her a pirate. Badriyya ties her black scarf like a bandanna, and she wears gigantic circular earrings. Her sumptuous smiles reveal a gleaming gold tooth. She brims with such a volcanic vivacity that I am continually taken aback by how diminutive she is of stature. Her shiny, black polyester gelabiyya houses a startlingly plump form. She sits smack in the middle of the sidewalk a few paces from the mouth of our building. Vegetables fill a large straw basket on her lap and surround her on both sides like mute, brightly dressed children.

We pass by her on our way to and from school. It is not long until she calls out greetings, trying to engage either of us in conversation. Slowly but surely we form a friendship with Badriyya. On days when walking Cairo streets has left me limp and disillusioned, I stop and chat with her on my way home from school, and somehow I always come away laughing.

She is Meg's favorite Arabic teacher. Every time they meet, Badriyya grills her on an arsenal of swear words and insults that has the rest of us envious and amazed. Meg, in her typically uninhibited oblivion, dishes them out left and right. She causes a very grim situation with a taxi driver whose mother gets the brunt of this newfound linguistic flair.

And although the sight of the cucumbers spread out on a torn piece of cardboard on the sidewalk does not prove appetizing, I start feeling obliged to buy something from her. Meg, too, starts showing up with vegetables we have no idea how to manipulate into edible dishes.

One day, Badriyya insists that we come over for dinner. We take the invitation to be an empty one, at first, and are surprised when she rings our bell after completing her day's commerce. She clutches her empty straw basket in her left hand. In an awkward rush, we change from sweats to jeans and sweaters, and follow her through an alley we didn't know existed and out onto Qasr al-'Ayni Street, where she stops a taxi. It isn't that far, but traffic is so congested that it takes almost an hour to get to Mohandeseen and wade our way along Arab League Street to its dim end.

The driver stops at the side of the road, and Badriyya reaches into her cleavage and produces the taxi fare, shooing us out. We are confronted by a towering temporary wall, one of those that has appeared all over as the metro is being extended. Construction goes on behind them all day and into the night. At the same time, the walls cleverly mask the living conditions of the areas behind them. Badriyya walks with rapid conviction to a sudden, murky gap in the wall, and disappears through it; we follow, suppressing the sudden urge to clasp hands.

This is Boulaq Dakrour, the face of a Cairo some might prefer to veil. Filthy children peer out from dark alleyways. Hovering flies dot the trash-lined pathways. The buildings seem almost makeshift, some without roofs, incomplete, others listing and crumbling. Some are of homemade bricks, the hay sticking out of them at prickly angles. The distance between buildings is negligible; at certain points we have to walk single file.

Women in austere *khimars* and patched sling-back sandals pick their way along muddy pathways that border impassable irrigation ditches. A rancid stench wafts up from what water is visible between the emptied koshary bowls and the puffy array of colored plastic sacks. Gray-faced men populate dirty, crowded cafés, their eyes crusted over with a festering defeat. There are no tea glasses before them; the emptiness of the tabletops emits a collective silent cry.

We immediately attract an entourage of harsh-angled children with shining, inquisitive eyes. They follow along behind and beside us shouting, *What's your name?* and laughing like little exploding geysers. Badriyya guides us with her small shoulders thrown back, a smile on her face that says she is thrilled to have caused such neighborhood uproar.

She happens to look back at us with a grin as I am about to light a cigarette. The grin is devoured by an instant, fierce frown, the first serious look I have seen from her. She reaches for me, pulls the cigarette from between my lips and places it on the tiny shelf where my ear attaches to my head. *You mustn't smoke in the street. Do you want people to think you're a prostitute?*

I certainly don't; I wait.

Badriyya stops before a door in a building that groans with age. A vegetable cart is pressed close against the outer wall of her home. A few soiled cabbage leaves litter the rough wooden belly that lies forlorn and exposed in its loitering emptiness. Long leather straps dangle in the dirt like the splayed fingers of a dead man's hand.

Badriyya disperses the children with a hail of rapid-fire insults that I cannot decipher. She pushes open the door and we enter a tiny one-room apartment. In one corner is a screen behind which is a hole-in-the-floor toilet. In another corner sit a bed and a wardrobe. A rust-stained sink leans woefully against one wall. There are no windows. The dirt floor is covered with straw mats.

Welcome, welcome, she says, putting her empty baskets next to the door.

Do you live here all alone? Meg asks.

Badriyya nods to my translation. *My husband was killed in a bar fight.*

We rush to utter condolences, but Badriyya waves us off,

almost impatiently. *He was a son of a dog anyway. He would take my earnings and spend them on the whiskey. When the money ran out he would drink the* sphinga.

Meg looks at me; I shrug. I know the word to mean "sponge," but don't understand what it has to do with drinking.

You don't know sphinga? Badriyya grins. *This is when the bartender wipes down the spills on the bar with a sponge, then squeezes the liquid in the sponge into a glass for the idiot who has no money but still wants to drink.* She nods vigorously, as though to banish our skepticism. *Yes, yes. Disgusting, isn't it? This was my man. And so I am not pining for him, eh?*

His family came to me after the death, offering to marry me to his brother. I swore at them, telling them that his brother was the only man in Egypt worse than him! She stretches her arms widely. *And now I'm free to live as I want. No one says to me, "Where are you going, where have you been?" And if I want a man, I can see any man I please.* . . . She bursts into laughter then, crossing to the wardrobe and pulling out a bloodred teddy. *What do you think?*

We laugh. *Gorgeous*, I say. Meg nods her agreement. We both try to envision Badriyya, minus headscarf and billowing black gelabiyya, her gold tooth flashing in the Red Light, decked out in her lingerie.

The black overgarment seems to be something of a dress code for women of Badriyya's bearing and economic circumstances. Between bustling steps, though, another hemline peeks out from beneath it. I ask her, *Why do you wear the black gelabiyya over your normal clothes all the time?*

She looks at me as though I am daft. *Modesty, of course*, she says, unzipping the gelabiyya to reveal that her brightly colored under-gelabiyya has a plunging décolletage. She shimmies out of the black garment and hangs it on a protruding hook. *The food should be here any moment now.*

Her sentence is not ended when we hear a soft tapping on the door. The food arrives in dented aluminum pots, stacked carefully in a threadbare tote bag. The bearer of food is Badriyya's only niece, Lubna, who enters in a long white *khimar*. Her face is perfectly round, and her pale lips are bee-stung plump. Her honeyed eyes are bordered by a web of long lashes. A bright smile consumes her features.

Lubna's apartment has a kitchen, Badriyya explains. Seating herself on a straw mat, Lubna interjects that she had wanted to entertain us in her home, but her aunt insisted on hosting us at hers. She pulls the lids off the dishes she has arranged on a wide tray before us, as Badriyya joins us with four wide spoons and bowls.

You like camel? Badriyya asks us.

I feel myself blinking rapidly. *Hut hut hut.*

It looks like any other meat, poking out of the bowl, all brown and boiled.

Meg casts me a self-satisfied, vegetarian look. I am stuck trying to explain Meg's position on the souls of animals and why they shouldn't be slaughtered for our sustenance. I give up soon and just say, *It's against her religion.*

This is respectfully accepted by the two women, and Meg's portion is added to mine. I smile gratefully. No one else has any meat in her soup, just pale broth with an occasional onion floating about.

We sit on the floor in a hunched, slurping circle.

Badriyya describes to us how she awakens every morning at four in order to be at her supplier's by five. She loads up with as many vegetables as she can carry and then rides the bus to Garden City.

Meg asks her why she picked that particular sidewalk.

Badriyya responds that it is a respectable neighborhood, and that ours is an exceedingly clean sidewalk.

But Lubna hears this explanation and bursts out laughing.

Tell them the real reason, she says.

Badriyya glares at her a moment, and then chuckles wickedly. *Well. There was a man—*

A married man, Lubna interjects.

—who liked me very much. And I liked him. Everything was fine for a while until his wife found out.

Lubna laughs with thin fingers pressed against her lips to mask the morsels in her mouth.

Badriyya smiles and continues, *There was a fight—*

His wife beat her until she bled, Lubna supplies helpfully.

—so we decided that we better not try to be together in the neighborhood. He was working in the butcher shop around the corner from your building in Garden City. So I moved my work there in order to be close to him, at least by day.

Meg and I work to imagine a love story wherein Badriyya is the obsessed heroine.

So what happened? I ask.

It went well for two years.

And then?

Badriyya looks away.

Lubna answers for her: *He died. Tuberculosis.*

Meg and I murmur condolences. We all sit silently for a moment.

And you stayed in the same place? I say finally. *Despite the memories?*

Because of the memories, replies Badriyya, appearing to enjoy the melodrama a little.

And because of the customers, adds her niece.

And because of the customers, echoes Badriyya, flashing that pirate smile at us.

As we are leaving, Lubna yanks hard at her fingers until she has removed two small rings, the kind you might find in a gum machine, pushing one onto Meg's ring finger and one onto mine.

What's this? I ask, protesting.

This is nothing. I'm ashamed of it. Just a little gift. So you'll remember us and come again. She and Badriyya both embrace us warmly, pressing kisses against our cheeks, sending us out into the night wrapped in blessings.

We had gone empty-handed.

❧ ❧ ❧ ❧ ❧

It is only the flu, but I am certain I'm dying. I moan wretchedly, not attempting to suffer in silence. Meg is disgusted by my vomiting, and although she nobly nurses me through the night, she is relieved to go to school in the morning.

Huda comes over to return my Billie Holiday CD. I can tell she was not particularly moved by it.

She looks at my matted hair and waxy skin. She calls her mother for backup.

Together, they form a mothering invasion that leaves the flat reeling. They do not hide how appalled they are by our living conditions. The dust, the Stella beer bottles, the sticky, slick dishes in the kitchen sink.

They stare at my bed. The sheet is gray, and much of it seems lost in the fat-man indentation. *You never thought to flip the mattress?* Huda asks.

I really never had.

They boss me into a corner and heave the mattress up and over. It emits a cloud of dust as it flops into place. Karima tsk-tsks and sends Huda across the hall for a clean sheet and blanket. I think of all kinds of protestations, but am too nauseous and feverish to speak.

Karima forces me bodily into bed and tucks me in, then disappears into the kitchen. I hear her clanging about and uttering orders. Huda goes to her apartment and comes back several times. I doze and awaken to hot fresh-squeezed lemon juice with honey for the nausea.

I doze and awaken to boiled mint. Also for the nausea.

Chicken soup, with real chicken in it. Not the Campbell's chuck-nuggets.

A clean, cold washcloth on my forehead.

Karima has worked up a sweat, and her headscarf is stowed somewhere. Her short black hair is frosted with gray. She has rolled up the sleeves of her dark, polyester blouse, and the skin of her arms is smooth and hairless. She clucks and pats and calls me her soul, and I am happier being sick than I can recall having been in health.

After one nap, I open my eyes to see Karima entering the bedroom with a steaming incense pot on a long brass chain. She starts moving it in circles above my head. She speaks very quickly and softly. The look in her eyes is so intent that I dare not move, cough or fan away the thick fog pouring over me.

She exits, moving briskly despite her bulk, without a word spoken directly to me, and I look a question at Huda.

She shrugs, as though it's obvious. *You've been struck by the Evil Eye.*

That's why I'm sick?

She nods, biting back a smile as I try not to retch from the smell of the incense.

Silly me, I whisper. *I thought it was a virus.*

Someone is envious of you, or wishes you harm. It happens.

She does this to you every time you get sick?

Oh, weekly. She did it when I didn't get pregnant the first month, and now that I am, she does it to keep me and the baby safe.

I had not understood Karima's smoky mutterings, and Huda explains that her mother had been chanting the last two *surahs* of the Qur'an. She'd added to this a saying: ʿAyn al-hassūd fīhā ʿūd which translates as "May the eye of the envier be struck by a lute."

The smoke has almost dissipated when Karima reappears. This time she holds a piece of paper in her hand, cut roughly in the shape of a person. In her other hand she holds a straight pin.

She nods at me, then starts poking holes in the paper doll. *In the eye of Huda,* she says, glancing at Huda, who grins at me. *In the eye of Karima,* she continues. She names the entire family, and anyone else she can think of who might know me.

Again, she leaves the room without explaining her actions.

Huda informs me that her mother will set fire to the paper, and toss it in the sink, and that's the end of that.

I ask Huda if the doll is supposed to be me.

Huda smiles. She tells me that by using the pin and saying all the names, it's as though she's disabling the evil intentions of whoever might look at me and think a bad thought, even inadvertently. Preemptive strikes. By putting the holes in the symbol of me and then burning it up, she's acting out the worst that could happen.

And you believe in all this?

Huda perches on the side of the bed, pulling at the little lint balls on the blanket. She lists examples of Eye incidents: You are talking on the phone with a friend who has the Eye. She is upset because you tell her a handsome man has come to ask for your hand, while she has gotten no proposals at all. Immediately after hanging up with her, you sprain your ankle. Someone comes to visit, tells you how lovely the apartment is (all the while being jealous of your good fortune), and right then a lightbulb shatters.

Pregnant women are particularly susceptible to the Eye from infertile women, and if stricken, can deliver stillborn children. Mothers of obtuse children cast it on clever children at test times, causing them to become ill and miss the test, or worse, flunk it.

Huda shrugs. *It's a good explanation for a lot of unfortunate occurrences. And such measures by my mother are her way of expressing that she worries about you and loves you.*

Just then, Meg comes in from school. She is walking dazedly about the flat, looking for some evidence that she's in the right place.

They entrust me to Meg. As she goes, Karima places a warm palm against my cheek. Her molasses-colored eyes glisten with care. *Get better*, she says. *I'll come and see you tomorrow.*

I tell her not to trouble herself, but she silences me with a frown.

I fall into a comfortable sleep, fed, loved and fortified, at least for the moment, against the Eye.

❖ ❖ ❖ ❖ ❖

She returns the next day, certain that Meg's leaving me all alone to go off and attend her classes is proof that she is not a good friend. She reheats yesterday's soup, and squeezes a lemon into it for extra curative powers.

Huda has been sent out for groceries, and as I blow on my soup, Karima wanders about the quiet flat. She pauses for a moment in Meg's room, staring at the pictures she has taped to the mirror. I hear her tsk-tsking through the open French doors that connect the two bedrooms.

The pictures on my mirror are of my parents and my dog, nothing to draw Karima's scorn. But Meg's are all of school friends. Meg holding a frothing cup of beer, dangling on the neck of a boy in boxers. Meg at a formal dance, wearing a low-cut dress, receiving a kiss from her date. Meg in a row of bikinied girlfriends on spring break.

It is in the swiftness of a tsking that Karima's presence in the flat goes from angelic to oppressive. I can guess what she is thinking, and I am irritated by her judgments of Meg. I want to tell her I have pictures just as shocking.

She has no mother, this Meg?

I laugh uncomfortably, irritated. *Of course she has a mother. And her mother lets her behave this way?*

I don't want to get into an argument with Karima after all she has done for me. I swallow, unsure how to respond.

I know that girls are not purified where you come from. But surely a mother can insist that her daughter grow up to be . . . polite. She does not look like a bad girl, after all.

I blink at her. *Purified?*

كريمة

Karima

The Caliph 'Abd al-Mālik ibn Marwān (reigned 685–705) asked Kuthayyir (d. 723 C.E.) what was the most amazing event that occurred between him and 'Azza. Said Kuthayyir:

One year I set out upon the journey for the pilgrimage; so, too, did 'Azza's husband set out with her. Neither 'Azza nor I knew the other was there. When we'd gone some distance, 'Azza's husband sent her out to purchase butter for the food for his traveling companions. She began going from tent to tent until she entered mine, not knowing it was my tent.

I was sharpening arrows. When I saw her, I continued cutting as I gazed at her, unaware that I had sliced my own flesh to the bone several times—I felt it not, though the blood was gushing. When this became evident, she came to me and clutched my hand and began wiping away the blood with her garment.

—from *The Book of Songs*
ABU AL-FARAJ AL-ISFAHANI,
d. 967 C.E.

عبد المالك سأل كُثيّرًا عن أعْجب خبر له مع عَزّة فقال:
حجَجْتُ سنة من السنين وحجّ زوج عزّة بها ولم يعلم أحد منّا بصاحبه.
فلمّا كنّا ببعض الطريق أمرَها زوجها بابتّياع سمن تصلح به طعامًا
لأهل رفقته. فجعلتْ تدور الخيام خيمة خيمة حتّى دخلتْ إليّ وهي لا
تعلم أنّها خيمتي. وكنت أبري أسهمًا لي. فلمّا رأيتُها جعلتُ أبري وأنا
أنظر إليها ولا أعلم حتّى بريتُ عظامي مرات ولا أشعر به والدم
يجري. ولما تبينت ذلك دخلتْ إليّ فأمسكتْ يدي وجعلتْ تمسح الدم
عنها بثوبها.

I t was dawn when Nayna pulled me from my dreaming and into
her bedroom.

Come, *she said*, I have to measure your waist for a new
gelabiyya.

*In my grogginess I was happy. It had been a long time since I'd
had anything new. My twelfth birthday was still three months away,
but I wouldn't dare remind her.*

*She brushed her gnarled hand against my cheek, then put both her
hands around my waist. I had just started to ask what color it would
be, when she upended me. My legs stuck at angles into the air, my
head bounced against the hard ceramic floor. Suddenly I saw that we
were not alone. The same gypsy whom I'd seen Nayna speaking
with in the souq yesterday stood over me. The huge gold ring in her
nose shuddered in the muted light from the kerosene lamp.*

I was surprised. But not afraid. She was a fortune-teller, Nayna had said. Perhaps she was here to read my fortune.

Nayna was still holding my waist, telling me I was clever for not moving, for keeping quiet. I must show how strong and clever I was by keeping quiet altogether.

Then the gypsy jammed her elbow against the soft flesh of my inner thigh, opening my legs even wider. I didn't realize that the flash of cold light was a knife until I felt the cutting.

I tried so hard not to scream, but it shot out of me like an explosion, as though all of my insides suddenly flew right out of me. I kept right on screaming until Nayna let me wriggle out of her grasp and sit up. I saw my blood on the gypsy's hands as she pressed something against the open wound.

I had been the first that day. The gypsies came when the Nile rose, telling fortunes, purifying girls for money. There were three other girls in our building who screamed that day as I did. Nayna had insisted that the gypsy come to our house first; she had not wanted me to be awakened by their screaming.

She had not wanted me to be scared.

My mother had not been there in the room.

She was so sensitive, she could not bear to watch.

Nayna and my mother explained that I must walk for a few days with my legs open, so as not to chafe the area.

They had sent my father out to buy a chicken for me, and they fed me chicken all day long, so that I would get my strength back quickly.

Seven days later they made a wonderful party for me, inviting the whole family. Everyone gave me little gifts of money, patting me tenderly on the head and saying, "Congratulations."

Just as they did years later when I gave birth.

There was a shop in Sayyida Zaynab which specialized in tahara. A barbershop. It was cheaper to take the child there than to have someone come to the house. I was the only one done in the house. All the rest of the grandchildren, boys and girls, were taken to the barber. Nayna would supervise, then help the child to stagger home.

She left not one of us uncircumcised.

Of course it's still done today! Not like it once was, but it happens.

Usually at doctors' offices. It's cleaner that way.

Yusuf, a man in the office where I worked, his wife's sister is a doctor. She did all six of his children, boys and girls.

He would joke about it at work.

"We slaughtered the girl last night," he'd say.

And we all knew that they had circumcised another one.

It is necessary.

A woman left alone—unmarried, or her husband is traveling . . . This way she is calm. Not excitable. Not prone to stray. It is shameful not to do it.

Riham—Huda's cousin, remember?

Her in-laws don't know that she isn't. They only accepted her as a bride for their son after making sure. They asked her mother, and she lied, not wanting to let such a catch slip away.

They would be scandalized if they knew the truth.

To this day, only her husband knows.

Some men have it done to their wives.

What do you think of that?

My husband, God have mercy on his soul, was not like that.

He was angry.

He said that he had been robbed. That the gypsy had robbed him of me.

Because I felt nothing.

Sometimes they cut just a little bit. Sometimes a lot. The gypsy, she took it all, you see. The whole clitoris.

She left me nothing.

That area was for having babies. Only.

He could never get my interest. And as much as I loved him, I only tolerated that part of it to relieve his needs.

And for getting my babies.

I wanted to do it to Huda. It is shameful not to.

I was on my way with her to Nayna's.

But my husband said no. He swore to divorce me if I did it. There is *nothing* in the religion that commands this! *he shouted at me. Nothing!*

He said no man should suffer as he had.

I had disappointed him.

I never made him happy. I didn't know how.

But I finally said to myself, This is not so much my fault.

How could he really expect to find happiness when it was death that brought us together from the start?

It was a scalding, airless afternoon when her home collapsed. Karima had just descended from the electric tram, her dress disgracefully damp and her hair matted with sweat, when she heard a thunderous roar and the ground beneath her shook. She scanned the sky in terror for Israeli planes; the defeat of the *naksa* was barely a week old, she insisted desperately to herself as she craned her neck upward . . . surely they would not dare attack the city? It seemed that every person on Shaykh Rihan Street had paused as she did, peering into the simmering sky. Then, as though on cue, each one began shouting and running.

Karima stood paralyzed, staring eyes shifting from the empty sky to the commotion on the ground, conscious of a lone rivulet of perspiration inching along the length of her back. She held her ground, watching people flowing in all directions, and waited. No other tremors came, nor deafening sounds, and the street seemed to regain an uneasy calm.

That was when the cloud of dust became visible all the way out in the square, motionless, caught in a layer of hot, still air, and the shouting began to reverberate from merchant to child to passerby that a building had fallen.

She was seized by an echo reverberating throughout the span of her memory. Over and over, her father had predicted this day—or more precisely, invoked it, the better to ward it off. Whenever his mother complained about a leaking faucet or a faulty toilet, he would defend the place, "Don't you know we're living in a miracle building? That old scoundrel never got a permit to add three floors. . . ." This was the way that her father hid his fury at being duped—ever and always joking. His children always heard, "Stop your shouting! Do you want the whole building to fall down?"

She started to run. Past the Palace of the Republic and right onto Timsah Alley, where the commotion and screaming were even louder.

She stopped short at the sight. The rubble spilled all the way across the narrow street, with huge sections of jagged cement sealing off the entrance to the facing building. 'Am Galal's newspaper stand had been completely obliterated, the bent old man having sheltered in a doorway. Broken water pipes shot geysers into the unrelenting heat. Twisted iron bars poked out of the debris, and torn electrical wires snaked about like tousled hair.

The building had once been a two-story villa in the days of the empire. It was vacated at the start of the revolution, and soon refurbished with three additional floors; ten apartments were carved out of it. After years of valiant effort, the original roof had finally collapsed under the weight of the unlicensed additional levels, and the back wall and central stairwell were all that remained, the stairs still wending their way hopefully upward.

Already the wreckage was crawling with dusty, frantic searchers yelling the names of their neighbors or family members. Heavy blocks of cement were being hoisted aside. 'Abd al-Khaliq, the barber, a spare, bony man with a pronounced collarbone, stood alongside Sa'id the butcher, himself no less than seventy years old. The two struggled and heaved at a portion of a bathroom wall, the gas-fired water heater still clinging like a massive white leech to the lavender tile. A woman's screams could be heard beneath, and the two shopkeepers began shouting for help from passersby.

Karima watched all this with a tenuous hold on her nerves. She knew 'Adil and Amar to be at school. But her parents were surely at home, awaiting her return from work. The scream of an approaching ambulance pierced the heavy air.

She watched breathlessly as a small group pulled the bathroom wall off Um 'Esmet, her parents' neighbor one flight down. Um 'Esmet had apparently been on her way to bathe, for she wore only a thin robe, and her hair was uncovered and hanging loose. Karima was startled to see that the woman, usually seen in drab rayon scarves, dyed her long hair Mar-leen Monroe blonde. As she was helped to her feet, it became clear that her left arm had been badly broken. It hung at an unnatural angle, limp and bloody at her side.

Karima could barely contain herself. In desperation, she waded into the rubble. "Baba!" she shouted, peering into crevices and behind the remains of once-glossy oak bed frames and Ideal refrigerators. "Mama!"

It was Sulayman the grocer who began calling at her to get back. He had been digging with three other men when he spotted her shaky ascent up the steep center of the rubble. "*Ya . . . Anisa!*" He called to her to get down, to let him do the searching, knowing as did everyone on Timsah Alley that this was her family home. When she ignored him, he scrambled over to her, the sweat pouring out of his hair and dripping off his chin. He offered his hand to guide her off the pile of concrete, but she shook her head, waving him away. Sulayman looked left and right, at a loss as to how to reason with her. Everyone else was too busy to notice Karima's insistent trek. She slipped and almost fell, hesitated, then looked at him in dazed desperation.

Finally, he cupped her elbow in his palm and steadied her as she went. They worked their way to the back of the building, now a single bared wall that evidenced the decorating tastes of the four uppermost apartments. Karima's eyes scanned the remains. On the fifth floor, the family of the civil engineer Mahmoud al-Tonsi had stenciled a strange, wilted-flower sort of design all across their sitting room. Below, on the fourth, her mother's delicate rose-print wallpaper ended abruptly in an angry, serrated edge; the open air about it felt sinister. Karima continued her search below that optimistic wallpaper, clinging to Sulayman as she slid and stumbled. The gold-edged pale pink sofa, the velvet for which had been obtained through the black market during the Second World War, lay smashed under a section of ceiling.

She came to a halt, staring numbly at the sofa. Sulayman stood alongside her, then raised his head, listening hard.

She stared at him, straining to hear, her fingernails digging into the skin of his forearm.

"A woman's voice," he said, frowning, not wanting to feed her frail hopes. It had come from beneath his feet, and all that was beneath his feet was a steep pile of rubble. Karima looked down at the crumpled cement, bile rising in her throat, her stomach twisting. She renewed her cries, and this time was answered ever so faintly by her mother's voice.

Frantically, Karima started pulling away small pieces of concrete. Sulayman shouted to 'Abd al-Khaliq and Sa'id, who were sifting through the debris in other portions of the collapsed building; these in turn called to other neighbors. Each one who came to help dig would insist that Karima descend to the street, but she would not stop. She yanked and heaved with the men, at one point taking off her shoe and using the heel as a lever between two small but unmoving pieces.

Someone finally produced some long, thick ropes. With one rope, they tied the largest section of concrete to a car; with another, they anchored it to 'Am Mustapha's apple cart.

The wall groaned as it slid and bumped across the wreckage, coming to rest in the street with a bone-crunching thud. Two other portions of wall that lay at forty-five-degree angles had supported it. Lifting off the crowning portion allowed a shaft of sunlight into the darkness. The first thing visible was her father's favorite, cream-colored cardigan, nearly worn through at the elbows. Karima's breath caught. She squatted at the edge of the opening. Sweat slid off the tip of her nose and made tiny splashes on the hot gray rock. "Mama?" she called, squinting into the hole. "Baba?"

"Karima! *Al-hamdu lillah*. Karima, *habibti*, get us out of here. I think your father's hurt badly. Hurry!"

Karima raised her eyes to meet Sulayman's.

He was shaking his head, his wide eyes dark. "It's going to take a very long time."

The two angled portions of wall were leaning against each other in such a way that if one were yanked away, the other would crash down upon her parents. The only other option was to try to open a tunnel to them and pull them through it.

Two fire trucks had arrived by this time, and the uniformed men seemed to swarm over the debris. It was they who with their tools and numbers managed to tunnel beneath the debris until they reached Karima's parents. Selwa, who was conscious, slid carefully from beneath Gamal and slithered out whole and unhurt except for a few minor scrapes. Karima gathered her into her arms and covered her in relieved kisses, then led her to the ambulance to be examined.

Karima threaded her way back over the rubble to the place from which her mother had just emerged. A fireman crawled the six meters or so to reach Karima's father and was dragging him out ever so slowly. As soon as he was free, Sulayman heaved her father's bulky body into his arms and started to carry him toward the street. Gamal's arm flopped down, his knuckles grazing the torn wall. Red gashes appeared in the wheat-colored flesh.

Karima leapt to his side. "Baba . . ." She grasped the dangling hand in hers, pressing her lips against his bleeding fingers. Then she noticed Sulayman's shoulder. Where it supported her father's head, his white shirt was already soaked through with blood. "Baba," she said again, this time in a whisper.

Sulayman was panting hard, his chest rising and falling rapidly. He stared at her, even as he blinked fiercely against the drops of sweat sliding into his wide eyes. "I'm sorry," he said.

"No . . ." She looked from her father's body to her mother, who still sat by the ambulance. "No . . ."

She fought for breath and balance. She looked about at the scene. It seemed as though everywhere she turned there were women wailing and slapping their cheeks. Sweat-drenched men still pulled at tangled iron bars and heavy blocks of cement, trying to make sure no one was left in the rubble.

She watched an ambulance attendant fill his stretcher with the inert body of Hamada Ahmad, the four-year-old son of her neighbor Hebba. The child's whole left side was awash in blood, and his broken shinbone had pierced his thin cotton pants. Hebba had thrown herself on the ground beside the ambulance, shrieking in hysteria, tearing at her dust-encrusted hair.

Karima looked back at Sulayman, paralyzed, searching his strong features for guidance.

He swallowed hard, fighting to even out his breathing. "I will take him to the ambulance. You must tell her."

She looked away, blinking back tears.

"It will be all right, Karima," he said, using her name for the first time, his voice gentle. "It's God's will. 'We belong to God, and to Him we shall return,'" he quoted.

She watched as he made his way across the debris, stumbling only slightly under his heavy burden. She inhaled deeply, then headed for her mother, who was on her knees in the dust, desperately trying to comfort the young mother Hebba.

The formal parlor of Nayna's flat was wall to wall with sweating, black-swathed women. The air was heavy with the scent of cardamom and electric with the designated mourner's impromptu grief.

Karima sat pressed up against her mother, rubbing her back gently with one hand, resting her head on Selwa's bent shoulder. The thin handkerchief in her other hand was used equally to wipe away her silent tears and swab at her rapidly perspiring forehead. Her aunt Kawthar cradled five-year-old Amar on her lap, covering one of the girl's ears with her hand and whispering soothing words into the other. Amar was terrified by the weeping and moaning of Um 'Atrees.

Um 'Atrees, for her part, had taken center stage.

She clutched at her head, then raised her hands and eyes to the ceiling, bellowing, "My darling Gamal! So good, so kind! You were stolen from us! Oh, God! Oh, blackest of tragedies!"

Karima watched her curiously. It would have been wrong for the family to wail and slap their cheeks thus in mourning for her father. To do so would be to grieve over an act of God, and so to question it. Um 'Atrees, the neighborhood's designated mourner, considered herself a friend of Nayna's after their lengthy chats at the public baths. It was she who had taken their collective grief on her own shoulders. As a favor to the family, she would even forego her usual fee.

The woman's teeth were short and uneven, ending too quickly in large, purple gums. Her cheeks were flabby and pallid. Large dark crescents skulked beneath pale eyes. Plump, arthritis-gnarled hands were host to ten gnawed fingernails. She reeked of cooked cabbage and raw garlic.

"That man was an *angel*!" she cried, although she had never met him. "The darling of his wife, the darling of his children, his poor children! Oh, the misery, oh, God! What a black and cruel day this is! *Ya Allah!*"

Karima sighed. At least the performance kept her from thoughts of her own pain. Her eyes darted to the lace curtain that separated the formal parlor from the living room. The men sat in a large circle, drinking the thick, unsugared coffee, tasting in it a bit of grief's bitterness. The cigarette smoke hung in a thick haze, further obscuring some of the faces of the men. A meditative silence reigned over the room, broken only by the arrival of visitors greeting and being greeted with *salaams*.

She tilted her head, pondering them. She knew her father's sudden death was as much an opportunity to express the grief over the country's loss as it was anything else.

And yet . . .

She wondered why they could wail in the streets, begging the president to lead them and retract his resignation, but enter this home on the same day and stoically refuse to shed a tear for the man whose gentle friendship had enriched them for so many years.

Uncle Zayd had collected 'Adil and Amar from school. They'd entered Nayna's Sayyida Zaynab apartment to find the corpse washer standing in the living room, and the doctor just leaving after having signed the death certificate. Amar was content enough to play with her cousins, circling her mother periodically to ask why she cried. Eight-year-old 'Adil fought a losing battle with tears, clinging miserably to Karima, his face buried in her neck; tears of loss brought tears of humiliation over the tears he could not contain. But when Uncle Zayd and his father's brother Yahya came to oversee the washing, he had slid off Karima's lap and followed them.

The corpse washer had worked quickly. 'Adil had stood, erect and dazed, as his father's body was gently laid out in Nayna's bedroom, washed with soft cloths, then wrapped in a pure white shroud. Karima had implored him to come away, but he stood as if rooted to the spot, soaking in every last possible sight of his father. There was a rush; these mute ministrations had to end and the body had to arrive at the family tomb well before sunset. Otherwise, they would have to wait until the next day.

As ever, bad news had traveled quickly throughout the alleys and streets, from shopkeeper to shopkeeper and neighbor to neighbor. The friends and family members of Gamal 'Izz al-Din, returning from their demonstrations in Tahrir Square, had gathered again by the time of the late-afternoon prayer. The muezzin's call echoed along Adri Street. The tones seemed too certain, too animated in the suffocating heat, as the mourners descended upon the flat in small clusters.

As the men gathered to accompany the coffin, 'Adil drifted into the gathering of women and wended his way to Karima.

"Come with me," he said, his voice low but urgent.

She smiled tenderly. "Uncle Zayd will walk with you. You won't be alone, I promise."

"His hand sweats too much," he protested. "Your hand never sweats."

She pulled him onto her lap, stroking his soft, wavy hair.

He continued, "I want you to come. Please. Why won't you come?"

"*Habibi*. You know girls can't walk in the procession," she said, gently trying to dam up his tears with the first two knuckles of her index finger. "What if I forget myself, and start crying out loud or sobbing? They say Baba will suffer in his tomb for every time we moan and shout for him." She pressed warm, firm kisses against his wet cheeks. "Go on, now. I'll watch you from the window."

Reluctantly, 'Adil disentwined himself from her arms and joined the men in the street. They patted him on the head, murmuring gruff condolences. Each time he looked up at the window, Karima blew her little brother a kiss and cemented an encouraging smile across her lips.

The men formed a somber, shuffling procession behind the plain wooden box. Eight men lent their hands to supporting the casket, to switch off with eight others along the way.

Once in a while, a man in the line would say, "*Allahu Akbar,*" and all would echo him. But other than that, the line was silent as it went, each man murmuring to himself as many memorized *surahs* as he could recall.

Karima watched numbly as the box carrying her father inched slowly out of sight, only allowing her own tears to spill over once she became certain that 'Adil, his small hand lost in Uncle Zayd's, had vanished.

"Too young," Um 'Atrees was braying, yanking at her black gelabiyya. "Too young, my Lord, to be stolen from us."

And so it went until late, late into the night.

The doorbell at Nayna's apartment chimed slightly off-key. Karima was browning spiced ground beef at the small gas stove when the bell echoed in the kitchen. Her mother and Nayna were preparing zucchini for stuffing at the small kitchen table. Karima laid aside the thick wooden spoon and walked to the door. She expected to see 'Adil or Amar home from school, but found instead the boy from the grocery holding a large box of chocolates and a folded piece of paper.

Karima extended her hand and read the note quickly. Her eyes widened, and she looked from the boy to the note several times, before saying, "Wait here."

With great deliberateness she walked out of the entryway and down the hall, her mind aswirl. *Sulayman,* she whispered to herself.

She stared at the chipped tile of the hallway, seeing only the tall, crowded shelves of the grocery and the quiet young man who stood behind the counter. She had only ever seen him in the light cotton button-down that clung to the muscles of his back when the heat of his small grocery got the better of him. He was much taller than she was, and his shoulders were broad. Substantial eyebrows hung over wide onyx eyes and heavy lashes. Sulayman had always been polite to her, if not excessively shy, rarely looking her in the eye when she entered.

She walked into the kitchen, her head slightly cocked. "Mama!"

Nayna and Selwa looked up, startled. "What is it?" they both demanded, knives paused like scalpels midcut.

"There's someone at the door. . . ." Karima began.

Her mother shook her head. "I've had about all the visitors I can stand for the rest of my life. It's been two weeks. The man is dead, may God have mercy on him. They never know what to say, and always end up talking about the war and the loss and the shame of it all, as though somehow that's a light subject in comparison. Enough already!"

The knife shook in her grasp, and Karima gazed at her mother. Selwa's grief was tidal, but somehow she resisted giving herself over to it completely. Karima felt her eyes suddenly swim with tears, wondering if she could ever be so strong. She pushed the tears away for now, whispering, "It's not that kind of visit."

Selwa looked up at her daughter curiously. The girl looked flustered. She looked at Nayna, who narrowed her dark eyes. Selwa set aside her knife. "Just what kind of visit is it, then?"

Karima shoved the note at her.

Selwa gave it a cursory glance, and then said, "Read it to me, girl." She could write her name and divine her letters, but only with difficulty. Nayna could do neither.

Karima took the paper again and swallowed. "*Sulayman Nazmi Harfush and his mother request the opportunity to pay a visit to the Anisa Karima and her family at the time that is convenient for them.*"

Selwa stared at her daughter. "The *grocer?*"

Nayna went back to coring a fat zucchini, shaking her head and tsk-tsking softly.

"Do you have some sort of agreement?" Selwa demanded.

Karima threw up her hands as though halting before a pointed gun. "I had no idea."

Selwa nodded. "So that's why he's been sending all that food over since the funeral."

"Will you talk to him, Mama? See what he wants?"

Her mother raised her eyebrows. "See what he wants? It's a good bet he wouldn't be coming to ask about my health." Selwa leaned back in her chair, watching Karima closely. The girl's suitors had been many, and she had refused every one. Gamal had been at an utter loss as to what to do with her, but he had sworn never to pressure her. And now here she was suddenly visibly interested in . . . Sulayman! Or was it that in her grief, she was vulnerable to the first one who came knocking? Why, the man hadn't even waited the forty days after Gamal's death! Did he think she was desperate?

"Girl, this is hardly proper," she said at last.

Karima toed the floor in silence. She couldn't explain why she was interested to hear the grocer's proposal. She hadn't thought about him before at all. Perhaps it was too soon after all, and she wasn't thinking clearly. Or perhaps the air had been too death-swollen these days, and thoughts of love and marriage were a sweet intrusion.

Selwa shook her head. "I don't understand you."

Karima shrugged again. "There's no harm in hearing him out, is there?"

Selwa drummed her fingers on the table, looking to Nayna for input. The older woman's eyes were crinkled up at the edges; her lips were pursed in an effort not to smile.

Selwa squinted, studying her. "What?"

Nayna looked up, her eyes laughing. "Marriage is a matter of Fate. Who knows what will move the heart of a young woman?"

Selwa looked at her mother in disbelief. She rubbed her eyes. "Where is Gamal when I really need him?" she asked the pile of peeled vegetables. "Tell the grocer and his mother to come tomorrow afternoon," she said to Karima resignedly. "We'll hear them out."

Karima was not altogether surprised to find that Sulayman looked terribly handsome, if somewhat stiff, in his suit and tie.

After delivering the tea to Sulayman and the two mothers in the parlor, Karima paced the kitchen floor. She had blushed furiously, despite her best intentions, upon entering with the tray. Now she raked over each brief moment she had spent in the room, wishing somehow that the outcome would differ, that she would have appeared coolly impervious to the situation's implications.

Every time she looked at Nayna, her grandmother would rivet her eyes on the task at hand. Exasperated, Karima yanked out the chair across from her and sat down. "Do you think it's bad that he didn't wait until after the forty days?"

Nayna smiled. "Do you?"

Karima thought about this for a moment. "I'm not sure. It either means he's very much in love and can't wait another second, or he feels really sorry for me. Or . . . or he thinks I'm desperate and wants to take advantage of the situation." She looked at Nayna thoughtfully. "But I don't think he's that kind of man."

Nayna tucked a wisp of hair into the black scarf she always wore knotted at the nape of her neck. "What kind of man do you think he is?"

Karima closed her eyes, revisiting the tiny grocery in slow motion and sifting through every *good morning* and *good afternoon* that she had received from him. Her mind leapt ahead to that day, the sweat dripping off his skin and the heavy, dust-choked air, and the way his eyes had looked as he'd said, *It will be all right, Karima.* Despite it all, she had believed him. She opened her eyes to look steadily at Nayna. "He's a good man. And honest. And strong."

Nayna nodded in silence.

"I can't explain it," Karima said. "I don't know; it's just this feeling I suddenly have about him. As if I'm supposed to be with him."

"Marriage is a matter of Fate," said Nayna once again, adding a minute shrug.

They heard the front door click into place and Selwa's even step on the hallway tile. She entered the kitchen slowly, carrying the visitors' offering of a tray of sweets.

Karima leapt out of the chair. "Well?"

She laughed. "Well what? We drank tea."

"Did you like him? What did he say?"

Selwa brushed by Karima to reoccupy the just vacated chair. "He's obviously a . . . sensitive young man."

Karima knelt by her mother's chair. "Meaning what?"

Selwa inhaled deeply. "Meaning that . . . he said that he

knew it was inappropriate to come so soon, but he has been terrified that you would agree to marry someone else in the interim without ever knowing his intentions."

Karima absorbed that, then said, "And?"

"And he had no reservations about saying that the *naksa*, followed so soon by the death of your father—for whom he had the greatest respect, he says—made him realize that life is uncertain. He has admired you from afar for a very long time, and decided that it was now or never."

The three women exchanged looks. Thus far, all was perfectly reasonable.

Karima pressed her mother. "And?"

"He has saved enough money to buy a reasonable apartment in the part of town of your reason-tempered choice."

Karima narrowed her eyes, thinking. "And?"

"And he has a two-year degree in commerce, but chose to open his own store instead of working for the enrichment of others. He has worked like a madman ever since, and with the grace of God," she made a dramatic pause before continuing, "a few years after the two of you are married, he'll be able to open a second grocery, and then a third, and someday he'll buy you the grandest villa in Heliopolis."

Selwa stopped, watching how Karima would digest this information.

Her daughter frowned at her, wide-eyed. "How about his mother?"

"Quiet like him. Could be a good sign . . ." She looked at Nayna. "*Could be trouble*," the two said together, laughing deep, knowing laughter.

Karima smiled despite herself. It was good to hear them laugh.

"She was impressed with your beauty," Selwa added soberly. Then, with a wink she added, "I believe she was noticing your excellent childbearing hips."

Karima rubbed her hand over her eyes as Nayna sniggered. She bit back the desire to snap at the two women, more sisters than mother and daughter, and demand they be serious at such a moment. Instead, she asked, "So how did it end?"

Selwa smiled. "I gave him permission to visit you formally, pending your approval, after the forty days are up, and I told him we would consider his offer."

Nayna was nodding in approval. "That's the right thing to do."

Karima bit her lip. It *was* the right thing to do. She couldn't explain the sense of urgency she felt.

They asked about him along 'Abidin's Timsah Alley. Nayna and Selwa had walked from store to store, from 'Abd al-Khaliq the barber, to Sa'id the butcher, to 'Am Galal the newspaper seller and Mustapha the fruit vendor. One after another, the merchants of Timsah Alley extolled Sulayman's virtues. Colleagues and competitors alike rushed to praise him. Sulayman was respected for his honesty, envied for his intelligence and loved for his modesty and eagerness to lend a hand in any difficulty, big or small. Each man claimed that if he had a daughter of marrying age, he would beg Sulayman to marry her.

Sulayman was a man of few words. Often in the period of their engagement, he and Karima would sit in Nayna's parlor sipping mint tea, their silence amplifying the clock's ticking.

Other times, they would talk softly of the world. He was always surprised to find that people could be so harsh with one another, that his fellow merchants would cheat each other, that a man could strike another man in anger before even giving him a chance to explain. It all seemed worse after the *naksa*. All that Sulayman dreamed of was a quiet place to rest after a long day's work . . .

. . . *And*, he would add, his face reddening slightly, *someone to fill that place with light.*

· The apartment that they found was located on a dead-end street in Dokki. It was a good area, fashionable, even, although the building was already over a hundred years old. Nayna warned her not to put on airs. But Karima was not the type. For Karima, the most important thing was the flat. It was a spacious, first-floor apartment with high ceilings and tall French doors. The two bedrooms overlooked a small open-air market, but the inner rooms were all peace-filled and inviting. The full bathroom had a deep, mammoth tub, and the living room was positioned so that by day it was filled with light.

No, Sulayman was not given to declarations of love and undying passion.

But often, as they sat in Nayna's parlor, Karima would look up to find him watching her, and the expression in his dark eyes was quite enough.

The wedding took place just six months after her father's death.

The air on the roof of Nayna's building was cool that night, with gentle breezes testing the resilience of the women's hairspray. Long folding tables had been arranged near the door leading down to the apartment, holding huge pitchers of strawberry juice and heavy trays of cakes and sweets. Colored lights had been strung from poles along the rim of the rooftop. The small band huddled in one corner, settling in as the oud player tuned his instrument.

Karima herself had overseen many of the arrangements, from the flowers behind the *kusha* to the placement of the tables and the songs to be played.

Karima swore she would not hire a belly dancer, considering it low class and out of fashion. The young unmarried girls could dance, and the men. That would be enough. Nayna had been scandalized. *What kind of wedding did not have a dancer? What would the neighbors think?* Karima assured her that Nayna herself would be more than welcome to dance if she felt the atmosphere lacking. At that, Nayna rapped the bride's knuckles with her wooden spoon and declared her impolite.

Nayna stewed all the way up to the wedding night, recanting at last when she saw her eldest granddaughter in her wedding gown.

Karima wore a sparkling white sheath that hugged her curving form closely. A thin tiara of rhinestones crowned her flowing ebony hair, anchoring the silk-trimmed veil. Black velvet eyelashes rimmed her wide eyes, and a soft pink gloss shone on her full lips.

Sulayman rose when she appeared in the rooftop doorway, his long fingers curling around the arm of the chair. He stood as though paralyzed while she crossed the length of the roof.

She returned his gaze steadily as she walked. Something within her was still surprised that the man she had chosen was this one, with the dark walnut skin and the slow smile.

The laughter at Karima's wedding celebration spilled off the rooftop and echoed through the neighborhood. The guests ate and sang and clapped their hands until well after one o'clock in the morning.

With much fanfare, Karima and Sulayman climbed into the back of her uncle Zayd's prized Chevrolet Impala, and started out for Dokki. As the engine roared to life, she leaned out the window and waved up to the balcony, where her mother and Nayna were standing.

Both women waved back, glad that the distance was such that Karima would not see their tears.

Sulayman clasped her hand firmly as they walked through the small courtyard of the building. She was keenly aware of their combined footfalls on the cement paving stones that led to the doorway. Some floors above them, a loose shutter creaked, caught in a teasing night breeze.

His hand was shaking; the key rattled softly against the lock before finding the keyhole.

As he closed the door behind them, he pulled her close. Her cheek pressed up against the light wool of his suit jacket, and she inhaled deeply as he circled her with his arms. He went to kiss her hair, but the tiara put him off. He kissed instead her forehead, then tilted her chin upward so he could kiss her lips.

She responded to his kiss, pressing her glossed lips against his, exactly as Nadia Lutfi had kissed 'Abd al-Halim in *The Mistake*. She imagined how she looked, her strong, tall husband clasping her to him, her hair cascading down her back. Yes, it was surely just as she had envisioned.

But when she felt his tongue slide between her lips she pulled away, surprised. It had never occurred to her that someone might kiss in such a way. He pushed his lips against hers again, swiftly, and she tasted her own fear mixed with his warm saliva. She placed her hand against his chest.

"I'll make tea," she whispered, desperate to regroup.

"I don't want tea," he said, lacing his fingers into her hand and pulling her close again. He pressed wet kisses against her neck.

She felt her body go rigid.

He felt it, too. "What's the matter?" he asked, frowning.

She pressed her hand against her temple, as though to banish a persistent headache that was blocking the flow of her thoughts. She groped for words. "We . . . we're standing in the hallway. . . ."

His face relaxed into a gentle smile. "Of course," he murmured. Still holding her hand, he led her through the sitting room and into the bedroom.

He turned on the light and they surveyed the room together. Everything stood as though breathlessly awaiting their arrival. The woodwork preened beneath its slick lacquer, new and untouched. The wardrobes swelled with her blouses and nightgowns and undergarments, all folded and pressed, stacked or hung in precise rows. Her lipsticks and eye shadows, perfumes and powders all stood at attention, carefully aligned on the vanity table's glass surface. The bedspreads and pillowcases she and her mother had stitched were smoothed and resmoothed on the wide bed.

The only thing that seemed out of place was an unadorned white cloth. It lay suggestively on the bedside table, next to the lamp with the dangling lavender fringe. She did not know when it had been left there. Perhaps it was Nayna's doing. The three of them had been there together that morning, putting finishing touches on the furnishings and kitchenwares.

Karima felt herself biting her lip as she looked at the towel. She had heard joking references to such a thing on several occasions in the past few months, usually from her aunts. But the words had been vague, and Karima, easily embarrassed, had never pressed for details. Her mother had only shaken her head and looked away each time, trying to conceal a sad smile that Karima understood to indicate her mother's constant ache for Baba.

And this afternoon, when her aunt Kawthar had taken her into her mother's room and locked the door, then used the sticky *helawa* to pull off all the hair on her limbs and most private areas, Karima had only concentrated on enduring the pain. "Just getting you all cleaned up," Kawthar repeated throughout the ritual. Karima was humiliated at being so exposed before her favorite aunt, and she blinked back tears a few times that Kawthar misinterpreted as tears of pain. She chided her for being such a baby, then spit on the rubbery mass in her hand, kneading it to soften it and make it more workable.

Now Sulayman watched Karima stare at the white cloth.

"Are you scared?" he asked, wondering suddenly if she knew its purpose.

She turned wide eyes to look at him. She had paled beneath her carefully drawn makeup, and he searched her features for the pliant, desirous woman he had conjured so often in his loneliness.

He found only a frightened girl in a woman's dramatically curving body.

"I won't hurt you," he said earnestly.

She smiled then, but her relief faded as he brushed a hand along the satin of her gown, cupping one of her breasts. She could not keep from backstepping, and his hand fell to his side.

He moved to the edge of the bed and sat down, his dark features drawn together pensively. "Do you not want me to touch you at all?" he asked, swallowing his frustration.

"I—" She turned away, angry with herself and embarrassed. Why hadn't she ever thought to picture this part of it, to prepare herself? She had drawn so many scenes in her head, but they were always far, far into the future. She had imagined them laughing on the beach in Alexandria. She had seen herself tidying their small apartment. She had posed in front of her mirror with a pillow beneath her nightgown, and envisioned the imprint of a small foot extruding from the taut skin of her stomach—as she had seen once when her aunt Kawthar was overdue to deliver.

Making dinner, making tea, talking softly into the night.

But this awkward, startling intimacy . . . It was as though her mind had blocked out even the possibility of such things, such nearness.

She felt tears spilling out of her elaborately lined eyes as she tried to arrange in her mind the imminent events. She knew he would have to see at least a portion of her naked body. And touch her in all the places that Kawthar's painful depilations had prepared for him. Proof of this touching would somehow imprint itself on the white towel. And somehow, if she endured it all patiently and quietly, in nine months she would have a baby to cuddle and coo over and press against her breast.

Sulayman watched her suppressed sobs with a sigh. He tugged at the uncomfortable necktie as he stood up. He laid a hand on her shoulder. "Please. Please don't cry," he said. He would try a new tactic, the one that Sa'id the butcher had insisted was the cornerstone of wedding nights all up and down Timsah Alley.

But it's forbidden, he had protested.

And Sa'id had punched him gently on the shoulder. *Think, man. Religion is easy, not hard*, he quoted. *Our Lord understands these situations. He knows that sometimes a man needs a helping hand.*

"Why don't you wash your face and change into a night-gown so you can be more at ease?" he said. "Come out and sit with me in the parlor and we'll talk awhile."

He waited until she had gone into the bathroom before he wriggled out of the suit and into his undershirt and pajama bottoms. He walked into the kitchen and reached into the depths of the refrigerator, where earlier that afternoon, still nursing reservations, he had hidden the recommended purchase.

When Karima emerged in a soft pink nightgown and matching robe, she found Sulayman seated on the formal couch with six bottles of beer lined up in front of him. He had opened one, and was dividing it between two of the crystal stemware glasses.

She gaped at him. "Alcohol?"

He smiled at her, patting the couch next to him. "To relax us both," he said.

She did not move from her spot in the doorway. "You want me to drink alcohol?" It never occurred to her that Sulayman would entice her down forbidden paths.

He sighed again, fighting for patience. "Karima. Come and sit next to me," he ordered.

She complied, staring at him in bewilderment.

"It's our wedding night," he said, his voice gentle, his eyes warm. "Won't you toast our life together?"

She couldn't say no to this. Timidly, she stretched a hand to accept the foaming brew.

The towel proved the evening's success, even if the events remained vague in Karima's memory.

They did not travel to Alexandria or Marsah Matrouh for a honeymoon; Sulayman could not leave the store. But Karima did not mind. She took the allowed month's vacation from her job at the Ministry. In this period, she cooked every dish she had ever encountered at Nayna's or her mother's. She puttered about the small flat, cleaning and recleaning, arranging and rearranging.

Late in the evening, after Sulayman's return from the 'Abidin grocery store, after dinner, they would sit side by side on the small veranda. He would recount the events of his day in detail, and she would listen intently. He would ask her opinion on ways to deal with customers defaulting on credit, or suppliers unfairly raising prices. She was always surprised when she realized that he was expecting some sort of comment from her. She would protest; she knew nothing of such things. But Sulayman would insist. He would tug playfully at her long, thick hair. *Didn't I marry you so I'd have someone to talk to? What good are you otherwise?*

He was only partially joking. For while Sulayman was loved by his colleagues as the man who would lend a compassionate ear to any problem, he never spoke of his affairs. The world had shifted and contorted beneath his feet, and he had learned not to trust. He wanted desperately to carve out of the world's uncertainty a peaceful place, and to pour his trust and belief into the woman who shared it with him.

And so Karima learned to listen. Of her wifely roles, confidante was by far the easiest to perform.

And then, nine months to the day, Omar was born. No baby had been more beautiful, with cheeks like ripe persimmons and his grandmother's jade eyes. But he was wakeful and demanding, and he never allowed Karima to sleep more than two hours at a time. Ever so subtly, Karima began skipping the veranda chats. All she wanted to do after dinner was sleep a few moments before her next session of walking the living room floor, singing any song she could think of to the baby in her arms.

Sulayman, as proud as he was of his strong, handsome son, fell silent once again. For it was in this period that he discovered with certainty that the only way to make money in the country had become to cheat, and the only ones attaining the success he had dreamt about were the ones who were stealing it. Sulayman, incapable of dishonesty, found himself to be a failure.

He would enter the bedroom quietly after having sat alone on the veranda, and survey the curving outline of his wife's form. She lay, her arm bent, the baby's head cradled on the soft flesh of her upper arm as he nursed, both of them deep in sleep. A sigh would escape from him as he crawled beneath the blanket.

Sulayman pulled the newspaper away from his face and stared at her, unblinking. "How?"

She swallowed. "I—" She felt tears start to pool in her eyes.

He shook his head. "You threw away the pills again?" His voice was soft, measured.

She nodded. "I thought . . ."

He interrupted her. "You thought if you put me before the reality of it, I would change my mind? Like last time?"

She bit her lip, seeing that she had been wrong.

He rose from his chair, folding and setting the newspaper aside with a chilling deliberateness. He held out his hand to her. "Come with me."

She looked up at him, confused.

He shook his outstretched palm at her, insisting. "*Yella.* Get up."

She took his hand and stood up.

He led her slowly into the kitchen, where her mother stood

before the stove, stirring a boiling chicken. Tiny Huda was sitting beneath the kitchen table, thumping an empty pot with a wooden spoon.

"What do you see?" Sulayman asked.

She started to reply, but he silenced her with a glance. "Wait; there's more," he said, leading her to the children's room, where Wagdy and Omar, six and seven respectively, were bickering over the use of the three-wheeled fire engine. It was Omar who was in tears, though, as he had just been clubbed in the face with the truck. Over the din, Sulayman asked her again, "What do you see?"

Karima sighed, and was about to begin her defense, but he held up a finger. "One more thing." He pulled her across the tiny hall to their cramped bedroom. He reached for the trousers that were dangling from the hook on the back of the door. He tugged his wallet from the back pocket.

Handing it to her, he said, "Open it."

She stared at him, then gingerly opened the wallet, as though expecting something to jump out at her.

"What do you see?"

Other than a few crumpled slips of paper, it was empty.

"Nothing," she said.

"Exactly," he replied, plucking the wallet from her hands and shoving it back into the trousers. He sat down on the edge of their bed. "Listen to me, Karima. I'm a patient man. But I'm tired. No matter how hard I work, every day I'm just a little bit poorer, and even more tired. I know you love children. I love children. But three is enough, may God keep them safe for you."

"God would never forgive me," she whispered.

"God knows the difference between sin and adding another mouth to starve a whole family."

She pulled away to regard him. His hair was gray streaked,

his eyes hung with half-moons of darkness. His favorite
leather slippers dangled off feet that were lined with protruding purple veins and falling arches. His strong, wide shoulders
were beginning to stoop ever so slightly.

She looked away, tears sliding down her cheeks.

He caught her wrist and pulled her to him, resting his head
tenderly against her sternum. "There are only two things I
want in this world, Karima. A little peace and a little of your
attention. That's all I want, and God is my witness. Can't you
save a little bit of yourself . . . just for me?"

*And so I did it. And although I had never felt the baby move within
me before it was torn out, I've imagined that it moves within me
even now. And that it is a girl like my Huda. And that she is so
angry with me for not letting her be born . . .*

Every day I pray for forgiveness.

I never forgave Sulayman for asking me to do it.

*And God, as though to avenge Himself of the wasted life,
caused Sulayman to waste his life in work that never produced for
him another store or more profit than what our family needed for
survival. And he sits home now, with swelling feet and a sputtering
heart.*

*My second son left me to live and work abroad, because he can-
not make enough here to live better than a beggar. Instead of four
children, then, I have but two who are close enough to kiss.*

She shed tears of pride and relief when Wagdy had finished
college with reasonable marks. She immediately took to arranging his next steps, and her mind was cluttered with possible
brides, and what bracelets to sell to help him start saving for an
apartment, and which people to talk to about getting him
appointed somewhere.

And now she found him sitting at her feet, kissing her hands, telling her that he had gotten a visa to the United States to take the CPA exam. Cold fear flooded her veins.

Amreeka. A million miles away. How could she care for him there, and make sure he was fed and safe?

Wagdy's smooth-shaven face was flushed, his honeyed eyes looking up at her, pleading, as his soft, round lips moved quickly, speaking rapid words that shredded her heart.

"I will take the test, and then I will stay and work there. Khalid Mahmoud has a little restaurant there where I can work without papers."

"No—"

"Just until I can save up some money—"

"No—"

"So I can open a business here, and buy a flat so I can marry . . ."

Karima was shaking her head. She covered her face with her hands, to blind herself from the sight of his pleading eyes.

"I beg you, don't cry. Mama." He was kissing her hands, trying to pull them from her face. "Please, you know I don't want to go . . ."

"No one comes back from there," she was saying.

"No, I swear. Just for a few years. So I can come back here and have a chance."

"You'll find work. I'm going to call your uncle Zayd, and he'll help you find a good position."

"There is no work. Better men than I are patching their shoes."

"The store—"

"You know the store is just barely enough to support Omar and his family. A little left over for us, with your pension from the Ministry . . ."

She let out a sob, and he kissed her forehead, continuing, "We already sold the car for Omar's apartment. What will we sell for mine?"

"My gold—"

"*Might* be enough to get the things Huda needs when it comes time for her to marry."

"Oh, God," she said, knowing it was true. She looked down at him, and saw that he was scared as much as he was hopeful. She clutched at him, then, and held him to her chest, dripping tears onto his soft hair, breathing him in.

She heard him say, "I can *help* this way. I can make in a month what I would make in a year here. I can buy you that air conditioner you've always wanted. . . ."

"I want no air conditioners. I want you in my arms."

"It's the chance of a lifetime, Mama. Do you know how hard it is to get the visa?"

She learned, then, that it had been a conspiracy. He had been planning the trip for months, had applied for the visa and gotten it well before the final term examinations. His great-uncle Zayd had loaned him half the money for the ticket. Omar's wife had pawned half of her *shebka* for the rest, on the sworn guarantee that it would be replaced by something far more chic and expensive within a year.

They had left off telling her until three days before he was to leave.

Three days! Three days more to fill her eyes with the sight of him. Three nights to stand over him as he slept, to watch the rise and fall of his chest.

Not enough time. Not enough. If only she had known! If only she had known that she would lose him, she would have weighted the past, fleeting lifetime of time with him so much differently.

She would have held him closer, harder, nearer, so she could imprint the feel of him on each inch of her tear-sodden skin.

She wept constantly. At first sympathetic and solicitous, Sulayman grew frustrated with her weeping and began trying to ignore it.

She stood over Wagdy's vacant bed, and whispered prayers that God might find him in that vast unknown and guard him from harm.

She drifted from room to room, inconsolable. He had turned his back and walked through the security station. He had not ripped up that wretched ticket and run back into her embrace. The wound this left she could not bind, nor could she find a cooling salve for it in her wanderings through the apartment's dimness.

Omar had married and moved away; this had its own pain, but she could endure it. Wagdy's leaving felt as though a portion of her soul had been sliced away. Now she cast swollen eyes on her remaining child, and a new fear descended upon her, a fear that awakened her from the few moments of sleep she stole. She recognized a seething danger within herself. If Huda, too, were to leave her, then she would have nothing; nothing would be left of her.

And the fear was that she would rather enfold her daughter in her arms and hold her until she smothered.

❖ ❖ ❖ ❖ ❖

Silence fills the room, and Karima's voice is only a mind echo.

I watch the gauzy drapes at my balcony submitting to the whim of a crosswind.

She has seen her story pull tears from eyes, as the moon calls forth the creeping tide.

She has looked at me as if to say, *Why do you cry? Do you think, perhaps, that you are more your own than I?*

❖ ❖ ❖ ❖ ❖

I sit at the kitchen table drinking tea; Meg stands before the stove. A bright blue flame licks at her pot of lentils. With one hand, she wields a wooden spoon, stirring slowly. Her other hand guides a cigarette from her lips to the ashtray by the sink in long, contemplative ellipses of spidery smoke. One of her Grateful Dead CDs fills the living room with sound that drifts into the kitchen in low waves. Her hair is woven in a loose braid that hangs between her shoulder blades; it swings, evidencing her otherwise imperceptible movement to the slow rhythm of the music. Rather than release cigarette or spoon, she hunches up alternating shoulders to push escaping strands of hair from her eyes.

The window beyond her, the one that peers out over the building's spinal cord, is curtained by a layer of gray dust. The light that filters through it is dim; the flame beneath the lentils trembles and swells, seeming to devour what light survives in the small kitchen.

I have told Meg all that Karima told me. I have spoken quietly, aware of the words forming in my mouth, aware of the way they taste upon my tongue, and the way they feel sweeping past my teeth.

Meg has listened in smoky silence, intent on the lentil soup she is making—for me, she says, free on this quiet Friday to attend to my ailments. It does not occur to her that the smoke might nauseate me; I don't mention it. I feel foolish for any ache I have ever harbored. I feel weak.

And then, angry.

She turns, observing my moist eyes, as I speak of "purification."

How is it that mothers do it to daughters? I say at last. *That they could even consider it . . . ?*

Meg turns the knob beneath the soup. The flames fade with a sigh. *Do you think it means they love them less than mothers should?*

I rake my fingers through my hair, hearing Karima's voice— "*We have never been apart . . . I could not endure it.*" I shake my head. *So what is this concern, then, with making a little girl worthy of some eventual man? . . .*

Meg hands me a steaming bowl of soup and a wedge of lemon to squeeze into it. She reaches for a bottle of water from the refrigerator, then sits across from me pulling her knee to her chest, resting her chin on her knee. She, too, seems to be feeling out each word before it escapes her. *Same ultimate reason, different methods.*

I stir the bowl, questioning her with my eyes.

She wrenches the top from the bottle. *Why do women pay to have their fat vacuumed out or their wrinkles scraped off or breasts built for babies filled with gelatin?*

I stare at her.

To be worthy. If not to get the man, then to get the gaze. To be the worthiest among women.

I frown, weighing her words.

She holds up a slender hand, tilting her head toward the living room. *Listen . . . listen to this bridge . . .*

I watch her drift away with the music, then rest her eyes again on me. *I think we've all been fed the same poison,* she murmurs. *We just suffer from it differently.*

I lift the spoon to my lips, blowing tiny ripples across its contents before tasting them. The soup scalds my tongue; stuck, I swallow the spoonful quickly. It sears all the way down my throat.

* * * * *

Um Kulthum is a phantom hovering over the streets of Cairo. A legend in her own time, she reigned for decades as the most beloved Arab singer ever. Firm in her peasant roots, she was a fierce defender of indigenous Arabic music, a passionate lover of Egypt. Her monthly Thursday concerts, broadcast over the radio, cleared the streets as families gathered; one song could last more than three hours as her mighty contralto improvised and experimented with the melodies of love songs, songs of loss, songs of patriotism. Ever primly conservative in her dress and comportment, still she would feed off the energy of the crowd, exciting her listeners to a frenzy. Nasir would address the country *after* her concerts, the only time he could guarantee an audience. After the 1967 defeat, she traveled the Arab world, giving concerts, donating the proceeds to the government. Four million people turned out for her funeral in 1975.

Four million.

Not a day goes by when I don't pass one shop or another that has Um Kulthum singing away within. Her voice is deep, black water reflecting a star-washed sky. It is the scorching breeze that mocks sweating skin. It is the fraught laughter of those who long, reveling in memory.

The butcher, his paunch spattered pink, chops and hacks away as Um Kulthum insists, *Taste love with me, sip little by little of the passion of my heart, which has yearned for you so long!*

In cafés, men with fast-thinning hair lean over backgammon boards, their lips moving along with words like, *After the joy of being with you, my love, I'd have no regrets if my life were taken . . .*

At Baba Abdu's Koshary Shop, a gaunt young man stands

behind two gigantic twin pyramids, one of rice, the other of elbow macaroni. He slaps huge ladlefuls of rice, then elbow macaroni, then brown lentils into plastic koshary bowls, topping them with chickpeas and fried onion slices, dousing them in sauces that range from tangy to liquid suicide. His barely mustached face is studded with rivulets of perspiration; between orders he taps his ladle against the countertop, in time to a song that goes, *You planted and tended in the shade of my love the branch of hope . . .*

I stop to buy a few tapes from Karim's grocery.

Ah . . . Suma. He says the diva's nickname appreciatively as he sees me poring over her section. He stands with me and helps me choose. *She sang this one in France,* he says, pulling out one called *"Al-Atlal"*—"the Depths." *They went crazy for her there, you know. She was known throughout the world as Egypt's ambassador, the Star of the East.*

He hums a moment, pondering the selection, then picks another tape and presses it into my hand. *This one, this is so beautiful. You will not believe your ears. The songs that ʿAbd al-Wahab wrote for her are the best . . . and this is the best of those.*

Amal Hayati, reads the cover. My Life's Hope.

They stopped playing her music in the first days of the Revolution, he says. *It was assumed that because the king had loved her so much, the new, free government would want her banned—she was a reminder of an older era. When ʿAbd al-Nasir heard of this he went into a rage. "Shall I take an army and destroy the pyramids? They too were of an older era!"*

He was crazy about Um Kulthum, says Karim, sighing the sigh of a lover bereaved. *God rest them both.*

✦ ✦ ✦ ✦ ✦

A trip to the Sinai is our spring break respite from the city's intensity. We are a small group of students who, uncertain of our exact destination, board a bus for the desert at 'Abbasiyya Station. The bus is filled with a strange scattering of people: an old man in a red kaffiyeh, deep wrinkles scrawled haphazardly across his face; a few emaciated soldiers in camouflaged jackets that dangle wearily open; a woman swathed head to toe in black, her eyes barely visible through a thin slit, accompanied by a dark, mustached man who engages one of the guys in our group in an animated one-sided conversation.

Endless expanses of parched yellow sand are dotted by random billboards extolling the virtues of Cadbury chocolates and Pharoah ceramic tile products, Mobaco cottons and the omnipresent Pepsi-Cola, which, due to the inexistence in Arabic of the letter *P*, is ultimately pronounced "Bibs." The air that pours through a few opened windows is thirsty air; it smells of scarcity.

And suddenly, we are at the edge of the world, and the passing into infinity requires only a step into its waiting waters. We disembark at a village called Basata on the rim of the Red Sea. Sinai is home to many sparkling five-star resorts with Italian-tiled chalets and jet-ski rentals, but on a student budget, the Bedouin village of Basata, offering sun and water and shelter from the nighttime sands, is all we require. *Basata* means simplicity, and as a way of life, it has conquered this portion of the planet. There are about fifteen huts made of straw, with braided rag rugs on the sand floors. They are spaced out across an expanse of satiny sand that nestles against a blue taffeta sea.

Beneath the water's gently pulsing surface slides a carnival world of creatures. Impossible fish, kaleidoscopes of color, dart among the eternally groping reefs. Only reluctantly does the snorkeler abandon that netherworldly palette.

Mahmoud, the Bedouin concierge, offers us marijuana for breakfast and grills fish over an open fire for our dinners. His skin is Nubian black, his hair long and rough. He is thin, wiry—his ribs push against his skin like coils ready to spring. His wide eyes exude a Mad Hatter energy. He walks the white sand with a scrawny camel called Fawzia, bestowing upon the lurching tourists on her back a rapid running commentary in the language of their choice. He is chat-fluent in most tongues, illiterate in his own.

Mahmoud watches as I claw at the contact lenses in my eyes. Especially at night, the desert sands blow swift and remorseless, and leave the unseasoned with streaming eyes and sand-caked hair.

You can't see me without those things? he asks.

I can see you, just . . . you know, you'd be all fuzzy.

Fuzzy?

I shrug. *Not clear.*

So why do you have to wear them?

Bad eyes.

What, you sick?

No, short vision. Can't see far.

He shakes his head with pity. *All Bedouin have perfect eyes.*

Why?

He makes a sweeping gesture that encompasses the sea, the sand, the russet mountains. *No walls.*

Every night, Mahmoud helps us build a small fire not far from the water's edge, and we gather, sipping warm Cokes and talking. We talk of the things that college students talk of, those winding discussions that can devour a night and defy summary. We smoke the joints that Mahmoud rolls, and watch the campfire lick at the darkness.

Nights in the Sinai are rich in starlit silence, interrupted only by the call to prayer resounding off the gently sloping mountains and the inscrutable face of the sea. We are reluctant to spash as we swim in that still water, idly pursuing puddles of moonlight. The stars over Basata leave little room for the sky, so numerous, so bright. I float on my back, staring heavenward, tasting promises fulfilled in a warm, whispering sea.

❖ ❖ ❖ ❖ ❖

One gray Friday morning, when I had left Meg still sleeping, I return from getting my Toblerone and paper and find Huda about to descend in the elevator.

Huda usually spends Fridays in Dokki. Ehab retreats to his family home in the morning; he will pray the Friday prayer with his father at their neighborhood mosque and appear at Huda's later that day, when the family gathers for a large afternoon meal.

She insists that I accompany her to Dokki and will not take no for an answer.

I leave a note for Meg, and grab an extra box of cigarettes for Huda's grandmother.

The whole extended family is expected today, and Mama Selwa and Huda are in charge of preparing a big dinner while Huda's mother deep-cleans the apartment. They insist that I should spend my time with them lounging on the couch, watching soccer with Huda's father, but I demand to be allowed to help.

Our first task is to procure the fowl.

Huda beelines through the teeming souq and in no time we are standing before a dark, tiny shop stacked floor to ceiling with flimsy wooden crates. The floor is littered with feathers. The sidewalk on which we stand is aswarm with savvy street cats vying for strategic positions. A man stands within the shop, blood-spackled and grim. Chicken blood on his hands, on his careworn jeans, some splashed across the once-white apron, and even a few specks on his thick mustache.

After returning Huda's greeting, he gestures with his long knife, asking in a gravelly voice, *Which ones do you want?*

I stare at the wee faces peering out of their cages.

What do you think? Huda is asking me.

I shake my head, at a loss. I watch as she chooses three from two different crates, wondering what characteristics one seeks.

On or off? he asks.

Off, she answers. *Feathers,* she explains to my quizzical look.

Of course, I say.

I do not watch as he kills and plucks the birds. But I do get to carry the bag, their still-warm carcasses thumping against my leg as I walk.

I return to the Dokki flat a shaken carnivore. I watch as she rinses the naked birds and takes to cleaning them, pulling globs from inside their corpses, then plopping them into a pan, grating an onion over them and sliding them into the oven. Efficient.

What, you don't have chickens in America? her grandmother demands of my curious stare.

Yes, but only the cut-up, plastic-wrapped kind.

Mama Selwa harrumphs. She sits at the kitchen table with her glasses balanced precariously on the tip of her nose, stuffing grape leaves.

Having secured the chickens in the oven, Huda joins her grandmother in the task at hand. She takes a tiny portion of the spiced rice and lays it on half of a leaf, folding it with a rapidity I hadn't thought possible.

I put aside the wooden-handled half-moon blade that I am using to cut up raw *molokhiyya,* thinking I can maybe shirk my current task and catch something of their leaf-rolling technique. *Molokhiyya,* I learn after no small amount of later research, translates as "Jew's mallow," which I've never heard of anyway.

Huda looks over at my handiwork. *No, no,* she says. *Still much too thick. You must make it very fine. Very fine.*

Caught, I return to rocking the knife back and forth in the small pile of greens. *Molokhiyya* soup is very good, although I cannot describe it beyond that it has a sort of snotty consistency.

I mention this, and Mama Selwa only shakes her head, asserting once again that if I didn't slip her cigarettes, she'd never abide my presence.

She is weaker today than usual, but she bristles at any attempt to get her to lie down. A half-smile never leaves her lips, and I am sure I hear her humming under her breath.

I make this observation, and Huda supplies that it has been a while since they have all gathered. Mama Selwa's other two children, Amar and 'Adil, will be here with their families. I am lost for a moment, calculating. As if reading my mind, Huda describes the scene at the home of her great aunt Kawthar, Mama Selwa's sister, when her nine children and their families crowd into an apartment far smaller than this one.

I watch Mama Selwa's face, loving its look of tenderness. *So how did you get away with having just three children?*

She pulls her glasses off and lets them swing from their chain. She sighs deeply and looks at me with what I realize is the first serious look I've ever received from her. Pain has slid over her gaze like clouds over a bright night moon. *I had twelve children,* she says. *Twelve.*

سلوى

Selwa

My eye, let your tears rain down, constant, copious rain
    like shining strung pearls.
I remember him as night's darkness deepens
    and my heart is cleft, irreparable.

—AL-KHANSA',
d. 646 C.E.
Tomader bint 'Amru ibn al-Harith
(from her *Diwan*)

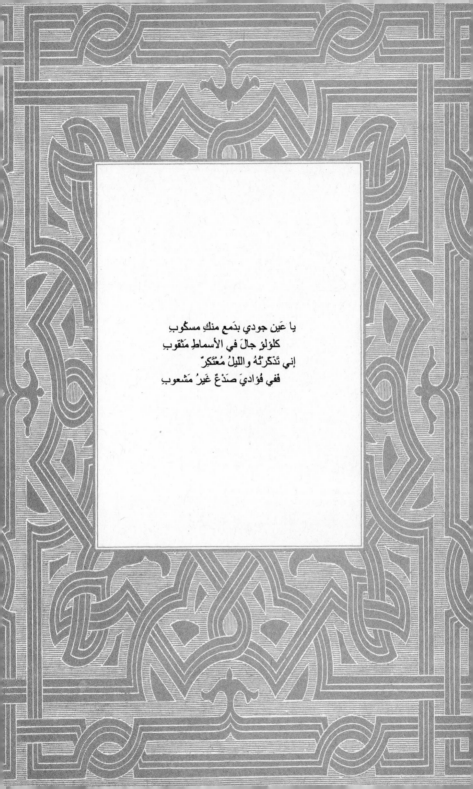

يا عَين جودي بدَمع منكِ مسكوبِ

كلؤلؤ جالَ في الأسماطِ مَثقوبِ

إني تَذكّرتُهُ والليلُ مُعتَكِرٌ

ففي فُؤاديَ صَدْعٌ غَيرُ مَشعوبِ

It was only two weeks after her sixteenth birthday when Selwa's father pushed open the door to the room she shared with her three younger sisters. Her father inserted his fast-balding head and squared upper torso.

He studied Selwa a moment, thoughtfully, then said, "*Mabrouk.* I've picked your groom."

Her sister Kawthar was sitting behind her on the bed they shared, raking a brush through Selwa's waist-length ebony hair. They looked at each other in astonishment. "He'll be here soon to read the *Fatiha.* Go help your mother in the kitchen."

Selwa fought for breath, but she did not cry as Kawthar had immediately begun to. She recognized Baba's succinctness. It meant he had thought a long time about the subject, and wasn't open to further discussion. She thrust aside a choking dread, unlacing her fingers from Kawthar's smaller ones, and rose from the bed.

Kawthar still held the hairbrush. Fearful tears fell onto the woolen winter blanket.

Selwa walked down the dark hall into the kitchen. The apartment was unnaturally silent, what with the two younger girls and baby Zayd napping and Baba in the parlor with the newspaper.

She paused in the hall, glancing in to where he sat angling the paper to catch the late-afternoon sunlight as he pored over the articles. She sighed soundlessly and continued walking.

When she arrived at the kitchen door, she stood watching as her mother pulled feathers off the strawberry hen, which had only that morning been skittering about in the cage on the building's roof.

Nayna felt her presence, turning slightly to look over her shoulder at her eldest daughter. "*Mabrouk*," she said gently. She turned back to the sink, her hands a blur of motion.

Selwa stared at Nayna's back, unable to move, teetering a bit and holding on to the rough wooden table for support. "Baba said I should come help you."

Nayna nodded. "We'll make some *konaffa* for them to eat with the tea. Let me just get this into a pot and onto the stove so it can take its time cooking for dinner. You know where the dough is, *hayati*, go on now, and start it up for us."

Selwa caught her breath. It was rare for Nayna to call her that; she was almost too efficient for affectionate nicknames and coddling. *Hayati. My life* . . .

Selwa stared at Nayna, and realized that she was rigid with repressed emotion. Her profile evidenced that her small lips were pursed into a hard line, her thin nostrils were flared, and her spine was hard and straight. Nayna's dark eyes bored directly into the hen, a ferocious gaze.

Selwa was her mother's greatest help, and with only thirteen years between them, her closest friend. She knew that Nayna's fierce silence indicated the depth of her grief at their imminent separation.

Swallowing an almost immobilizing fear, Selwa crossed to the icebox. She raised the heavy wooden lid to take out the pan of thick cream. She set the pan on the table and, still propping up the lid with her shoulder, rifled about for the long strands of *konaffa* dough that she and Kawthar had bought two days ago from the sweets seller on the corner of Khayrat and Mubta Dayan streets.

She smeared the bright yellow clarified butter along the insides of a shallow aluminum pan, then divided the *konaffa* dough into two halves.

Ya Rabb . . . she whispered to herself. *Let him be handsome. . . .*

She spread the heavy cream over the half she'd placed inside the pan, then layered the other half of the dough above the cream.

Ya Rabb . . . Let him be kind. . . .

She poured more clarified butter over the top of this, and set the pan in the oven.

Ya Rabb . . . Let him love me . . . madly. . . .

Taking sugar and water, she set about boiling them into syrup for the pastry.

She knew her mother watched her from the corners of her eyes, and she heard her deep, drained sigh.

Finally, Selwa could bear the silence no longer. "Do you know anything about him?" she asked, stirring the syrup.

Nayna carried the long knife and a mesh bag of vegetables over to the kitchen table. She brushed aside the traces of *kon-affa* dough that lingered on the tabletop and sat down.

She took so long to answer that Selwa paused in her stirring to look at her with expectant, anxious eyes.

Nayna carefully cut the stem off an onion, then smiled reassuringly at her daughter. "I hear he is a good man," she said, her voice even. "From a good family." She made four cuts in the skin and then rapidly pulled away the peel to expose the onion's moist white meat. She blinked fiercely and, with a sniff, lifted her chin and straightened her thin back.

Thoughtfully, Selwa took in her mother's slim form before turning back to the stovetop. "Yes, but . . . is he a nice man? A handsome man? What does he do? Does he have money?"

Nayna shook her head, her knife halving the onion with a swift, sure motion, then chopping it into precise, matching cubes. "All I know is that he saw you one day at your father's shop. He reappeared the next day to ask for your hand, and your baba has been thinking it over for several months."

Extinguishing the burner beneath the pan of syrup, Selwa walked over to the table. "So he saw me . . . and he liked me?" She sat down, picked up a tomato and stared at it distractedly. Her memory was working furiously, skimming over the many faces she'd encountered over the past months when running errands for her father at his fabric shop.

Nayna nodded, blinking her wet eyes. "I think he's a merchant of some sort. He lives in 'Abidin."

Selwa looked up then, relieved. Not so far after all!

Her mother knew her thoughts. They were her own. She glanced at her with a tender smile, their eyes locked, then she went back to her chopping. "You see, it will be all right," she said. *"In sha Allah."*

Picking up the paring knife, Selwa took to cutting out the stems of the tomatoes with a deliberate slowness that would normally have agonized her mother. But today Nayna did not chastise her; she busied herself instead with filtering out the tiny bugs and small stones from the large burlap bag of rice.

"What about his reputation, then?" asked Selwa after a long silence.

Selwa watched her mother's face closely, watching the question pulse through her, watching her set her expression as she prepared to respond. Nayna was the co-wife of a man who loved women.

The neighborhood was electric with the news of Baba's latest relationship, this time with a dancer called Amina Zubayd. His attempts at discretion were halfhearted at best. Feasts of information were repeated to Selwa via her neighbor Sanaa, whose mother gossiped incessantly.

Although the total meaning was lost on her, she knew that her father was celebrated as a generous patron of the arts. His dancer friend wore baubles that caused other women to pause, fainthearted with envy, as she passed them on the street. So beautiful, so garish, so . . . much. *Feddan* after *feddan* of family property in the countryside had been tenderly strung about Amina's neck. Still other *feddans* had been poured down her graceful throat from Casino al-Layl's seemingly limitless stock of imported champagnes.

Nayna endured these things in straight-backed silence. She was an expert at conserving her energies. *Such is the nature of men, after all,* Selwa had heard her murmur to Sanaa's mother, from behind the rooftop clothesline. *Weak. He is his own destruction.*

She could have shrieked and slapped her cheeks as some women did. But what would she and her children gain? she would demand of Um Sanaa. Had his barren first wife gained anything by protesting the marriage to Nayna, or the large, airy apartment he had purchased for his new family?

And because he had never hurt her, nor had the children ever gone without food or clothing, Nayna felt no need to complain. However, her concern for Selwa forced her to ask whether he had come to know this Gamal 'Izz al-Din through his business dealings or from the cabarets.

The reply had been that Gamal was not the sort even to enter a cabaret.

Selwa received this news thoughtfully, trying to envision the man in question. She was so caught up in her imaginings that she almost forgot the *konaffa* baking in the oven. She rushed to the oven door and, clutching a rag, pulled it open and removed the pan. She set the steaming pastry on the cracked marble countertop to cool, then ladled the syrup over its golden surface.

Knowing the visit was upon them, she filled the dented teapot with water and set it on the burner, then went about preparing the tray for the tea service.

When they finally heard the rap on the door, she stared at her mother for a moment, her eyes wide and blinking rapidly. Nayna nodded, knowing she could not prevent her from trying to get a look at her future husband.

Selwa rushed the tea service into the parlor and placed it carefully on the chipped marble coffee table. Baba waited until she exited before going to answer the door.

Kawthar was already entrenched outside the side parlor door. Selwa squeezed her sister's hand, then sank onto her knees next to her, peering through the keyhole.

She watched as he entered the parlor, clutching his bright red fez in his hand and laying it carefully on the couch next to him as he sat. Without the refuge of the fez, his head sighed under thinning hair.

She trembled from the effort it took to make no sound, to see and hear as her father and Gamal sat talking. She bit her lip as she watched her intended sip at his tea. Occasionally he would take a bright white handkerchief from the breast pocket of his suit jacket and mop at his wide forehead. His skin was as dark as 'arq al-sus, and his eyes seemed to be skulking under heavy lids. His cheeks drooped under their own weight, giving him a melancholy look even when he smiled. His stomach protruded generously from his girth, and the hands that clutched the teacup were large and thick-fingered.

She looked and looked, insisting to herself that she would not rise from her knees until she found some appealing characteristic. Surely there was something . . . But just as she had surrendered, and began telling herself that at least he looked distinguished in his gray gabardine suit, his laugh rang out, deep and warm as summer sunlight on her skin.

A man with such a laugh cannot be all bad.

She sighed soundlessly and raised her eyes to meet Kawthar's. Her sister's china-doll features were confused by a mixture of fear and pity, unsure as to whether to offer encouragement or commiseration. Selwa herself did not know. Gamal seemed kind enough. And she trusted Baba not to bring her a bad or cruel man. But surely he could have found someone a little younger, a little more handsome?

It was all she saw of him until the night of their wedding.

On that day she rose early and slipped out of the house. She walked down the cool cement stairs to the rush of the street. She listened intently to the tapping of her own shoes against the uneven brick road, skirting donkey droppings, discarded newspapers and rotten vegetables rejected from the vegetable sellers' carts. The calls of merchants and their ever-bargaining customers peppered the air, along with the squeaking of the grease-thirsty wheels of donkey carts. The mosque of the Sayyida Zaynab presided like an expansive queen over the main square, and as always a vast crowd of pilgrims and worshipers was milling about, the pilgrims themselves anxious to do business before heading home.

It had been several years since she had been there; she'd been only a little girl clutching Nayna's hand.

Now Selwa walked through the women's entrance, draping her hair with a loose scarf. She removed her low-heeled shoes, leaving them on a large mat in a sea of others, most of which were crude country sandals. The gilded tomb was centered in the mosque, straddling the women's and men's areas so that both sexes could come close enough to work their fingers into the delicately curved grillwork surrounding the remains and whisper their pleas, their lips brushing against the cool brass.

She waited patiently for an opportunity to squeeze in close enough, observing the weeping women who clung to the grating. She listened to their pleas:

—*O Granddaughter of the Prophet, please give me a son.*

—*I beg you, save my baby from the fever.*

—*Um Hashim, let my husband live another year, so we don't starve this winter.*

—*I lost my little girl at the souq; Sitt Zaynab, show her the way home.*

Gingerly, she wedged herself in among the desperate, praying women. She pressed herself against the tomb, her forehead touching the grating, and whispered her only prayer: "Let him love me like I long to be loved."

Um Hasanayn was waiting when she returned to the apartment.

Selwa felt a stab of fear. Such visits never boded well for her.

What the midwife lacked in knowledge, she compensated for in intensity. Um Hasanayn did nothing without invoking God and the prophets, and every once in a while King Farouq. She was constantly in demand throughout the neighborhood, and as such she swelled with self-importance. She was on call for births, circumcisions, home abortions, menstrual complications—including cramps, crabbiness and crying jags—yeast infections, frigidity, stretch marks, depilation, hymen reconstruction and, above all, gossip. And while Selwa was not fully aware of all Um Hasanayn's functions, she had enough experience with her to find her repugnant. She was constantly red in the face, due to her insistence on moving rapidly despite her immense mass. Bulging ankles spilled over the flimsy slippers that she wore everywhere, never bothering with actual shoes, not even in the depths of winter. Her gelabiyyas were inevitably sweat-stained, and strained to their endurance to contain her bloated backside and bulging breasts. A huge gap stared out from between her gray front teeth, causing most of her words to hiss, and adding to what Selwa considered her sinister air.

Um Hasanayn greeted her as though she were a beloved niece, dousing her in kisses and compliments, pulling her arm and indicating that she should sit next to her and chat.

But Selwa only smiled politely and retreated to her room, where Kawthar was trying on her own dress for the wedding. She turned to Selwa amid a waterfall of pink lace. Her eyes were wide. "I heard them mention *helawa*."

Of all the wedding rituals, she at least had a little background on that. She had seen her mother boiling down sugar water with a drop of lemon juice until it thickened. Then she would pour it out onto the ceramic of the kitchen countertop, leaving it to cool into a rubbery putty. She would fashion from the mixture balls that she worked between her fingers until they were soft and supple. Then she would flatten one of the warm, sticky balls across the skin of her arm or leg, ripping it up rapidly to remove all the hair.

What Selwa had not imagined when they called her into her mother's room is that the hair on her head was all they were willing to leave her with. Nayna abandoned her to the chuckling, gap-toothed midwife. Um Hasanayn's hands were rapid and sure, but the pain of the hair being yanked out by the roots was nearly intolerable. Selwa could not help but whimper as she was pulled and prodded.

She sat later in the bath, exhausted from the effort it took not to cry out. She had feared that she would terrify Kawthar and her little siblings if she yelled. The sugary remnants on her skin melted away in the warm, soothing water, and she had not realized how satiny her skin was beneath the light dusting of hair she had lived with all her life. The water beaded and rolled off her arm when she held it up.

She looked at the length of her body in the water. She knew she was as beautiful as Fatin Hammama or Shadia or any of those movie stars. That day last year when she took Baba's morning sandwich to him at the shop, hadn't Baba's friend implored him to let her go to the studio, or at least have her picture shown around?

Of course Baba had laughed politely then, to the man's face. As soon as the man left the shop, Baba swore at the memory of him with curse words more foul than any she had ever heard before.

He had slammed his hand down on the wide metal desk, adding yet another dent. *Does he think my daughter, my daughter, is a slut to be mixed up in the cinema?*

And then, she remembered, he had turned to her and looked at her a long while, as though seeing her for the first time. He nodded slowly, smiling gently, and motioned for her to sit on his knee, the place she had occupied for hours at a time when she was younger and would visit him like this in the shop. He tugged at her long, silky braid, gazing into her cool green eyes with something akin to alarm. *What is this, where did all this beauty come from? You grew up so quickly.*

She knew Baba loved her best—best of all the girls, anyway—because she looked just like his mother, whose light skin and green eyes proudly proclaimed her Turkish origins.

You could turn the Egyptian cinema upside down, you could, he said tenderly.

It wasn't long after that, that he pulled her out of school, telling her that her mother needed more help around the house.

And now . . . this.

Her mother sent Kawthar to call her from her bath to begin to have her hair done.

She dried herself slowly, watching the sunlight filtering in from the slats of the shutters and skating over the still-steaming water. She relished a moment of peace.

Surely Gamal will treat me like a movie star. Hadn't he fallen in love at first sight?

Her hair was piled high atop her head; the miniature buttons down the length of her back had all been buttoned. Long silk gloves drifted to just above her elbows, and precariously high heels enveloped her small feet.

Even Shadia, Darling of the Screen, paled in comparison.

Nayna looked at her for a heavy moment, frowning, her wide gray eyes threatening to brim over. It was this gaze that terrified Selwa more than any other single event before her wedding. She knew somehow that Nayna was frightened for her, but couldn't or wouldn't do anything to stop what would transpire.

That silence roared in Selwa's ears. If Nayna couldn't even speak to her, couldn't prepare her for what was to come, she knew that it must be particularly awful.

Selwa felt the optimism seeping from her body.

She closed her eyes for a moment, wishing sincerely that she wouldn't have to open them. She steeled herself, knowing there was nowhere to run, no lamp-cowering genie waiting to spirit her away.

She nodded, and Nayna opened the bedroom door. Immediately, the apartment was filled with screeching ululations. They accompanied her as she mounted the stairs to the roof, where she had only last week been hanging laundry and giggling with the neighbor's daughter. Now that rooftop was unrecognizable, decorated as it was with flowers and nearly overwhelmed with rented tables laden with kebab and *kofta*, cakes and rice pudding, and large pitchers of mango juice. Upon seeing Selwa attain the final step, the belly dancer motioned to her drummers to increase the rhythm, and she took up the dance with renewed frenzy, her waist moving back and forth with near-blinding speed, the fringe of her costume shaking wildly as she writhed, swerving through the crowd of guests.

Slowly, Selwa was led to her place, a large, thronelike wicker chair, the twin of the one Gamal occupied. She did not at any time since emerging from her bedroom raise her eyes to meet any guest's gaze.

She sat perfectly still in her chair as Nayna and Kawthar fussed over her dress, fluffing and arranging so that the tulle and lace would be visible to all. She did not look at Gamal, only stared distractedly at the way his pant leg sustained the slight bend of his knee.

The guests lined up to congratulate them, the men shaking Gamal's hand, the women kissing Selwa's cheek with such intensity that it did not take long before she felt her cheekbones to be bruised.

The dancer circulated over the entire rooftop. Selwa shot sidelong glances at her now and then. She wasn't bad; Selwa, dancing in secret, with Kawthar humming and drumming on the bed frame, was better.

Selwa and Gamal sat thus, presiding over but somehow excluded from their own wedding feast, for what seemed hours. Finally, her mother came and pulled her gently to her feet. Gamal followed as they left the rooftop and descended the narrow stairway to the brightly lit apartment.

The ululations seemed to have reached a fever pitch, exploding off the rooftop and resounding off the minarets of Sayyida Zaynab's mosque, and surely echoing all the way to 'Abidin Palace.

Selwa was surprised to see two of the drummers from the dancer's group thumping away and grinning madly outside the bedroom. The door swung open, and Um Hasanayn appeared in the room's dim light.

Selwa felt her knees buckle, and she leaned heavily on Nayna, fighting for breath. Gamal and his mother followed them into the room. She did not hear the door close over the sound of the drumming. Um Hasanayn and Nayna sat her down on the edge of the bed and started to undress her, laboring over the tiny buttons, even ripping off a few in their impatience, until Selwa stood at last in only her thin silk slip. She had never been so naked before a man, and only rarely before Nayna herself.

She looked up at Nayna in confusion—*I don't understand,* she said, but Nayna would not meet her gaze. *It will all be over soon,* was all her mother could say.

Selwa looked at Um Hasanayn, who was humming along with the mad beating of the drums. She looked to her mother-in-law, who was staring at her, a cold, scrutinizing look. And finally to Gamal, who was staring at the floor, a deep frown etched across his features.

And suddenly Nayna was holding her down, and Um Hasanayn was pulling at her underwear. Selwa shrieked in surprise and fear, and started to struggle. It was then that her mother-in-law joined the small group on the bed, to aid in holding the squirming bride. Um Hasanayn forced Selwa's thighs apart and she felt the midwife's fingers enter her, cold and probing, and then she felt the lancing pain as the fingers shattered the thin barrier within. She stared wildly at her mother, but Nayna's head was turned. Selwa looked down to see the burgundy stain snaking from between her thighs to drip onto the white sheet.

Her screams were masked by the ululations of the three women and the relentless thudding of the drums.

So that was why they stood outside the bedroom door . . . The realization crept in on her like a visitor entering a dreamscape.

The drummers were not posted outside the door to celebrate her marriage.

They were there to drown out her screams.

Nayna, still unable to meet Selwa's eyes, patted her hair gently, whispering something that she could not hear over the drumming. And suddenly she was gone. The other two women pulled the stained sheet out from under her, gently, and Selwa understood then that the sheet was to be displayed to the wedding guests. The drummers apparently accompanied them on their rounds, for the noise level in the room abated little by little, until Selwa could hear her own sobbing.

Only Gamal remained in the room. He moved silently to the bedside, stretching a hesitant hand to touch his wife.

"Don't you touch me," she hissed, as she curled in on herself in pain.

"I'm sorry," he said. "If I had known, I would have insisted that it happen differently. But Mama . . . well, it's the only way she knows." His voice was low and gentle, and despite her warning, he ran his hand along the skin of her arm and took her hand, pressing it to his lips.

She turned her head slightly to look at him. Their eyes met for the first time, and she found his to be warm and kind, glistening softly in the low flame of the kerosene lamp. She felt her sobs begin to subside, although tears still slipped out of the corners of her eyes.

"I promise you, I'll never let anyone hurt you again," Gamal said.

He did not approach her until, two weeks later, she invited him to. Nine months after that, she gave birth to Karima. She was the first child in two generations to be born without the help of Um Hasanayn.

Forty days after Karima's birth, Selwa was pregnant again.

But then it began.

She was still nursing Karima when her second child, a boy, was born dead.

Selwa stared down at the tiny, limp body that was still

connected to her own by the long, curling umbilical cord. She looked up at Nayna in fast-brewing despair, working to contain a hurricane of astonished grief.

Nayna grasped Selwa's shoulders with hands still wet from the birthing. Her voice was urgent and insistent. "Tears will sour your milk. For the sake of your beautiful little girl, do not cry. God has a reason, Selwa, even if it isn't clear to you now."

It was in this period that Selwa came to love Gamal more deeply than she had ever hoped to. He would rush home from work to lend his hand to hers, to make sure that she would not strain or tire. He would carry the eleven-month-old Karima on his back, making the most peculiar neighing sounds, until both mother and daughter dissolved in laughter. Night after night he would stand with her in the kitchen as she chopped and sliced and boiled and seasoned, regaling her with stories of his coworkers and the injustices they suffered at the hands of their wives and mothers-in-law. Gamal was prepared to say or do anything to keep Selwa's mind off their stillborn son. So it was that he developed a talent for talking incessantly, and a repertoire of anecdotes for which he gained fame.

And at night he would press his lips to her ear and whisper words that she had never even dreamed of hearing in those days when she pictured herself the movie bride of Shukry Sarhan or Rushdy Abaza.

My princess.

My soul.

My bright night moon.

Forty days later she was pregnant again.

Six more followed the second boy's death, each child dying either still within her or only a few weeks after birth. The longest any of them lived was two months. Every time, Selwa listened to the entreaties of her family, burying her pain in some distant place within her, knowing that surely, surely God had a reason for such cruelty.

Until there was Shams.

He was perfect. Silky black curls and luminescent blue-gray eyes. His skin smelled like warm butter, and his legs and arms were rolls upon rolls of soft, fat flesh.

He lived a month.

He lived two months. And then three. And then a year passed, and more, and he walked and laughed and began to shout portions of words, clapping when he was understood and his needs were met.

Shams could not fall asleep unless Selwa lay next to him, their noses almost touching, their breath mingling. Then he would drape his smooth arms around her neck, his tiny fingers meeting in the soft waves of her hair. Never having sung in her life, she was surprised to find that little Shams loved her voice. He insisted that she sing to him until he drifted off to sleep:

> *When is Baba coming?*
> *He's coming at six o'clock.*
> *Is he walking or riding?*
> *He's riding a bicycle.*
> *Is it white or red?*
> *It's white like cream.*

Sometimes she would linger, tasting his breath, until long after he had slept. Gamal would come and whisper to her, "Isn't he asleep? Come on, then . . ."

And she would loose herself from her son's sleeping clutches reluctantly, regretting then that for which she had been so often grateful: Gamal's continuous desire to be near her, to sit talking late into the night, to lay his head on her chest and enumerate every detail of his day as she stroked his hair.

Sometimes she didn't feel that she had enough love to go around. Perhaps, she often told herself, perhaps that's why the others did not survive. *I would never have been able to give Shams all the love he needs if I were tending to seven others.*

She was grateful, too, that Karima could be of so much help. At ten, she could care for Shams well in the coming period when the new baby came.

If this one, too, lives, she thought, offering up a few whispered prayers while rubbing the knot of pain in the small of her back. *If he lives.*

She had been scrubbing the parlor floor when it happened.

Karima was spooning yams into Shams's mouth, humming happily and savoring the early September breezes sweeping across the tiny balcony off her bedroom. Shams sat curled in the bend of her arm, happily accepting each sweet spoonful, laughing at the faces that she made as she fed him.

It was then that the neighbor woman Fathiyya opened her balcony door and witnessed the scene. Fathiyya's son was slightly older than Shams—almost two years old. But he was weak and sickly, his skin always loose and yellowish, and they were constantly calling for the *hakim* to come and attend to him.

Karima felt Fathiyya's gaze and looked across, a distance of not more than four meters. The woman's scarved head was cocked, her lips pursed, and her eyes seemed to burn into Shams's soft, warm body.

With a start, Karima jumped from the folding chair and took refuge in the bedroom, sealing the balcony doors behind her, mumbling, *Allahu Akbar, Allahu Akbar, Aouzu billah min a-shaytan ar-rajim*, into his satin hair.

But no manner of prayer would help.

The very next day, the dysentery settled in Shams's stomach, and within a week he was dead.

Dead of the Evil Eye.

Selwa crumbled. The baby she was carrying was born in a river of tears. She would not touch him, or hold him even to nurse him. "Why should Shams die and this one live? Why *this* one?"

And he, too, died, despite Karima and Nayna's frantic efforts, a week after his birth, only two weeks after Shams.

Unnamed.

Selwa had closed in on herself. She did not eat or speak, she did not offer up her chest for comfort or companionship; she would not listen to cheerful stories of coworkers or anyone else. She did not brush her waist-length hair, or outline her bottomless eyes with kohl. She did not bathe.

She only lay dripping silent tears onto that smooth cotton sheet, imagining the tiny arms, warm against the skin of her neck, and tasting the measured, buttery breath. Her tears would not cease. All the unacknowledged pain of seeing so many tiny corpses had welled up into a tortured, heaving sea.

The cotton-stuffed mattress on which Shams had slept still bore the stain of months and months of tears.

It was Nayna who came to her at last. Angry. Her black eyes flashed.

"Do you think you're the first?"

She was standing in the doorway, her spare, black-cloaked form imposing in the dimness.

Selwa did not answer.

"I lost six babies. Six. Do you think I didn't grieve for them?"

Selwa curled in on herself, draping her thin arms over her ears to seal out Nayna's words. "My babies . . ." she moaned softly.

Nayna sighed sadly then, and crossed to the bed, pulling some of the matted hair out of Selwa's face and smoothing it back. She sat down next to her on the bed. "Look at you. What are you doing to yourself, child?" she whispered, stroking her hair. "Are you trying to kill yourself?"

"I am dead. Pieces of me lie dead before me. My flesh. I don't have anything left," she sobbed. "Nothing. I am empty."

"No woman is ever empty," Nayna said. "You are life. When it is fragile, when it is miserable, when it is beautiful, you brim with it."

"Even if I can't give birth to a healthy child?"

"Even if you *can*."

Selwa was silent a long time, considering this.

"Don't you see now why babies are flesh from flesh, and not just dropped in our laps? So in loving them we have to love ourselves. We get to discover it, if we missed it before."

Selwa turned her head to look up at her mother.

Nayna continued to caress her hair, her tone chiding even as she smiled, saying, "Karima deserves more from you than this."

"Karima," Selwa murmured hoarsely, a sudden regret shuddering through her. Somehow Karima had crept out of Selwa's mind, cowering in the shadows of her grief. Karima, whose own shivering grief for Shams and the new baby had been completely disregarded. The girl was present to rub a cool, damp cloth across her mother's skin, or bring sugary tea or trays of ignored food. But Selwa had not touched her or spoken her name aloud for months, as though the girl were an apparition that would vanish if acknowledged.

"My little girl . . ."

Selwa sat upright in the bed then, the rapid motion making her eyes swim in blackness that dissipated with a warm finality. She stared down at her body, the way the thin nightgown stuck to her sweating skin, the way her hands had grown thin, the nails split and uneven. She pressed her palms to her cheeks and her cracked lips, as though tracing the features of a stranger.

Whispering prayers of thanks, Nayna slid from the bed and crossed to the heavy green shutters, unlatching them for the first time in months. Selwa squinted against the hot amber light, then inhaled deeply.

"Karima!" she shouted, her voice scaly with the residue of sobs. "Karima!" she called more clearly. "Karima!"

The rapid smacking of Karima's bare feet against the hall tiles preceded her. She skidded into the room, her features set in a now habitual expectation of pain. She stopped short, stunned, at the sight of her mother sitting up and smiling.

"*Hayati*," Selwa whispered, and her daughter fell eagerly into her embrace.

My life.

232 · Carolyn Baugh

*I had two more children, after that. 'Adil, because God was just
with me, even though I had called Him unjust, and Amar, my
moon.*

Mama Selwa is drained from talking, but the deep aluminum cooking pot is filled with tidily rolled grape leaves. She
steals a cigarette from me and sneaks away to smoke it in the
bathroom, the one place where Karima will not intrude on her
and smash it out.

Huda looks at me sadly, and I know she counts every day
with Mama Selwa as a gift. *It won't be long, they say.*

I feel my own eyes brimming.

Death and life are so closely interwoven, I cannot gauge the
distance between them. How desperately I want to feel death
out, divine its features, in order to bar the door when it arrives.

✦ ✦ ✦ ✦ ✦

Early March brings Ramadan, and the tone and tenor of the city's song shift perceptibly.

Strain colonizes passing faces about half an hour before sundown. Patience ebbs, and the desire to be safely ensconced in the home, surrounded by the emanations of willing pots and pans, takes on tidal proportions. Drivers push irritably at their accelerator pedals, only to be forced to jam the brake, sandwiched in the crush of homeward commuters. The mighty buses barrel recklessly through red lights and traffic posts long since abandoned by apathetic officers. The passengers within rest their heads against the aluminum frames of open windows; their faces suggest they are convinced they may never return home at all.

The corrugated metal doors of shops come crashing down, one after another, until the streets resemble the faces of fearful children who have clamped shut their eyelids against invisible monsters; the eyelids wrinkle and tremble with the effort of remaining closed even as the longing to peek pricks at them.

Little by little the streets swallow up their human ornaments until at last the *adan* pours out into the stilling air. And then comes a surreal hush, when the massive, shifting city folds in on herself, her voice wafting out in soft whispers from between the slats of closed shutters.

Walking along on deserted sidewalks, I hear cutlery clanking against china and the low hum of indistinct conversations. A lone taxi streaks through the empty streets like a thoroughbred released into rolling countryside. Even the *bowwab* has sealed himself into the tiny room off the building's entrance; the tall, thin door is closed in stark defiance, daring any resident to impose on his meal with a trifling request.

Ramadan appeals to me. All which is taken for granted is rendered temporarily off limits. The thirst-quenching cup of water, the morning glass of tea. The breakfast bread and cheese, the afternoon Turkish coffee, the heavy, endless late lunch. The cigarette smoked in anger. The cigarette smoked for the sweet sake of smoking. The pleasures of the flesh. The particular release found in cursing out of wrath.

All of these are placed just out of reach, postponed until the magic hour in which the *adan* returns the forbidden to the realm of the permissible. Ramadan demands investigation of the dispassionate way in which the day is passed and recognition of the fragile nature of existence and its sustaining elements. Food and drink and passion. To explore their absence is to taste true hunger; for believers, it is to know and know gratitude to God.

Ramadan nights tremble with an intensity of energy. Some Cairenes pass the night at mosques in prayer. Some linger at home hypnotized by the month-long nightly soap operas. But it is the "Ramadan tents" that hold the most popularity.

Hotels, coffee shops and restaurants all scramble to construct the most entrancing atmosphere. Colorful Arabesque cloth is hung from thin tent poles. Within, the aroma of Turkish coffee and flavored *shisha* smoke intermingle, weaving scented shrouds around tables filled with conspiring lovers or laughing groups of friends.

Nights within the Ramadan tents blaze like shooting stars aware of their rapidly approaching finale. Sometimes a popular singer is featured on the list of entertainment, and he or she is forced to forsake the safety of the studio and warble over the din of swift-walking waiters and raucous knots of young men, a flirting woman's peals of affected mirth and the tapping of the *shisha* attendant as he tends to the blazing coals that heat the cherry or canteloupe tobacco.

And by two or three o'clock in the morning, if not intending to dine in where they are, the *shisha* smokers and *sahleb* sippers call for their checks. The *suhur* is a meal taken just before dawn. Most often the meal is *foule*, fava beans, known to be cheap and filling. Of the multitudinous *foule* venues in the vast city, the most remarkable is the one called al-Gahsh.

The Gahsh lies at the heart of Sayyida Zaynab, an area of Cairo that sprung up around the huge mosque bearing the name of the Prophet Muhammad's granddaughter. The shop sits on a typical Sayyida Zaynab corner, a bead in a weary necklace of grime-conquered storefronts.

People from all walks of life appear to eat there. Slick Mercedes-Benzes, bruised bicycles, duct-taped flip-flops—whatever the mode of transportation, the customers flock to the Gahsh. The crowds, especially during Ramadan, are overwhelming. The narrow streets around the store are clogged to the point of impassibility, with cars parked along the side of the road, and a line of cars halted at loggerheads with a more daunting line of cars going the opposite direction.

Patrons line up to wait for a seat at wide wooden tables that have spilled into the street. Those who cannot wait spread newspapers across the hoods of parked cars and eat standing up. Servers who cannot read or write make rapid-fire mental accountings of the checks for groups of ten or fifteen. *Foule* with ghee, *foule* with olive oil, *foule* with fried eggs . . . side orders of felafel and fiery pickled lemons. Warm 7-UP, or at least a drink vaguely resembling 7-UP, in a glass bottle that has been refilled and resealed over and over.

The aluminum bowls are dented. The *foule* itself is a mucky mass of uninviting brown that when glopped onto a bit of warm pita bread, redefines sublime. But it is less the taste and more the gathering that is particular to the Gahsh. Rich and poor beneath a waxing Ramadan moon, cheerfully filling the last crevices of their stomachs before submitting to another day of obedient deprivation. In the moments before dawn, taxi drivers and investment bankers savor as one the sweetness of a draught of water, the earthy reassurance of a bite of bread. Gratified, humbled, elevated, united, the group disperses into the city's waiting embrace, to snatch a few hours of sleep before the start of a working day.

✦ ✦ ✦ ✦ ✦

It turns out that Huda and her sister-in-law 'Alia have been conspiring against my eyebrows for some time. They organize an intervention.

I am in no mood for socializing after battling the crush of Qasr al-'Ayni and then dragging myself and an armload of groceries up all five flights. But Huda is leaning out of her half-open door, her protruding belly testing the resilience of an otherwise loose yellow nightgown, her long hair dangling and glistening with oil. She frowns with mock menace when I tell her I'm too tired; she beckons me inside. I hear 'Alia say something from within, the words not quite reaching the hallway.

Huda blushes. *And bring your cigarettes*, she says in a low voice, suppressing a laugh.

I sigh and open the door to my flat, shoving the groceries inside. I cast a blistering glare at the impervious elevator before stepping into the warmth of Huda's flat.

'Alia's children are with Karima at the Dokki flat. 'Alia is sitting on the couch, her toes splayed widely as fuchsia polish dries. She rises to kiss my cheeks, and I smell the rich, nutty scent of the oil in her hair. She is wearing a thin-strapped tank top and cut-off shorts. I realize that with Huda's husband tucked safely away at work, the two are having a spa day.

But we shouldn't smoke around Huda, I am saying to 'Alia. *Because of the baby . . .*

Huda waves me off impatiently. *I think by now you've noticed the pollution outside. A little cigarette smoke will only build up her immune system.*

"Her"? You got the ultrasound?

She nods, her eyes shining.

I throw my arms around her, careful not to bump her midriff. *Mabrouk!*

Huda disappears into the kitchen to make the tea while 'Alia rapidly dispenses with the small talk, accepting my still-reluctant offer of a cigarette.

She coughs a little, waving at the smoke that she can't quite inhale, then delves into the subject at hand.

I can help you with those, she starts, a slightly devious smile dimpling her smooth cheeks. She is regarding me steadily, wondering if I will take umbrage at her implication.

I finger my furry brows, startled. I'd never considered pruning them. Curious, I compare our eyebrows. Hers arch like squatting spider legs, thin and precise.

I submit.

'Alia talks to me as she charts her design with an eyebrow pencil. *My sister's husband is in Amreeka, you know. The only way for him to stay there was to marry an American woman.*

I pull my head back slightly to frown at her. *He's married to your sister and an American at the same time?*

'Alia shrugs slightly. *My nephew has leukemia. My sister quit her job to care for him. My brother-in-law was not making enough to support the children and pay for his son's medicines and treatments. He walked the length of Egypt trying to find a second job. He was a junior journalist at* Al-Ahram. *When a group went for training for a month to America, he broke the visa and stayed. He has a bachelor's degree in journalism, but he works there in a gas station.*

I say, *But how can your sister stand to have her husband married to another woman? Doesn't she love him?*

'Alia sighs, puffing on the cigarette and sipping at the tea Huda has brought. *Madly,* she answers. *And she is the love of his life. They were neighbors, and he loved her since they used to play together in the street. Seven months after he started working at the gas station, the immigration people passed by his work, looking for him. They had gotten a tip about an illegal alien. But it wasn't his shift. His supervisor there, an American woman, she called him to warn him. He called my sister that night to say that he was coming home, that otherwise they would put him in prison for God-knows-how-long until they deported him.*

She begged him to stay. She begged him to do whatever it took, even if it meant marrying anyone he could find, but that if he came home her son would die.

She told him if he killed her son, she would kill him.

At this point, 'Alia is looping a long thread about her index fingers and pulling it into a triangle with her teeth. She comes around behind me, telling me to rest my head on the back of the couch. She leans over me again, and the rapidly twisting thread makes a buzzing sound as it yanks out my offensive extraneous eyebrow hair. My eyes water fiercely and I whimper, squirming.

Huda scoffs gently, and I feel like a wimp.

It is over quickly, and I sit up, brushing off the tiny hairs that litter my face and the couch cushions. 'Alia hands me a mirror, but I do not yet look, eager for her to continue the story now that her mouth is thread-free.

What is your sister going to do? I ask.

What can she do? For now, today, her son is alive, and her other children are happy and healthy. What more could a mother want?

A woman could want her man all to herself, I say.

'Alia smiles indulgently. *For poor women, there is not often the luxury of being "woman" before being "mother" or "wife" or "sister" or "daughter."*

Alia holds up the mirror, insistent now that I look. My

face is strange to me, a new openness accompanying the tidy crescents.

What a difference! she remarks, triumphant, as Huda murmurs approvingly, calling me a moon.

We grin at each other. Women for a while.

✦ ✦ ✦ ✦ ✦

There is a mountain in Cairo . . . or perhaps it is just a thwarted attempt of the land to slip earth's bonds and stretch heavenward. These are the Muqattam Hills; some insistent English mapmaker changed the literal translation of *mountain*. Reached only by a long, curving, rutted street, a demoralizing trek for a puttering taxi, the view from atop the Muqattam's precipices is sweeping. As such, the area has been developed, with lavish villas filling the streets along the rim, and sturdy blocks of apartment buildings fleshing out the mountain's humpback.

Along the craggy edges are areas where cars park and passengers emerge to sit as close to the edge as they dare, knees folded firmly against chests, and drink in the view. Lovers come to stroll the winding street of the periphery that is lined on one side by mansions and the other by sheer drop-off. Arrogant, eternal-looking edifices on one side; cool, empty space over harsh red rock on the other.

Wiry boys amble along carrying metal buckets that thump against their thighs. Within the buckets are warm bottles of soda chilling dazedly over a few filthy ice cubes. For a few piasters, a boy will release the carbonated jinn from the bottle with the opener that dangles from his belt loop. For a few piasters more, he might stoke the suffering of tortured lovers by singing one of 'Abd al-Halim's love songs in a clear, reedy voice.

Onlookers breathe the thin, still air and stare out over the city. By day the city looks tranquil and immobile from such a height, a benign, borderless maze, poised to receive well-meaning wanderers. By night, she is a gilded carpet of fireflies, rolled out beneath a low-hung moon. Lighted minarets and the soft swells of domed mosques create the anchoring points of a seductive sensory web.

I, hovering at the edge of a misshapen mountain, am not awaiting the hermit's wisdom. I tilt my head, listening; the ascending moon breathes a silver blessing over this shifting stillness.

* * * * *

Meg and I have spent an April afternoon in the Khan al-Khalili, topping it off with a jaunt to Karim's grocery for necessities. We return to number 10 Hasan Murad in a haze of exhaustion, our hands pleated with the marks left by our heavy plastic bags. After pressing the elevator button several times, Meg leans her forehead against the grating. *I hate this elevator,* she says.

It hates us, I reply, starting to turn toward the stairs.

No, she says. *Not today. I believe that our good friend 'Abd al-Latif needs to reevaluate his building maintenance policies.*

She starts walking toward the small room off the foyer. Remembering the taxi driver fiasco, I follow her uncertainly. She knocks loudly on the closed metal door.

No answer comes.

She knocks again, looking at me. *How do you say* I hate your elevator *in Arabic?*

I open my mouth to reply, but the door creaks slowly open. 'Abd al-Latif's thin wife stands regarding us. *What is it?* she asks with a visible weariness that shames our bazaar tiredness immediately, fiercely.

Meg asks for the *bowwab.*

The woman shakes her head. *He's gone to the village.* Her tone is resigned, heavy.

Meg hesitates. *Is he coming soon?* She points to the elevator's ornate iron grating and the empty shaft behind it. *The elevator . . .*

The woman observes us, working her bony jaw. *He's gone to the village to spend the month with his other wife.*

Meg looks to me for translation, and I mutter the words

quickly, wanting to question the gaunt woman to make sure I heard correctly, while knowing that I had.

Meg and I exchange a wide-eyed glance.

The woman sighs, looking at our packages, and points to the bench her husband usually occupies. *Sit there while I get the electrician,* she says, shuffling out of the gaping mouth of the building's entrance in flip-flops that were once pink.

Meg obeys immediately.

We could just walk on up, I say. *We made it this far, after all.*

Meg shakes her head. *Can't budge.* She starts rooting about in the bags. *Where's the Cadbury?*

I offer her one of the bags in my left hand.

She pulls out a few bars of milk chocolate. *Now, in your lifetime, have you encountered a woman more in need of chocolate than Mrs. 'Abd al-Latif?*

Admitting that I have not, I sink down next to Meg on the *bowwab*'s bench to await his wife's return.

يسرية

Yusriyya

Whenever I touch her, it is as if dew settles upon my hand,
and from my fingertips sprout green leaves.

—MAJNUN LAYLA
c. eighth century C.E.
(from *The Book of Songs*, volume II,
Abu al-Faraj al-Isfahani, d. 967 C.E.)

تكادُ يدي تَنْدى إذا ما لمسثُها   ويَنْبُتُ في أطرافها الورَقُ الخُضرُ

Sunlight poured over the ripening corn, threatening to boil it on the stalk.

Yusriyya squatted in the shade of the *sifsah* tree, wiping her neck with the hem of her gelabiyya. She breathed deeply, aware of the hot sweat marking trails along her backbone, inching along her scalp, pooling at the backs of her knees. In the distance she could hear women's laughter frothing above the thudding of men's iron tools slicing through the tender green stalks.

She had slipped off to draw the bucket up out of the well, and now she rested for a moment in the gauzy shade. She would return to the group to help gather and separate the ears of corn from their stalks, then load the harvest onto carts drawn by patient donkeys. For now, though, the earth beneath her bare feet was cool and pliant, while a breath of wind seemed to have sought her out at last.

She stared out at the green fields and the line where the date palms brushed the blue sky. It was not green in the city, they told her. There were only buildings in every possible direction. No wells that surrendered up cool, sweet water, and no velvety brown earth in which to burrow hot feet on a hotter day.

Yusriyya sucked the moist air into her lungs and stood up. There was no point dwelling on it. What was done was done. She could have refused him. But she had agreed.

The village was unanimous: 'Abd al-Latif was a fine catch. He had gone penniless to the city and returned laden with gifts and conveniences for the family dwelling.

Yusriyya had noticed something more, though. There was an element in his eyes that had not been there before. She would watch him pass, always amid a tight knot of men. His gaze was deeper, cooler. It seemed now to possess a metallic aloofness that observed the village without settling back into it.

Yusriyya weighed that gaze as she leaned into the *sifsah*'s lower boughs. She rested one cheek against the smooth bark. *I won't be that way*, she thought, curling her toes into the earth. *I will come back as I left, and race my sisters through the fields, and weave myself into the tall grass, and lay as I have always lain on moonlit nights—with my head in a cradle of moss and my whole self flung starward.*

She reknotted the scarf at the back of her neck and replaced the clay vase at the edge of the well. *He's a good match*, she told herself again. Her father was so proud that of all the village girls, 'Abd al-Latif had come to ask for Yusriyya's hand.

After all, Yusriyya's were good, strong hands. She began to

walk toward the group of women, a smile curling across her face. There was money to be made in the city. She had seen it with others who had gone and come back, but most of all with 'Abd al-Latif. She worked side by side with the men in the fields, matching them hour for hour in the sun. She, too, could work for money in the city, money that would help her father raise his nine remaining children, that would let him catch his breath for a moment, and sit still long enough to savor a night sky . . . the way he had when Yusriyya was still little and his lap was her throne.

Ah, and perhaps someday, when she had seen her brothers and sisters wedded and content, she would buy for her father an Arabian horse, black like the moonless sky, and she would watch as he rode it through the village, his head thrown back, not bowed.

He was a horseman, her father. He could break the fiercest mount, and the wealthy in their mighty winter mansions would send for him to teach their children to ride. He went, gentle and spare of word, and returned home late at night to extract the splinters from his pride in stiff silence.

They called Cairo the Mother of the World.

My own mother is long dead, she said to herself as she walked, the flat of her palm grazing the silken crowns of the cornstalks. *I will seek out this mother and nestle deep, deep into her embrace.*

Her father walked into the room as she tucked the last of her things into the vinyl suitcase. He shooed out three of his youngest daughters, who had been trying on Yusriyya's delicate white veil each in turn. She stood, and the two exchanged a long gaze.

His face, the skin as sun-browned as a ripe date, creased

into a forlorn smile. "Your brothers and sisters will miss you. I'm not sure how we'll get along without you," he said.

Yusriyya tilted her head. "Ekram can do everything I can. She'll take good care of you all."

"She's never known how to make a cup of tea."

"If you tell her gently how you like it, she'll come around. But don't be so gruff with her; she's sensitive."

"You're the smartest of the lot," he said, lowering his voice conspiratorially.

"Just the oldest," she answered. "Give them time."

He fell silent a moment, surveying the open suitcase and the bridal gown hanging in the armoire. "There was no one in the village good enough for you. This life has dragged all the good young men through the mud."

She had no response.

"You'll have a chance for a better life with 'Abd al-Latif. He's done well in the city."

She nodded. "You made a good choice, Baba. I agreed to it. Don't worry."

He stretched out a rough palm and patted her hair, then drew her close. He placed a kiss on her forehead.

"You are as beautiful as your mother was," he said softly. "Go and come back to us safely."

She dozed on and off, her head against the train window. 'Abd al-Latif sat still and alert next to her. He smiled at her, seeing how the previous evening's events had forced her sharp features to succumb to weariness. The celebratory rifle shots still rung in his ears. He himself had only stopped dancing when the guests began to disperse, fading back into the huts and low-slung buildings of the tiny village, and his mother came to place his new bride's hand in his.

Yusriyya had not cried when they departed the next morning. She only kissed each of her sisters and brothers in turn, and kissed her father's hand. A quietness descended on her as she settled into the truck's flatbed for the ride to the train station. As she waved, she filled her stores of memory with emerald green fields and shuddering palms, and the smell of molten sunlight spilling over dark, supple earth.

She followed him onto the train, surrendering to him her suitcase, which was bound tightly to seal the portions where the vinyl gaped. He settled her into her seat, uttering a few gentle words. He could tell that it was a good match, after all. She was as quiet as he, and surely would not demand much of him.

The face of the land contorted as they traveled, and the green began to grow sparse. Long, precise rows of scrawny trees stood linked by endless hoses, dripping precious water onto the sand, coaxing life out of nothingness. Yusriyya stared at these, her stomach twisting. She tried to steel herself as the spattering of trees grew more and more meager, giving way at last to tawny expanses of sand.

'Abd al-Latif leaned in to her to tell her that the city was drawing near. From her window, she could see the fierce blue of the sky dissolving into a murky gray as the buildings began to come into view. A hot pool of apprehension bubbled within her as she watched the window fill up with concrete.

Garbage lined either side of the track as they drew near to the station. As the train jerked to a stop, she peered out at the faces passing on the platform and found them to be set and grim. The train passengers stood as if one and surged out of the doors, elbowing each other and jockeying for position as they toted their assorted boxes, duffel bags and thick wicker baskets stuffed with food and an occasional goose.

She blinked over and over, trying to navigate the crush of people. She clutched 'Abd al-Latif's hand, allowing him to drag her out of the station.

"We'll take a bus from here."

She looked up at him, and let the calmness in his eyes steady her.

He smiled at her. "Get ready," he said.

The bus cannot be said to have come to a stop as people poured off of it and into the street. It continued to roll as 'Abd al-Latif pushed her forward. "Hurry!"

She ran alongside the bus, its massive wheels dizzyingly close to her sandals.

"Grab onto the bar!" her new husband was urging, and she watched as a lean man in front of her did just that. He grasped the bar and swung himself up onto the steps of the bus, just as hands emerged from within to pull him inside.

Yusriyya found her resolve and imitated this action easily. 'Abd al-Latif, laden as he was with her suitcase and the wide basket that he had slung over his shoulder, could not mount without difficulty. He shoved the suitcase up first, and she seized it and drew it inside. But by now the bus had picked up speed, and he had to sprint alongside it as he clasped the bar. With a leap he jumped aboard, and Yusriyya, the alarm evident on her face, sank her fingers into his strong forearm.

It had struck her during the few moments that 'Abd al-Latif was racing alongside the grumbling red bus that if they were to become separated, she would be completely lost. She did not know the address of the building that her husband managed, nor did she even know the section of town where it was located. She could not read, and she had no money.

Fear tugged at her. 'Abd al-Latif stood before her, his chest heaving, and sweat streaming down from under his head wrap.

"Don't lose me," she said, feeling utterly dependent on another person for the first time in her life.

His eyes were kind. "Don't worry. It isn't far now." He did not attempt, however, to pry her fingers from his arm for the rest of the distance.

Whenever the bus paused, which was often in the traffic-choked streets, exhaust billowed into the open windows, and Yusriyya pressed her nose and mouth against the sleeve of her shoulder as she swayed back and forth, one hand on her husband and another clutching one of the small nooses that dangled from the ceiling.

They passed massive mosques and what she could only assume was a vast church, with soaring crosses sprouting from its domes. Tall apartment buildings stood sandwiched together, with row after row of air conditioners jutting out from their dingy walls. Green shutters were sealed tightly against the sunlight. Nylon lines sagged under the weight of drying clothing.

The bus came to a halt in a morass of traffic and she found herself peering between the limbs of fellow passengers at the streets splayed out before her.

Yusriyya had never seen so many automobiles in one place, all panting in the sun, awaiting their opportunity to race off again down an opening in the traffic. There were huge, heavy cars with thick wheels and darkened glass. These dwarfed lame little cars with a freckling of dents across their rusting surfaces. Sleek black or silver cars that even she recognized as the revered Mercedes were driven by men in precision-knotted ties or women with carefully fluffed hair and long, glossy fingernails.

In the midst of all these, Yusriyya's eye settled upon a donkey taking advantage of the traffic jam to rest. The cart he drew behind him stood empty of produce, save for a littering of stems. His skinny driver sat cross-legged, cheek resting on his palm, the reins lying idle in his lap.

A knife sharpener stood with his wheel outside a butcher's corner shop. Yusriyya watched as he pumped the pedal with his foot and laid the wide blade against the swiftly rotating wheel. His once-tan pants were rolled up at the ankles, and the blackened soles of his feet were supported by green plastic flip-flops. His filthy face was haggard. But his hands were steady and deft as they held then flipped the blade.

He was neatly skirted by a slim woman in rhinestone-encrusted heels and skintight blue jeans whose tinted hair caught the fading sunlight as she passed. Yusriyya's eyes alighted on the woman and could not release her. The dark glasses on her face revealed nothing of her eyes, but her lips were plump and deliberately glossed. Her walk was swift and sure. Her slim hips were locked in an abbreviated but still obvious sashay. Yusriyya cast darting glances at the men around her and found three sets of eyes staring at the woman. She found herself glad that 'Abd al-Latif was facing the other way.

Suddenly the bus lurched into motion once again, and a man's body came flush up against hers. She wriggled quickly away, pressing closer to 'Abd al-Latif.

Finally he nodded to her, signaling that their stop was approaching. She tensed, trying not to imagine what would happen if her foot caught in her hem and she were to fall under the great balding tires of the bus. She followed 'Abd al-Latif down the steps. He pushed the suitcase into the street before leaping immediately after it. Yusriyya hesitated at the bottommost step, then sprang into the street even as a small group of men and women was fighting to ascend.

She followed 'Abd al-Latif onto a side street that curved,

disappearing out of sight. She walked slowly along, noting the bread seller with the small round loaves cooling on crate tops and the grocer ensconced in his tiny, overflowing shop. Gratefully, her eyes fell upon a few plots of earth out of which grew plants with drooping, dusty leaves.

'Abd al-Latif halted in front of a great, sturdy building, and Yusriyya allowed herself a moment to tilt her head backward and observe its height and breadth.

"Is all of this building yours?" she asked him.

"I'm in charge of the whole thing," he answered. "Come."

She muttered a *bismillah* as she stepped into the foyer. She cast a curious glance at the massive iron cage in the far corner. With its stark brown compartment and fat, snakelike cords stretching up and out of sight, it seemed to possess a menacing poise.

"Come," she heard 'Abd al-Latif saying again, and she turned to find him beckoning to her from out of a small door. She crossed to him, and he pulled the door all the way open. Within she discovered a pallet pressed against the wall, opposite a small sink and a single-burner gas stove. A cabinet clung uncertainly to the wall, and through the misted glass she could see a few plates and some small cardboard food containers. At the foot of the pallet was a small television propped up by a plastic table. A rickety partition divided this space from the floor toilet that was surrounded by a few ceramic tiles against the far wall. All was illuminated by a single naked bulb dangling from the ceiling.

The entire area was the size of a horse's stall.

She stared wide-eyed at 'Abd al-Latif, but he busied himself with unpacking the basket his mother had sent along. "You won't have to cook for a while, with all this food Mama sent," he was saying.

Yusriyya squatted down next to her suitcase. She laced her fingers into the rope that held the bag together as she tried to regulate her breathing. She said nothing.

He glanced at her. "If you want to rinse off, there is a hose on a hook by the toilet. Just try not to let the water splash beyond the tile."

She remained immobile. He had not even seen her fully naked on their wedding night. How was she to wash herself in this doorless place . . . or, worse, use the toilet?

At last he regarded her fully. "Is something the matter?"

Yusriyya evaluated his tone, questioning the edge she found in it. She weighed her words carefully before speaking. "Is this where we are to live?"

His nostrils flared slightly. "Had you thought it would be in one of the apartments upstairs?"

She looked away. "Did you tell my father that this is the way you live?"

He rose and came to stand before her. His words were slow and direct, void of emotion. "Your father was honored to have me to take you off his hands. You'll get used to this place. Believe me, the bigger the place, the more time you have to spend cleaning it. Now, go on. Rinse off and change your clothes and we'll eat some of these stuffed pigeons. Newlyweds must keep up their strength."

He started to unwind his head wrap when a loud knock came at the door. "'Abd al-Latif—we have a leak up on the fourth floor! The kitchen floor is sopping wet!"

He froze, and his shoulders sagged ever so slightly as he emitted a small sigh. Deliberately, he rewound the soft wool, and then headed for the door. "I shouldn't be too long," he said to her. "If someone else knocks while I'm away, just don't answer."

She watched as he disappeared through the door, and she was surprised to hear his voice take an obsequious tone as he conversed with the man on the outside. She listened for a while, and then heard their footfalls distancing themselves from the little room.

Yusriyya refused to let herself cry. She began unbinding the suitcase, as her eyes raked over the room. She fished out a clean gelabiyya from the bag, and made her way to seek out the hose.

There was not even a sliver of a window to let in the setting sun.

Sleep came in small chunks that night. The street sounds were harsh intruders, bombarding the little room that lay just off the foyer's mouth. The sound of car doors creaking open and slamming shut was a constant din. An engine backfired, and she was sure someone had been shot. She sat up on the pallet murmuring prayers, until 'Abd al-Latif patted her from out of his dreaming, muttering to her the sound's source.

Voices passing on the street were thin and strange. The accents of the city knotted words into new shapes, obscuring meaning for Yusriyya. She felt as though she listened to her native tongue through a thick, damp cloth. Conversations seemed to come in torrents. The summer-rain rhythms of the country were nowhere to be found.

The low pallet was not far enough off the floor to distance their prone forms from the skittering of bugs. Yusriyya was not the sort to fear an insect, but the city's creatures were dark and unknown to her, and she cringed at their shadowy scuttlings.

The bit of light that came from under the metal door was enough to illuminate the whole room. She lay on her side staring at the yellow shard, breaking off tiny pieces and tossing them onto the ceiling. By the time the call to dawn prayer exploded all around her, she had hung the whole night sky.

The steam was just beginning to ebb from the surface of the tea she had made him when 'Abd al-Latif's eyelids fluttered open the next morning. He found her squatting next to the slim cooking gas tank, observing him. Without even saying good morning, she asked, "When can I begin working?"

His eyes narrowed slightly. "What do you mean?"

"I want to work like you do, to send money home to my family. When can I begin?"

"The work of caring for children won't be enough for you?"

She inhaled slowly, then said, "Even if God allows it, that won't be for some time now."

"The cleaning work here is strenuous. You could be pregnant now."

"My mother gave birth while working in the fields. Once she delivered alone and bit through her own umbilical cord."

"A hemorrhage after one such birth is what killed her, if I recall."

All of this was more than they had spoken collectively since they had known each other. Yusriyya stared at her long, sturdy fingers. "I'm strong enough," she insisted.

"So we'll see," replied her husband, as he stretched and walked to the back of the room.

She slipped discreetly out the door and seated herself upon the long bench. The location gave her a generous view of the street outside and she tucked her legs up beneath her and settled in to watch.

Men carrying briefcases walked by, swiveling their wrists to consult their watches. She watched pairs of siblings en route to school in pressed uniforms, the elder clutching the younger's hand, and slowing impatiently to match the shorter gait. All of this was accompanied by a constant flow of cars, their shrill horns petulantly pricking the air as they demanded the right to pass.

Every so often the box in the corner of the foyer would ascend and then descend, ejaculating humans. A few regarded her curiously, but their steps did not falter.

One elderly woman paused to survey her, looking upon her not unkindly. "Could you be 'Abd al-Latif's new bride?" she inquired.

Yusriyya understood this, at least, with clarity. She nodded, just as her husband appeared from within.

The woman addressed her words to him, complimenting him on his choice. Yusriyya took in the careful curls of the woman's hair, and her trim, clean fingernails. She carried a folded newspaper beneath her arm and a large leather purse. The heels of her shoes were high—not as high as the sunglassed sashayer of the day before, but higher than Yusriyya imagined could be comfortable for a woman of such advanced age.

She was complaining of the heat, it would seem, and a leaking pipe in her bathroom. She motioned with irritation at the iron cage in the corner, and Yusriyya heard them both discuss the word *elevator* at length. At last the woman nodded to Yusriyya, and then she stepped out into the sunlight and was gone.

Yusriyya watched her go, then turned to 'Abd al-Latif. "Did you tell her that I could work for her?"

He laughed. "Sitt 'Awatif? She's had the same maid for fifteen years. Do you think she will be willing to train an ignorant girl like you?"

She sat, chided thus into silence for a while, then finally said, "I am a fast learner."

'Abd al-Latif turned to her in exasperation. "What is this chattering that's descended upon you all of a sudden? We were off to a good start!"

It was three days later, when 'Abd al-Latif was standing with the electrician who had come to fix the elevator, that a voice bellowed from the upper reaches of the building.

Her husband turned to her. "Go up to the fourth floor, and see what they want."

A fat, balding man in a sleeveless T-shirt opened the door and pressed a few pounds into her hand. "Get me some L&M's and six eggs."

She clasped the money tightly and hurried down the stairs. 'Abd al-Latif watched her descend. She crossed to him. "What is 'Ellandems'?" she asked.

"Cigarettes," he replied. "He smokes lights. A white box with blue writing. You'll find it at the grocer . . . make sure you tell him white and blue."

She nodded and headed out onto the street. She had been to the grocer's twice in the last few days, buying soap and small items with which to cook. He recognized her when she came in.

"What is it, girl?"

She cast her eyes downward. "White and blue Ellandems and six eggs, please."

The man sniffed. "Here's the cigarettes. The eggs are at the chicken seller's."

She took the box from him, regarding it steadily. It was indeed white, with blue writing. She surrendered to him one of the pounds in her hand, and he demanded two more. Reluctantly, she turned them over, and he returned to her a fifty-piaster note.

Clutching the box, she said, "Where is the chicken seller's, please?"

The grocer looked at her with distaste, snapping, "Do I look like a tour guide to you?"

She withdrew hastily and scurried back to the building, where she found that 'Abd al-Latif had not moved from his position by the elevator. "Where is the chicken seller?" she asked urgently.

He sighed. "Go out, turn left. You'll find him on your left before you reach the busy street, Qasr al-'Ayni."

She repeated these instructions to herself over and over as she darted down the street. The sweat was beading on her forehead, and the box of cigarettes grew slick in her hand. The chicken seller gave her a cursory glance, then asked gruffly, "What do you want?"

"Six eggs, please."

He put them in a small sack and accepted from her the remaining bills. He did not offer her change, so she turned and headed back to the building. She nodded to 'Abd al-Latif as she ascended the stairs. She saw his gaze detach from the electrician to scan her purchases, and he nodded approval.

Slightly out of breath, she pressed the doorbell to the fourth-floor apartment. The man reappeared, frowning.

"Took you long enough," he muttered.

Yusriyya apologized.

"Where's the change?"

"The change, sir?"

"There should be ninety piasters change."

"The vendors did not leave me with change, sir."

"Go to them for your tip then," replied the man, shutting the door in her face.

She stood, her chest still rising and falling rapidly, staring at the closed door. Walking slowly down the stairs, she revisited the grocer and the chicken seller in her mind, wondering which one had taken more than his due. *You have to be sharper than that,* she told herself. *You have to be faster.*

'Abd al-Latif was finishing up with the electrician as she resumed her place on the bench. He joined her. "How much did he give you?"

"How much should he have given me?" she answered quickly.

'Abd al-Latif shrugged. "Twenty-five . . . maybe fifty."

She turned to him intently. "How much do they cost, these Ellandems?"

"Two pounds fifty."

"And six eggs?"

"Ten piasters an egg."

She sighed, imagining the feel of the warm eggs as she slid them from beneath the satiny feathers of her father's hens. If she had had ten piasters for every egg she had cradled in her skirt as she walked from the hen house at dawn, she could have amassed a fortune. She enumerated on her fingers, adding the sums quickly, then said, "He cheated me. He took ninety extra piasters."

'Abd al-Latif nodded approvingly. "Now that you know that, he will not do it again."

She stood up. "Now that I know that, I will go back to him and get my due."

Her husband watched her in curious silence as she walked, straight-backed, out of the building.

The chicken seller surprised her by laughing.

"My husband is the *bowwab* of a huge building," she insisted, her tones low and measured, her eyes flashing. "Deal fairly with me, and I will do the residents' errands here. But if you cheat me, I will walk as far as I have to in the opposite direction."

"From that Delta accent, I'll guess you're 'Abd al-Latif's wife. All right, *ya sitti* . . . how much do you want back?"

She stood, refusing to move from the entryway to his store, watching customers come and go, until she could accurately tell him the varying prices of chickens sold live, butchered, with or without feathers; eggs; turkeys; ducks; and even baby chicks for raising. He returned to her the ninety piasters, and satisfied, she tucked them into her gelabiyya.

She repeated this activity at the grocer and the fruit seller, astonished at the latter's prices. Grapes that she only weeks ago was picking with her own hands were being sold for eighty piasters a kilo.

Day by day her errands increased, but the paltry sums she earned only served to make her restless. Each day she would ask 'Abd al-Latif to find her a maid's job in one of the building's wide apartments. Each day he would brush off her requests. The moon swelled and ebbed and swelled again.

It wasn't until the elderly maid from the third floor was carried away in a hearse that Yusriyya found an opportunity.

The next morning, she studied Samira *Hanim* as she walked a measured pace through the foyer. The woman's eyelids were swollen, and her features were heavy with grief. It struck her that a wealthy woman who would mourn so for a poor woman was a woman for whom she wanted to work.

A fierce determination settled over Yusriyya, causing her to spring up from the bench and approach Samira *Hanim*.

"Begging your pardon, *Sitt-hanim*. God alone endures," she said, by way of condolences.

Samira *Hanim* murmured her thanks, continuing on her way.

Yusriyya followed after her. ". . . But if you need someone to help in the home, please consider me."

Samira *Hanim* stared at her, her wide eyes taking a long moment to focus. "What are you saying, girl?"

'Abd al-Latif emerged to witness the scene, understanding immediately what was transpiring. He called his wife's name sharply.

Yusriyya did not falter. "I'm a fast learner and a hard worker. Please consider me," she repeated breathlessly.

Samira *Hanim* regarded her for a long while, looking between the two faces, Yusriyya's pleading one and 'Abd al-Latif's stern one. Her eyelashes fluttered slightly as she sighed. "What's your name again?"

"Yusriyya, *Sitt-hanim*."

"Yusriyya, come up to my flat this evening and I will show you what needs to be done."

An enormous smile broke over Yusriyya's features. "Bless you, *Sitt-hanim*. I'll be there. Bless you . . ." she repeated over and over, as Samira *Hanim* walked away.

Yusriyya felt the hot wave of anger emanating from 'Abd al-Latif before she even turned around. His face was dark and menacing as he resumed his place on the bench.

"How dare you approach the residents without my permission?" he hissed.

Drawing her legs up beneath her, she sat down next to him. She swallowed, then said as softly and slowly as she could, "I have asked you over and over to approach them for me, but you refuse. The only work you allow me is to run about the city for fifty-piaster tips, no different than the little children

living on the roof. You know my father, and you know his situation as well as I do. You know it's wrong to keep me from
working to help him.'"

She had addressed these words to his profile. His black eyes
still bored into the facing wall, unwavering.

"You and he are sons of the same earth. It is a matter of
honor," she said finally.

'Abd al-Latif did not answer her. But he did not, when evening came, prevent her from ascending to Samira *Hanim's*
already tidy flat.

Six months passed. It was rare that Yusriyya could regard the
moon to gauge the passing of time. But she knew its passing
from her cycle that did not, despite her husband's best efforts,
abate.

"You work too hard upstairs. You might already have mis-
carried," he said testily.

"Blood would come later than its time, if that were the
case," she replied simply. Although she longed for children of
her own, she knew well that such matters could neither be
rushed nor forced. Moreover, she had no desire to add a child
to the cramped room off the foyer that she so hated.

Each month, she would gather what money she had saved
and tuck it carefully into an envelope. Then she would ask
Samira *Hanim* to write her father's name and address in her
graceful, precise letters. On the letter within, she would ask
her employer to write that Yusriyya was well and happy and
that she sent her love and regards to her family.

"Only this?" Samira *Hanim* always asked.

"Only that," Yusriyya would reply firmly.

And although her employer repeatedly offered to unlock

for Yusriyya the secrets of the alphabet, Yusriyya was always so intent on finishing her work without neglecting her husband's needs that she would not allow herself the luxury of study.

It had not taken long for her to become indispensable to Samira *Hanim* and her husband, Ziyad *Bey*. She learned how to clean the spacious apartment quickly. It took a while for her to hone her cooking to their tastes, and to fully absorb the elaborate system of serving, but cooking for two was almost an insignificant task after cooking for ten. The tea that her father loved so much met with such approval that suddenly neither of her employers could tolerate drinking tea except from her hands.

They were very kind to her. Yusriyya knew this to be exceptional. Even as she would scrub the marble-tiled floors on her knees, she could hear the woman across the hall cursing her maid in the foulest terms.

Yusriyya was a gentle presence in the quiet flat. The couple's children were grown and married, and they spent most of their time in silence, reading the newspaper side by side, or watching television before succumbing to sleep. By day, Samira *Hanim* came and went on various errands, more often than not returning with gifts for her grandchildren. Sometimes she spent a day visiting lady friends; now and then she would host them for a morning coffee hour.

It was several months after Yusriyya had begun working on the third floor that she dared to make a suggestion.

"*Sitt-hanim* . . . begging your pardon, but if you were to buy some plants, I could tend to them. I know how to care for things that grow."

Her employer tilted her head, considering. She looked all about the place, before nodding slowly. "I gave up on plants long ago. They always died at my hands." She pulled several bills out of her wallet. "Go pick out what you want and have them sent over."

Yusriyya could barely contain herself as she entered the greenhouse down by the corniche. She sank her fingers into the soft potting soil, and pressed her face into the slick satin leaves of ficus trees and the buttery leaves of the poppy anemone. The plant seller was surprised to find her laughingly shaking the dark soil from her long fingers and handing over the better part of forty pounds. She gave him the address and departed, humming softly to herself.

The bougainvillea she placed on the balcony off the dining room, where it could revel in full sunlight. The black maiden-hair fern occupied the corner of the parlor, where its spidery fronds could whisper in the dimness. On opposite sides of the front door stood the twin pots containing velvet leaf plants, ushering in those who entered with their wide, heart-shaped leaves and delicate yellow flowers.

From the morning glories and anemones she would constantly tease new shoots, then transplant them swiftly into tiny clay pots. Samira *Hanim* would find a tender green sprout next to the kitchen sink or on her bedside table, and she would smile, grateful for the new life and the hands that enticed it into emerging.

It was but a year after she began working that 'Abd al-Latif lost his patience altogether. She returned from Samira *Hanim*'s flat one evening to find him packing his things. For a moment, her heart soared. He would take her home for a visit.

But he swiftly tamed her hopes. He was indeed returning to the village, but she would stay to care for the building in his absence. Moreover, his mother had arranged for him a marriage there—one that would, *in sha allah*, prove more fruitful a union.

Out of respect for her father, he would not divorce Yusriyya. His new wife was to remain in the village, and he would visit her periodically.

Yusriyya lay silently awake throughout the night, not speaking, not eating. She arose the next morning and prepared her husband's tea. She was sitting alone on the bench when he emerged, bid her peace and exited the building's foyer.

He did not look back.

She spent each night of his journey on the roof of the massive building. She lay soundlessly on the pallet, her eyes seeking out star shadows through the film of smog and haze, her whole self holding fast to a swelling and ebbing moon.

❖ ❖ ❖ ❖ ❖

The three of us sit in a row on 'Abd al-Latif's bench, watching as the electrician tinkers with the elevator.

Yusriyya licks the chocolate residue from her long, sturdy fingers.

It's been three years since he began going to the village, she says.

She has not been back to the village since she left it.

Her gaze falls on the chocolate wrapper in her hand. With a chocolate-free finger she traces the curling letters on the Arabic side. *In his absence, my time is more my own.*

She turns to us, a faint smile at last tugging at her lips.

Cad-bury, she says softly.

❖ ❖ ❖ ❖ ❖

Once in a while, we allow ourselves to wallow about on Arab League Street. We drift from Arby's to Baskin-Robbins or Pizza Hut to Cinnabon. We order Happy Meals at McDonald's, and construct long conversations between the Disney toys nestled within. We pause outside a tiny booth, jammed sidewalk to ceiling with CDs, and investigate the new arrivals from groups only vaguely famous before we left the States.

Inevitably, though, such evenings end at Faraghali's.

Located at the end of Arab League Street, it is open nearly twenty-four hours a day. Cairene promenaders predictably cap off their wanderings with the saccharine bliss afforded there. Car-side service brings the tall glasses to rolled-down windows. Groups of teenaged boys loiter about, leaning on vacant cars or the occasional tree, draining their glasses in gulps that strike us as blasphemous as we work to draw out the experience in slow, savoring sips.

The most famous and beloved of Faraghali's juices is the elixir known as Fakhfakhina. Fakhfakhina is a concoction of mango juice, strawberry juice, thin Egyptian bananas and fresh cream.

Nothing born of globalism's loins can compare to the sweetness of the mango juice flowing at Faraghali's. Nothing even comes close.

❋ ❋ ❋ ❋ ❋

And then there comes the day that Huda is possessed by a pregnant craving for kebab. She knocks on our door and insists she is taking us out.

Meg refuses on vegetarian principle.

Huda says, *Come for the atmosphere.* Ehab has gone off to attend to some sort of family obligation, and it will be the three of us. *Besides,* she says, *don't you know what happens to pregnant women whose food cravings go unsatisfied?*

Meg and I look at each other, imagining all manner of catastrophe.

An image of the craved food ends up as a birthmark on the baby.

That clinches it, of course. We can't have Huda's daughter spend her life carrying an image of kebab splashed across her forehead.

Across from the Sayyida Zaynab mosque, and next to the Cairo Institute for Qur'an Recital, there is a Narnian passageway. We notice people vanishing into it, as well as a steady flow coming out. Chevrolet Suburbans and the inevitable Mercedes are wedged between dusty Hyundais and Kias that have seen better days. Hard-eyed men argue noisily over the tips they expect merely for directing drivers into empty spots.

Huda threads her way between stalls piled high with toys and backpacks on one side, and a rainbow of headscarves on the other, until we emerge in front of an elegantly tiled storefront that declares, MUHAMMAD AL-RIFA'I, KEBABGI. Flanked on both sides of this swirling brass declaration are Qur'anic invocations to take the edge off the Evil Eye.

An assembly of men stands before a long grill stretching along the pavement outside the store. One of them coaxes chunks of meat onto long, shiny spears, another kneads ground lamb into *kofta*, another flips the spears left and right on the grill, distributing the effects of the fierce open flame. Others come and go, replenishing the stock with trays piled high with raw meat or carrying away the finished product laid out on thick beds of parsley.

The clamor is intense as orders are shouted to the grill; boys with stained T-shirts are directed to carry stacks of fresh bread and tiny bowls of *baba ghanoug,* hummus and yogurt salad to the waiting tables. Along the alleys that intersect behind the grill are tables with wooden chairs; each table is packed with intent diners.

As we wait for our table, Huda explains that al-Rifaʿi began with only a street cart. Out on the Sayyida Zaynab Square, in the position now occupied by the vendors, he would sell his product. Residents even complained of the smoke and smells emanating from his small pushcart. Little by little, though, he gained a following. The great actors and actresses of the Egyptian theater began making it a habit to patronize his cart after performances. He could not but expand.

Huda's story is verified by the walls of the crowded dining room behind the glass doors. The walls are dense with huge glossy pictures of the owner with ʿAdil Imam and Hasan Husni, Sherihan and Ahmad Zaki.

When we sit at last, we feel as though we occupy the corner of a massive hive. The side of our table is flush against the wall of one of the apartment buildings that lines the alley. Diners call out the names of servers with the familiarity of regulars, lobbing requests into the steamy air. A short, heavyset woman in a haphazardly tied scarf walks among them, flipping lids off of glass bottles of Sport Cola and 7-UP. Cats and kittens dart under the grill and among the tables, nipping at whatever morsels might have fallen.

When the mixed kilo of meat—half kebab, half *kofta*—arrives, Huda sighs happily. *Don't you want to try it?* she asks Meg, who smiles, shaking her head, content with the spicy *baba ghanoug.* As voices pitch and tumble, and plates clatter, Huda keeps placing pieces of meat on my plate, chanting, "*Eat.*"

The after-dinner tea is long in coming. While we wait, Huda suddenly seizes my hand and settles it on her belly. Beneath her thin blouse, I feel the taut skin shift and shudder. I jerk my hand away in surprise, then swiftly replace it. I watch my hand being moved, and I stare at her in wonder.

I've never felt a baby move before, I say.

Meg scoots her chair around to our side of the table and adds her hand to mine. Her eyes widen.

Huda is grinning. *I told you she wanted kebab from al-Rifaʻi's.*

The three of us sit, transfixed, as life squirms and stretches, testing its boundaries, impervious to the rush that resonates off the surrounding walls.

✦ ✦ ✦ ✦ ✦

Certain May days radiate with a heat that makes me grumpier than I have a right to be, and far less focused. Getting out of the elevator one afternoon after school, I drop my key. It slides into the crack between the floor and the elevator door, and I hear a faint tinkling sound as it tumbles downward and strikes the shaft's bottom.

Cursing, I walk down to the foyer, but the iron grating does not open unless the elevator is present, in which case the area behind will be inaccessible. I peer into the debris littering the ground, and it seems to me that the silver key peers back, mocking me, having bounced into the far corner.

In frustration, I rap on the *bowwab*'s door. No answer comes.

I sit on the bench for a while, then remember Yusriyya. I divine in which flat she is employed by the potted plants placed outside the third-floor door.

Shyly, I push the buzzer. Yusriyya herself opens the door, surprised to see me.

I'm sorry to bother you, but I'm having an emergency and 'Abd al-Latif isn't answering his door.

He's gone on an errand. It will be at least an hour, Yusriyya tells me gently.

A beautiful woman of about seventy emerges from an inner room. She is thin and well-tailored; her gray-streaked hair is pulled back into a perfect French twist. I apologize for disturbing her, and she can't help laughing sympathetically when she hears my reason.

She insists that I come in to wait for the *bowwab* or Meg's return from school, whichever comes first.

Her name is Samira, and I see instantly that she is a true . . .

lady. Her every movement is infused with grace. Her gaze is tender and welcoming.

Her flat is bright and unrumpled, each item of decoration solidly, assuredly in place—from the heavy silver boxes that evidence only a delicate wisp of the Kleenex within, to the crystal candlesticks and inlaid mirrors. The crown molding presides like a benevolent father over each orderly room, and the carpets sprawl in expansive pride, their designs worn with age but still able to preen above the marble tile. The chandeliers gleam from the entryway and over the long dining room table, their crystal pining for hot light to cast across the room in lacy showers. I take it all in, as I hear her ask Yusriyya to bring us tea. I sink appreciatively onto a sofa covered in sage green silk, and she seats herself in the armchair next to me.

We chat over mint tea drunk from nearly translucent china. She asks me to describe the events that led to my being her upstairs neighbor. She listens politely, nodding and asking the pertinent questions at all the appropriate points, giving me a few gentle smiles. But it becomes clear after a few minutes that her mind is elsewhere.

Have I intruded on you at a bad time? I ask, watching her closely, noting a slight shaking to her hand that causes the teacup to trill as she places it on its delicate saucer.

No, darling. She pats my hand in a way which suggests that she is really steadying her own. *You are welcome here at any time. I live alone, you see, so I am hungry for company.*

Where is your family?

My son and daughter are both married, with families of their own. They visit once or twice a week.

I remember Yusriyya having mentioned the man of the house. *And your husband?*

She flinches visibly and does not reply, only stares at me unseeingly.

I'm sorry, I say, realizing with a start that her black clothes were not New York chic, but rather mourning dress.

I watch in astonishment as her amber eyes pool with tears that begin snaking down her cheeks.

[Majnun's] father said to him:

"Cling to the curtains of the Ka'ba and ask God to cure you of your love for Layla."

So Majnun clung to the Ka'ba's curtains and cried, "Oh God, increase my love for Layla, and increase my attachment to her; do not ever let me forget the memory of her!"

And then his passion overwhelmed him entirely, and disorder settled in his mind, and he could no longer hold fast.

—from *The Book of Songs*
ABU AL-FARAJ AL-ISFAHANI,
d. 967 C.E.

ثم قال له أبوه: تعلَّقْ بأستار الكعبة واسأل الله أن
يعافيك من حبّ ليلى.
فتعلقَ بأستار الكعبة وقال اللهم زدني لليلى حبًّا وبها
كَلَفًا ولا تُنسيني ذكرَها أبدا!
فهام حينئذ واختلط فلم يَضبط.

They had no pictures together. Oh, there were a few group pictures, laughing, eating, toasting. But they had never posed together before a camera . . . as a pair.

This had struck her with breathless desperation as she withdrew her fingers from his for the last time.

Her mementos were many. The cocktail napkin on which he'd set his glass that first afternoon on the veranda of the Meridien.

The glass from which he'd drunk one night at a dinner party she'd hosted. She'd tucked it away unwashed in the depths of the china closet. When the house was still and vacant, she would pull it out and press her lips to its rim.

The pen she had plucked from his breast pocket, with which she always wrote. Once, when Suhayr was in high school, the girl had taken the pen to school with her. It was the only time Samira had ever slapped her daughter.

And, of course, there was the thin gold band with the two small diamonds that he had given her. He couldn't inscribe in it their names, as on a typical wedding band, so he'd had the jeweler write only *Amal Hayati*, "My life's hope." She'd hidden it until her mother died, then claimed to have found it among her mother's things. She never showed the inscription to anyone. She wore it on a chain around her neck, never once removing it.

But she had no pictures. Nothing to prove they were ever a couple in the way that only the wordless intimacy captured by a picture can.

They had decided never to put anything in writing. Love letters were too damning if discovered. In the beginning, when she could not contain the brimming of her heart, she had poured it out onto paper and sent it to his office. Unsigned. Without return address.

But he had burned it. Rightly. He had realized that a time like this one was possible. When the eyes of those who could never possibly understand would pore over his things, filtering, sifting. Weeding the trifles from the things of importance. Judging, throwing away. Raking through a life.

It should be me, she wanted to scream. *Oh, God. Why couldn't that horrible, heartbreaking task be mine?*

This wasn't the plan.

"You are a moon," Ziyad whispered, kissing the nape of her neck as he fastened the clasp. The necklace was the same one he had presented to her for their engagement, and the gold felt bulky and chill against her flesh. She had not worn it since their wedding. Thoughtfully, she ran her fingertip along the intricate braiding, pausing at the row of sapphires that gleamed coolly, unchanged since that night.

Samira nodded, turning from side to side as she scrutinized her figure. She laid her hand against her stomach; peculiar, still, that there was no swelling ledge for it to rest upon. It had been so long since she had dressed up to go out, the motions themselves felt only vaguely familiar. Here she was, then. Looking not noticeably different, save for the missing bulge. As she gazed upon her features, she acknowledged that she did not *feel* all that different.

He watched her studying herself in the mirror, and assumed her to be criticizing her swollen chest and still slightly inflated belly and hips.

"You're perfect as you are, you know," he said, trying to pull her to him.

She shook her head wryly. "A few more kilos," she said, before allowing herself to be drawn into his embrace. She laughed as she felt his hands float to the gentle curve of her spine. "We're *late. . . .*"

"We wouldn't be recognized if we weren't," he answered.

The baby's cry pierced the stillness, and Samira moved to go to him.

"Amina will take care of him."

She paused. "I know," she said, reaching to straighten his already straight tie. "I'll just kiss him good-bye."

"I'll tell the *bowwab* to get the car ready." He took his cigarette case from the vanity table, and walked slowly from the room, his gray suit clinging to his frame in a way that struck her as particularly fine. She smiled slowly to herself, and went to take Marwan from Amina's spindly arms.

The old woman complimented her on her beauty, and Samira uttered a blessing in return as she laid her cheek against the baby's forehead. She inhaled deeply, savoring his warmth and the smell of his skin. She pressed her lips against his satiny black hair, and then carefully returned him to Amina, her stomach twisting slightly. The appeal of the evening out bolted and swelled within her. The certainty that Marwan would need her, would need to nurse and curl himself against her, and that his needs would go unmet for several hours, burrowed deep into her, threatening her resolve.

She exited the apartment in an aching agitation, and walked the three flights down instead of awaiting the elevator. The slick oak banister slid along beneath her light touch, curving almost unobtrusively to match the spiral descent of the marble stairs. You need this, she whispered to herself. He'll forgive you for a few hours for yourself.

She felt strangely light, too light as she slipped into the front seat next to Ziyad.

"Ready?" he asked.

She nodded, masking her uncertainty by squeezing his hand as it rested on the gearshift.

They had missed the *zeffa*. The bride and groom—both coworkers of Ziyad's—were already installed on the *kusha* by the time Samira and Ziyad arrived. Rima had promised to save them a place at a table far enough from the musicians that they would be able to talk. She had missed Rima's wedding, having gone into labor the very night of the event, a full two weeks before her due date. The newlyweds had only returned from their honeymoon three days before, and Samira had never even seen her best friend's husband. All she had heard were happy tales of the month in Cyprus, sweet stories that poured from Rima like a gushing fountain as she'd kissed and squeezed Marwan the day before.

Now Rima stood glowing by the chairs she had saved, her

hair hanging loose and straightened over thin, bared shoulders. She waved to get their attention, and Samira and Ziyad weaved their way between the tables, nodding and smiling to acquaintances.

Hasan stood when he saw their approach, and extended his hand to greet Ziyad first. Samira watched with curiosity. Hasan was of average height, only slightly taller than her, and several centimeters shorter than Ziyad. She remembered Rima's descriptions of him from their first meeting. He was a distant cousin who came all the way from Alexandria for their introduction. Rima had agreed instantly to the match, and they read the *Fatiha* only one week afterward, designating the wedding date for six months later. Samira had watched Rima rushing like a dervish between dressmakers and furniture craftsmen and real estate brokers, making all the necessary decisions without Hasan's opinion. He was wildly busy at work, she'd said, trying to prove himself worthy of the promotion that would allow him to head up the Cairo branch of the architecture firm. In fact, they only saw each other six times in those six months. Following each meeting, Rima would regale Samira with his anecdotes and tender words and lavish gifts.

Here he was, then, with a wide grin and ready laugh. Samira did not consider him particularly handsome. The beginnings of a belly whispered over his belt, just barely taxing the bottommost visible button. His nose was slightly too large for his face, with overly wide nostrils accentuating the thinness of his lips. His hair, though clean and naturally straight, was curiously shaggy and unkempt. Thick, black eyebrows raged across his brow, nearly linked by the untamable hairs between them. The only remarkable feature was his eyes, and even this Samira did not realize until he turned them directly on her, shaking her hand firmly.

They were clear as fresh honey and infinitely bright.

"Rima has told me a lot about you. I'm honored to meet you," he said. He inclined his head slightly, clasping her hand, and looked into her eyes. A shuddering sense of recognition passed between them, surprising Samira. She withdrew her hand quickly, as though pulling it away from an open flame. Confused, she regarded his warm brown eyes warily, as though piqued by a riddle well-known to be futile.

The four of them talked throughout the evening, and soon Hasan had the rest of the table, all heretofore strangers, clutching their sides and dabbing at tears. Their laughter drew the attention of the other guests, but the group was oblivious. Ziyad and Samira almost forgot to approach the *kusha* to offer their congratulations to the bride and groom.

When the couple stood to dance, Samira felt Hasan's eyes again. Guiltily, she glanced at Ziyad and Rima to be certain they were watching the newlyweds before meeting his gaze.

Recognition. Or, perhaps . . . cognition. She knew this man without having known him. His whole being was mapped with perfect clarity across her soul. Known, as she was certain he knew her.

And with a sudden, violent surety, she knew that she loved him

She forced a coughing fit upon herself in order to tear her eyes away. Ziyad immediately took to patting her back, offering her his own glass of water. She continued coughing until she was hoarse, using this as her excuse that she did not feel well and wanted to go home.

Rima protested vigorously. "You finally get out to a party after staying home with the baby for forty days, and you want to leave early?"

Samira nodded, plastering a smile across her lips. "I get

tired so easily, Rima, you'll have to indulge me for a while. Besides," she added, glancing down at her swollen breasts, "I can feel that he's hungry."

Rima shrugged. "I cannot argue with a man's stomach," she said.

"I'll call you tomorrow," Samira said.

She offered her hand to Hasan without raising her eyes, muttering a clumsily rapid farewell. Politely, she and Ziyad said their good-byes to the three other couples at the table, then both slipped out the side door and into the still summer night.

"Are you all right?" Ziyad asked with a frown, pulling her hand to rest on his bent arm as they walked toward the car.

She nodded. "I'm fine. Just feeling a little guilty." It was not wholly a lie. "I imagined him crying for me and not finding me. . . ."

Ziyad patted her hand. "I understand. He's still a newborn, after all."

They continued on in silence, the ride home only punctuated by Ziyad's contemplative chuckle as he recalled various things that Hasan had said.

Marwan's cries were audible from the elevator before it had even stopped fully. Samira pushed open the iron grillwork, fumbling for the apartment key, and arrived at the door to the flat in a near run. Amina was pacing back and forth with the miniature bundle in the middle of the living room. The cracked soles of her feet slapped softly on the cold tile floor. She was muttering prayers and cajoling the child with whatever phrases struck her, all to no avail. The bottle of buffalo milk lay on its side, spurned, on the sideboard; a tiny puddle dripped onto the dark cherrywood.

Samira gathered Marwan into her arms, asking Amina to

unzip the blue taffeta dress. It fell to the floor in an indecorous heap, and she stepped out of it quickly as she carried the baby into the bedroom, pressing him to her straining breast.

That night, for the first time in a long time, she pulled out the prayer rug that had been her grandmother's. She laid it carefully on the thick carpet of the bedroom floor, then padded out into the hall. Ziyad was snoring in his chair, the *Ahram Daily* draped over him like a tent. The newspaper rustled softly, in time with his rhythmic exhalations.

She continued down the hall, glancing into the kitchen as she passed. Amina was curled up on her pallet, having assured herself that her employers did not wish to have a late dinner.

Samira opened the tap in the bathroom and let it run for a while as she stared into the mirror. The reflection looked altogether unfamiliar to her. There was a brooding fear in her amber eyes that she had never seen before; a galloping panic that seemed barely contained by the dark rims of the irises.

But what disturbed her even more was the terrible hope she saw lurking there. Like a starving man offered human flesh for survival.

She plunged her hands into the cold water, splashing her face repeatedly before beginning her ablutions. "*Aouzu billah min al-shaytan al-rajim* . . ." she repeated over and over, seeking refuge from the whisperings of Satan. But even as she murmured the words, her mind's eye was sculpting Hasan's face. In the bathroom's tiled dimness, she tried to rinse her eyes free of him, but he would not budge. The words slipped emptily from her tongue, hollow, hissing whispers in the dimness.

Later, still on her knees on the frayed silk rug, she fought tears.

Oh, God. I did not realize my loneliness until I recognized myself within this man's skin, and saw that I have been lost from me all my life.

Oh, God.

Anything but this.

The dream she dreamt that night was that he enfolded her in his embrace on a bed of white sheets, and she pressed her lips against the smooth, warm skin of his shoulder. There was no touching beyond this. Only a curious peace.

And so it came about that Samira became a haunted woman. For out of every still corner in her home, Hasan would emerge to murmur discontent.

She had wanted nothing more than to love Ziyad and bear him strong, handsome children. Her life had been neatly tucked and aligned, whispering along at a placid pace. Idyllic. Ziyad himself denied her nothing. He was sensitive and solicitous, rarely going out without her, and never spending long nights with his friends in the casinos and cabarets. Never leaving her, as so many other wives were left, bored and neglected. He'd made her the envy of most of her friends.

She loved him. How could she not?

But his touch was suddenly something to be suffered, rather than the sweet solace she had once sought.

It was hard to stay away from Rima. She was persistent. When she felt she was being rebuffed, she embarked on strident campaigns of guilt and manipulation, badgering and demanding until Samira acquiesced and appeared for the dinner or cocktail party or wedding in question.

Ziyad, too, saw no need to curtail their social schedule, as great portions of his business were done over scotch and soda.

And so, a few times each month, she found herself shaking Hasan's hand, returning his smile and responding to the assault of his gaze with only tremulous, darting glances. As though brushing her toe across the surface of a quicksand mire.

It was four months after their first meeting that they finally spoke privately.

The balcony was still, a warm wind rumpling the trellis's wide *liblab* leaves in lackadaisical gusts. She had only put one foot out of the French doors when she saw him leaning against the rail, swirling a quarter glass of J&B idly over melting chunks of ice.

He looked up suddenly, sensing her presence. He stared at her wide-eyed, as if she were perhaps an apparition.

Samira was forced to ask herself if she had secretly suspected he might be here, sulking uncharacteristically just beyond the pool of light from the open balcony door. She could not rule it out. "I don't want to disturb you," she said. "Just . . . the smoke is too thick in there. . . ."

He exhaled audibly, straightening. "I—I've been waiting for you," he said finally.

She was shaken by his response, and she felt suddenly wary of being alone with him. She paused for an interminable moment, watching him stare at her, then cast a quick look over her shoulder. *Go back inside. Go back.* But the pull of the night air was surely reasonable enough an excuse to be standing out there. She left the balcony door widely ajar as she moved to the railing.

The river ran slow and black beneath them. On this side of Zamalek were only a few anchored houseboats casting ribbons of light across the Nile's surface. She could not deny that she envied Rima this apartment. "You have a beautiful view," she said, breaking the silence.

Hasan looked at her, frowning in thought, clearly searching for words. He parted his lips as if to speak, then sealed them only to part them again. All that emerged was another long exhalation. His gaze barreled through her.

She felt winded, and her knees seemed to have locked. She knew he was begging her to understand an infinite need, a need that words could not hem in. She found herself shaking her head, slowly at first, and then rapidly. "Please," was all she could whisper.

He closed his eyes then, and when he opened them it was to stare into his glass. "I love you," he said. His tone was slightly resigned, as though he had been in the midst of panning for words more precious, and the current had suddenly risen and swept them away. Now, conscious that any party guest might invade the moment, he resorted to these. "I love you," he said again; by repeating them he would make them sufficient.

Her response was rapid. "No," she said firmly.

He looked at her fiercely then, and his face surprised her. He stretched his hand as if to clutch her arm, but planted it firmly on the balcony railing. "Yes," he insisted. "Yes. I do."

"You—I—Rima is my best friend." She cast her eyes into the crowded room, lowering her voice further. "My *best friend*, Hasan."

He did not respond for many moments, his eyes scanning the mute water. At last he spoke, and his voice was heavy with a tiredness that surprised her. "She is dead."

Samira wasn't sure she'd heard him correctly.

"They're all dead," he continued. "Going round in endless circles. The same gossip and sniping and dinners and parties."

Samira listened intently, certain then of what she had only suspected: that Hasan masked his disinterest in his engineered marriage with laughter.

"But she loves you," she found herself saying.

He sighed. "She loves me, and she has no idea who I am, and she doesn't even try to find out. Rima has never been anything but good to me. Do you think I want to hurt Rima? Do you think this has anything to do with her? Samira. Samira, I love you. I know you love me. I know it."

"Please, Hasan. Don't say anything more. We'll both regret it."

"I will never regret that I'm in love with you. From the very first day I saw you I loved you. I know you felt it, too. I saw it in your eyes. I saw in your eyes that you know exactly who I am, without a word being said. We are the same soul, cleft in half. I found you. I can't let you go now. I found you."

"Oh, God. Don't do this."

"I love you."

She looked at him in electric silence. "I have to go," she said hoarsely, pulling herself out of his gaze with effort, rushing through the French doors and into the smoky parlor.

He was right, of course, she thought to herself as she watched Rima, deep in conversation, rest her hand on her newly protruding stomach. Hearing Hasan speak so frankly only added greater depth to a well already impossibly deep.

What kind of woman are you? she chided herself, sipping distractedly at her wine. *What kind of friend? What kind of mother?*

Stretched alongside him in the bed, Samira would run a light hand along the soft contours of her son's sleeping form, begging him to move her with the same intensity as this stranger did. Marwan would reach for her in his sleep, groping about for her breast, and clutch at her with two tiny hands. Tiny nails would dig into her exposed flesh. A tenderness would crest within her as she nursed and cared for her son, but it was like cool water dashed against the desert floor. Walking through the motions of her life without Hasan left her singed and dusty and possessed by a demon thirst.

She surprised herself daily with the depths of her pain. To Samira it was completely inexplicable. To feel such fear and longing, foreboding and desire. Confusion hovered about her like a persistent shadow, clinging even in darkened rooms.

One morning, she left Marwan weeping and protesting at being consigned to Amina's care. Samira rode a slumping taxi deep into the ancient crannies of Old Cairo, to a grubby shop just beyond Abu Serga Church; she sought a well-known herbalist. On a wild hope that all that had happened was the result of the Evil Eye, she requested to be treated with incense. She sat hopefully as the smoke billowed over her, engulfing her, and she insisted to herself that her needs were modest and simple. To love her husband and son and live a simple, uncomplicated life. She did not desire fame or fortune, indeed could do without what comforts she had—if only she could go back to that contented shore she had occupied before looking into those eyes. Those mercilessly beautiful eyes.

Desperate, she tried to pray. But her attempts to concentrate would only end in tears sliding from her eyes as she knelt, palms heavenward, begging for mercy from the contortions of her mind.

No mercy came, and no respite.

Finally, at Camellia's dinner party, he cornered her by the hors d'oeuvres table.

"Meet me," he said, smiling jauntily for whomever might be watching them from across the room. "Just . . . just talk to me. I just want to be near you for a little while. Please. I can't bear this any longer."

Just . . . to talk.

She stared at him, feeling her stomach tremble and writhe at the thought of it. She recognized her pain etched across his face.

She met him at the Meridien on a warm, tranquil day. The terrace jutted out dramatically into the heart of the Nile, offering a sweeping view of both banks and the massive Qasr al-Nil Bridge. The afternoon sun dripped diamonds onto the river's rippling surface. Gulls coasted above the billowing sails of feluccas.

He sat at a table by the rail, the wind skating through his hair, his face toward the great glass doors. Waiting.

She felt her heart swell as she made her way across the marble terrace to the chair he rose to pull out for her. She sank into it, relieved, feeling as though perhaps her legs might not have carried her any farther. She looked at him freely, drinking him in, overjoyed to be able to look without fearing that someone would notice. The Meridien was an oasis of foreigners—tourists and expatriates.

The two could breathe here, unrecognized and unafraid. At last.

"I was scared you wouldn't come."

She shook her head. "There is nowhere else for me to go. I can't escape my head."

"So you think of me, too? Tell me."

She told him in a rush of words that she had not intended but could not suppress. "I am possessed by you. I don't understand it. I don't know why. I just . . . want you near. I want to hear your voice every day, all day. I want to . . . sleep next to you and watch you dream."

"Aaaah." He settled back into his chair with a contented smile across his face. As though he had been longing to hear just those sentences. He was silent a long while, savoring the way her voice had sounded, the way the wind had tossed those strands of hair that escaped her tight chignon. The way her eyes had looked straight into his. How she had let him see her wholly by allowing him to look deeply into those wide eyes of sparkling amber. *Samira.* He said it over and over, staring at her, delighting in the ability to say it aloud. *Samira.*

When he finally reached across to grasp her hand, he did not let it go for even a moment. At times throughout their conversation, his grip would ease. He would lean back in the chair, tracing the lines of her hand with the tip of his thumb as he continued to cup her hand in his. Other times, he would lean forward, clenching her hand tightly as if for emphasis as he spoke.

They spoke distractedly that first day, tongues tripping over words they'd only imagined speaking aloud. They both knew they were trapped. Divorce—if Ziyad would grant it—would be scandal enough; painful for Ziyad, devastation for Rima. Remarriage to each other would be immediate ruin. For Samira, it would mean that Marwan would be taken from her. The law would not allow him to be raised by a man not his father. Even as she stared down at Hasan's hand, exulting in the heat of it, and the way that its warmth emanated along the entire length of her skin, when she closed her eyes she could feel Marwan's small one. The sharp, miniature finger-nails that she could only trim as he slept, that somehow seemed to need trimming all over again the next day . . . She could feel the way the hand clung to her as he struggled to a standing position, and she could see his arms outstretched as he begged to be lifted into her arms.

Marwan needed her.

Neither Hasan nor Samira had the ability to cause grief.

The sheer impossibility of it all weighed so heavily on her that she felt she would never be able to rise from her chair.

And yet.

She was alive. For the first time in her life she felt truly alive. She felt the cool river wind gliding across her body as though her skin were that of a newborn's. His touch had awakened her. His voice. His words. Their chairs that, as the afternoon progressed, had somehow inched closer and closer together until the bamboo arms touched.

"I love you, Samira. From the first moment I laid eyes on you I have been living every day with the hope that I will see you. When I go to bed at night, after having gone an entire day without seeing your face, my only prayer is that God will allow me to dream of you. And He hears me, I know it, for my dreams of you are so sweet that I can barely endure awakening in the morning."

She felt her breath catch. She regretted, then, the day; the sunlight against the softly lapping water was suddenly blasphemous. These words should have been spoken in dimness, as he lay with his head against her chest, her lips pressed to his hair. She had never wanted so desperately to hold him close as in that moment.

She stretched out her hand and placed it against his cheek. "I love you."

He took her hand and brought it to his lips. "I know."

They met thus for a full year. Twelve afternoons, one for each cruelly crawling month.

Her sudden, constant exasperation was noticed only by Amina. The old woman would stare, astonished, at Samira's retreating back, after unaccustomedly curt words were spat at her. The Garden City flat, in those moments, would feel curiously cold and bereft, as though in the grips of a surprise mourning. Amina, abandoned to her tasks with the echoes of reprimands stinging her withered ears, would reflect slowly on the exchange, faulting herself automatically while repressing a seedling rebellion that might have acknowledged that Samira, not she, was in the wrong.

Samira, for her part, moved about the house in a mist of suppressed emotion. The mist would part briefly, belatedly, and Samira could in random moments ruminate on her behavior, then realize with no small regret that she had been cruel. At those times, she would seek out Amina with an affectionate word or a small consideration unbefitting mistress to servant— the offering of a glass of tea, or a sandwich of the imported cheese she had bought for Ziyad. Once after recalling how Amina had shrunk from a hurled insult, Samira stood before the stove and stirred still-warm buffalo's milk and cornstarch, tender boiled rice and sugar into Amina's favorite dessert. When the woman returned from the souq, she found the tiny, delicate crystal bowls swelling with the cooling *ruz bi leban*, and Samira standing like a sheepish child, a nervous smile on her face.

Amina would accept these things without comment. An orphan, Amina had served Samira's grandparents and then been sent to the house of Samira's mother. Amina's reedlike arms had cradled Samira's newborn body and her lean lips had whispered cooing comfort in long hours when a weary household had slept. She had drawn the warm bundle against her thin chest and clutched her close until exhausted sleep overtook her. Later, when the baby had sprouted into a quiet, sensitive little girl, it was Amina to whom she turned for solace—rarely discussing, simply depositing dripping tears on Amina's worn gelabiyya, and when she had cried herself out, going on about the business of a child's existence.

Perhaps because of this, it was possible for her to allow her inner hellfires to singe Amina, while the rest of the household went generally untouched. Or perhaps, Samira thought one day as she watched the bent woman shuffle from room to room, she despised the woman for her virgin transcendence that seemed ever content to keep the tides of marriage and family flowing for others. Amina herself, ever dry and untouched, remained a silent observer on a distant shore.

Samira still clung to the idea that as long as she did not give herself to Hasan physically, she was not breaking the letter of her vows to Ziyad.

But then Rima called early one morning. "Have you seen the papers yet?"

Startled, she said she had not. Rima never paid any attention to the papers. What could it be? She imagined wildly that a photographer's camera had caught them at their table at the Meridien, hand in hand, heads bent closely together. Her heart beat rapidly, her breath shortened as her eyes scanned the apartment, retracing Ziyad's footsteps, seeking out where he might have left the newspaper.

But Rima was saying, "The judges ruled in the Amir al-Far case."

Samira exhaled, collecting herself, even as she spotted the rumpled paper abandoned on the dining-room table. Staring at it from across the room, she recalled that the story had been a sensational one, worthy indeed of Rima's famously short attention span. Amir al-Far, a minor importer, had returned home unexpectedly to discover his wife in bed with another man. As most traveling men of means were wont to do, he carried a small pistol in his briefcase. Before the surprised lovers could collect themselves, or even arise from their bed of sin, al-Far promptly shot and killed them both.

"What sentence did they give him?" she heard herself asking.

"Sentence?" Rima retorted. "He walked away free, of course. The six months he spent in jail awaiting trial was punishment enough, it appears."

It was not unexpected. Drastically reduced sentences were normal in these cases. Squirming within, Samira could only muster a soft *tsk-tsking*.

Rima continued sourly, "Of course if it were the reverse, and his wife had found *him* in the same position, and done the same thing, *she* would have hanged."

Fresh from his breakfast, Marwan tottered across the living-room floor. Amina pursued him, a damp cloth in her hand, attempting to wipe his face.

"Did they have children?" Samira asked.

"It doesn't say. I hope not, for their sake."

"Me, too," she murmured. "Me, too."

She cradled the receiver and walked over to the table, reassembling the paper so she could locate the front page. The picture showed Amir al-Far emerging from the courtroom, an unrepentant smile upon his face. Slowly, she traced the murderer's picture with her fingertip.

Victim of his wife's betrayal, he had been justified in acting as he had. It had been, after all, his home and his marriage bed. The law knelt before his honor.

Honor scourged, washed clean with blood. Benevolent judges. *Also men.*

Samira suppressed a wave of nausea as she stared at the grin on the man's doughy face. Slowly, she replaced the paper, regarding her ink-stained fingers as though they were divorced from her body. Her gaze traveled to Marwan where he sat pulling tissues from the Kleenex box. He smiled up at her, filled with pride. She swept him up and hugged him too hard, until he yelped in protest.

That should have been it, then. Samira said this to herself several hundred times a day. Isn't that warning enough? Warning that everything could be lost in a second, a heartbeat, the time it takes to pull a trigger? Not that she would be foolish enough to meet with Hasan in the home, of course, but still . . . She would find herself observing Ziyad as he chewed and sipped, bent and straightened, coughed and sighed and snored. Always she wondered, *Could he do it? Would he? Would he be justified?* Didn't he, after all, lay sole claim to her body?

But as she drove to the Meridien meeting, she realized at last that she had surrendered her heart and mind and soul to Hasan from the start. And these, for her, were the greater surrender, the greater betrayal.

The one for which they should both be shot.

To take him in her arms, then, and melt against his skin, and drown him in soft kisses . . . would only be an expression of what surged within her. Only a symptom, much as the cough to the consumption.

Samira was consumed.

Her step was rapid as she crossed the veranda to where he awaited her. She did not sit down when she arrived at the table, even though he stood waiting to push in her chair.

He looked at her, his features a question.

She gripped the back of the bamboo chair, steadying herself. "I will not waste any more time," she said simply. "Take me somewhere where we can be together."

They left her car parked at the Meridien. She cast a regretful eye at the hotel's tower, wishing suddenly for European passports that would allow them to check into the hotel without having to prove themselves married. But she smiled at him as he held open the passenger-side door to his dilapidated Citroën. She heard him sigh happily as he shut the door, grinning at the image of her in that seat. He seized her hand immediately, refusing to let it go even as he shifted gears.

She laid her head against the headrest, watching him drive, loving the glances he cast in the rearview mirror, the way he guided the car in and out of the traffic's current.

He felt her eyes, and turned to smile at her. She brought his hand to her lips and kissed his palm, pressing his long fingers to her cheek and holding them there.

Hasan took to shifting gears with his left hand, steering, when necessary, with his knees.

His friend's apartment lay in the Muqattam Hills, a new development then. Bashar spent most of the year working in the Arab Emirates, having bought this second apartment as an investment. She did not ask when Hasan had taken the key from him; she was simply glad that he had.

The streets were nearly deserted. An aged *bowwab* appeared from nowhere as Hasan fumbled with the key to the building's main entrance. Samira faltered, suppressing the desire to bolt, but Hasan greeted him with a confident smile. "We're here to visit Mr. Bashar," he said, pressing a fifty-pound note into the man's hand.

The sinewy old man stared at the bill as though it might devour his hand, then stepped aside. "Welcome . . ." he said with a pronouncedly nonthreatening, three-toothed smile.

The building was still largely uninhabited, and Bashar's fourth-floor apartment, though finished in the sense of tile and fixtures, was almost entirely void of furniture. There was a bed, although its mattress was still encased in plastic. A film of chalky dust coated the flat.

Hasan shut the door slowly, relishing the sound that sealed them in alone together. He inserted the key into the lock from within, then looked about regretfully. "If I had had some warning—" he began, his eyes gleaming in the dimness.

"It's paradise," she whispered.

They stood awhile, close but not touching, watching each other, listening to each other's exhalations.

"I don't know how to start," he confessed. "I feel like the seconds are vanishing, but I don't want to rush."

She felt her chest rising and falling rapidly, could hear her boiling blood pouring through her veins. When he finally came and put his arms around her, she emitted a little cry, as though she had been shocked. He did not misunderstand her; he pulled her closer, outlining his body with hers.

He disentangled the clip from her hair and gathered a handful, pressing his face to it and breathing deeply.

"Hasan," she said, clinging to him. "Take me to the bed."

He pulled back, his eyes blazing, his lips parted as he breathed in and out.

All he could find to lay across the mattress was a dusty cloth the painters had left. She watched as he shook it out, then spread it across the plastic. He looked at her, chagrined, then unbuttoned his shirt rapidly and fanned it out on top of the cloth.

She was laughing by then, and she crossed to him, running her hand along the smooth skin of his shoulder and down to the long, curling hair of his forearm.

"Paradise," she repeated, her eyes filled with him.

From that day on, the sound of rustling plastic would re-create for her the feel of flesh against flesh, slick sweat slinking along her arched spine and the exquisite echo of Hasan's voice: *Samira, Samira, Samira . . .*

She stood naked that day in the tiny bathroom, having left footprints in the gray film on the floor. The small, bare bulb fluttered to life, and Samira stared at her reflection, surprised by the woman looking back at her.

Her hair was disheveled and slightly matted, a few long strands clinging to her cheeks.

Her face possessed a lush glow, her features flushed and sated. Her gaze had deepened; her eyes were illuminated by a banked fire whispering within her.

Is this it, then; is this what it looks like? she wondered, dampening her slip under the faucet, and wiping the wet cloth across her thighs.

A tiny corner of the mirror displayed his place on the bed. His eyes did not waver as he watched her watch herself.

Her skin, parted from his, simmered in protest.

The telephone became her greatest enemy, mocking her cruelly when the voice on the other end was not his. Every ring had her racing to answer, whispering entreaties as she slid across the heavy marble tiles in her stocking feet. The first few times, Amina stared at her as though she'd gone quite mad. It was not long before the old woman became used to this new system, not daring to approach the telephone when her mistress was at home.

Sometimes, feeling certain he would call, Samira would not leave the flat for the entire day. She would drift about, trying to busy herself with any small task, tending distractedly to Marwan, her nerves constricting and twisting themselves into fraying bundles.

Not that their conversations could be anything but brief and benign, allowing for whoever might be listening from his company switchboard, or for Amina herself. They learned quickly to speak in a complex code of tones and banalities, such that a simple good morning meant, *I miss you. I missed you the whole night long. My pillow missed the warmth of your exhalations. My sheets missed the rumpling that your body would have made as you shifted and turned in your sleep.*

Still Samira prayed. Only now she did not cry. She begged for forgiveness, not for her love, but because her love was, by cruel coincidence, a transgression.

She tried so hard to be perfect in every other way. She denied her small family nothing, nor did she deny Ziyad's needs. When he suggested it was time for another baby, she clung to Hasan in tears.

What excuse could she offer, what justification for having only one child, when Ziyad was so eager for another? Even new acquaintances seemed keen to insist that two-year-old Marwan needed a sibling. Samira felt as though she were pacing in an iron-barred cage. No woman could get away with having just one child. But how could she give another child to anyone but Hasan?

Hasan, knowing as she did that they were trapped, only stroked her stomach lovingly.

"Anything which is from your body I will love as my own. Are we not one? Woman, I do not even know where you end and I begin."

But as her stomach swelled with life, she became more and more depressed. Her only moments of joy were when she lay in Hasan's arms.

Sometimes, after they had been together, she would not shower for days.

She could not bear to wash the traces of his touch from her skin.

Never once in their lifetime together did she spend a night in his arms. All they could ever do was steal a few hours.

Hasan rented the apartment from Bashar. Samira's decorations were sparse. She never left anything in it that could be attributed definitively to her, but at least it was a space they could call their own. Only once did she encounter a neighbor as she ascended the narrow staircase, and the greeting was formal and free of judging glances. They paid the *bowwab* well, but Samira never once looked upon him without wondering: If Ziyad came looking, would this man give us away?

They were always alert to the possibility that Ziyad had followed them or had them followed, or some acquaintance had spotted them entering or exiting the flat. Even in their moments of greatest intensity, each one was always listening for the slamming of a car door and hasty footsteps. The element of risk inhabited each moment they spent together, such that Samira began to ask herself, after many years had passed, if they would even recognize each other were they to be together in absolute safety.

Ah, but there was no safety except in his embrace.

Samira had changed, had become unknown to everyone, and therefore startlingly alone in the company of anyone but him. Because she could tell no one of the affair, lest the secret somehow emerge, she could speak honestly to no one. Whereas once she had divulged herself airily and easily to anyone, she waded into a silent pool where no one but Hasan could follow.

And so she would gather up her life into little pouches, opening them only for him when they met. Every whimsy, every bizarre dream or nightmare, each random anecdote about the children—small achievements, mistakes she'd made, scenes of anger and laughter and frustration. All of this she delivered to him in lazy whispers as they lay together, skin against skin.

She had never known that listening alone could be love. The simple fact that he was hungry to hear her voice, to know all that passed through her mind and washed over her senses, every tiresome detail of her life and every color-rich reverie, was at times more exciting to her than his touch.

How desperately she wanted to speak to him whenever a thought struck her. How painful to recall something she had meant to tell him, when it was too late and they had already parted.

There were times when her guilt overwhelmed her.

She would linger in front of the bathroom mirror, studying herself, appalled and amazed and weary. She would speak to herself in thin rationalizations. Her love for Hasan was not, after all, motivated by some crude ulterior motive. She had not been looking for love, had not been discontent in her marriage. He was not a wealthy man who showered her with gifts. He gave her only himself. He was not a poet or a revolutionary or a hero. He was just a man, more human a man than any she had known. A man whose heart beat within her chest, as hers beat within his. Who needed her more desperately than the children she had nursed.

She loved him. And she would lean her forehead against the mirror in defeat.

Once, she called him at the office, and they arranged to meet at the end of Pyramids Road. She parked her car on a side street and waited for him to appear. He opened the door for her, and she sank into the passenger seat.

"There are certain issues I can no longer hold at bay," she said. She spoke to him of actions, consequences, salvation, damnation . . .

Hasan had remained totally silent as she randomly strung together the rush of thoughts that tumbled from her head. His grip tightened on the steering wheel, his lips pursed, his jaw shifted from one side to the other. He listened as she wavered and retreated, doubted and writhed. They came to rest at a stoplight and he turned to look at her. Her eyes were swimming with tears that couldn't fall.

Only the penitent can really cry. The rest of us can well up. Release teases the eyes, mists the lashes, but scurries away at the last moment.

—Oh, God, teach me the desire for repentance . . .

He was unmoved by her guilty fears. His voice was tired: "Listen to me. I don't understand what you're trying to tell me. You give me facts and details; you tell me things I already know. If you think I take any of this lightly, you are wrong— so wrong. Do you? Do you think the reality doesn't claw at me every single day, every hour?"

He wasn't really asking. He continued:

"I have no choice. If you want to end it, if you can, if you can walk away knowing what you know of this, of us—then do it. I cannot. You are my whole life. Do you understand what that means? The only force that wakes me up and pulls me along. If I think that I can see you, even if in a room full of people, and never touch you, never pull you close, no: just see your face . . . that's enough. That's all I need. But take that away, and I am finished."

Too much, she thought. But as she studied his profile, she realized those were her words he was speaking. *We were one in need, one in pain.*

And yet . . . how could he be so fearless, God, how could he not fear the consequences? Isn't there always a choice?

Where had hers been—at what point could she have stopped and said, *no more?* Was it the night he turned that penetrating gaze on her, shaking her so deeply she couldn't breathe? Or when he began inhabiting her dreams? At exactly which point could she have banished the ache that had suffused her since that night, the longing that, even when he was near, wouldn't settle into peace? Because each moment together had been snatched from jealous Time and spiteful Reality. The *us* of which he spoke was a being that existed in a private world that was ephemeral at best, delusional at worst.

He felt her eyes and turned. He took her hand and pressed it to his lips. "You torture yourself with your thinking. As for me, it is all very clear. I will do whatever I have to in order to be near you."

She pressed her palm against his cheek, surrendering to that simplest of logic. And when she prayed, she begged forgiveness for loving him more than her fear of consequences. More, even, than God.

Their hours together would evaporate, dazing them and leaving them starved for each other. Every time, every single time, it was harder to release him upon parting.

The acting was difficult for her. To sit across from him at a dinner table, and have him look on her casually, was sometimes beyond her bearing. After seeing him look up at her, his body stretched out beneath her, submitting to her touch, seeing the emotion in his eyes as she moved over him, whispering her worship to his gentle replies . . .

After tasting his salt tears on her lips as he confessed the fears that haunted him . . .

After peering into his soul, as one might peer through the backlit shell of a bird's egg, to see the brittle fragility within . . .

It seemed to her that such things would diffuse into every gaze they shared.

Forever.

And so it went. She indulged her lawful husband, standing at his side through endless parties, laughing at his jokes, accommodating his routines, submitting to his desires soundlessly, coolly, grateful for the darkness of the room. During their rare arguments, she would struggle to be angry over the issue at hand, rather than lashing out at him for being the wrong man.

And she raised her children, loving them and listening to them, disciplining and entertaining them. It was not often that she fell into inexplicable furies, or broke into unwarranted tears—like the day when Marwan raised his voice to her, demanding to go out with his friends instead of focusing on his sliding grades, chilling her with his glare. Samira locked herself in her room, sobbing, clutching her knees to her chest and murmuring over and over, *I have suffered all of this for you. . . . For you . . .*

Ungrateful . . .

Ungrateful . . .

But she did not, could not linger in this state. She had recognized early on that giving in to it would bring a quick and not unsatisying insanity. Better to be lucid enough to carry on, lucid enough to drive herself along the winding path to the Muqattam Hills.

For thirty-three years she made a conscious choice every single day. Every day, she resisted the urge to put her hand in Hasan's and run.

They had talked about it. Once, when they lay wrapped in stillness, breathing slowly at last, in rhythm, she broke the silence with a soft whisper:

"I can't."

He turned over slowly, stretching his hand to push a lock of hair behind her ear.

"What?" he asked.

"I can't do it today. Today I can't send you back to her."

He looked into her eyes, his gaze wavering between her left and right eye, torn as to which one to dwell in.

"I don't have it in me today," she said. "It was all I could do to live until now, to survive up till this moment. I can't start all over again. I can't wait again. I can't be alive for one hour and dead for thousands. It's not enough. I need . . . more time."

He nodded. "All right."

She frowned. "What do you mean, all right?"

"Let's go. Let's do it. Let's just get in the car and go. We'll drive to South Africa. Or Morocco. Or China. I'm ready." He sat up and grasped her shoulders, his long fingers pressing deeply into her flesh. "Because I'm tired, too. I'm tired, and I just want to sleep in your arms and not have to keep looking at the clock. And I want to wake up in the middle of the night and find myself pressed against you. And I want to see what you look like when you first wake in the morning. And I don't want to share you with anyone, or hear your name on anyone else's tongue, nonchalantly, as though . . . as though your name were not sacred. . . ."

She was crying then, and he pulled her roughly to him, kissing her hair, clutching her. "I'm so tired," he said again, feeling the wetness of her tears against the flesh of his chest. "Samira. Samira. You are my whole life. Tell me what to do and I'll do it."

And she was his whole life. Except . . . for that whole other life he had. Yes, they could have gotten into his car and driven away forever. Leaving the people who needed them most. The people whose orderly lives depended on them playing their roles forever. Surely their aching need for each other could not be worth the pain they would leave behind them. They were incapable of such selfishness.

Surely . . . the guilt alone would have one day destroyed them.

And thus they grew old. Once in a while permitting themselves lingering looks across rooms full of chattering people. Clasping hands just slightly longer than normal when greeting or parting. No scandals or divorces had ruptured the rhythms of their children's lives; there were no awkward questions that needed answering when the families of potential mates came to tea. Dancing and clapping at the weddings of each other's children, their eyes would meet in gazes of bleak gratitude.

Darkly, Samira would explore his body for new gray hairs each time they met. Just as he would trace her increasing wrinkles with a tender touch.

There were days when she was content. Thankful. When she could curl up in memory, and sigh with a languid satisfaction. For she had already known more love than most women could ever hope for. Knowing that as much as she ached for him, he ached for her. And she would thank God in long, tearful whispers for having let her trail her fingers in Paradise's silken rivers.

But she could not overcome her greed.

Nothing was ever enough for her. If she spoke with him for a moment on the telephone, just to hear his voice, she would need to see him. And the needing would settle over her like a dark cloud that would not dissipate. And if she saw him, she would not want to part from him, sure that when they parted that time, she would crumble.

At last, a month ago, Ziyad died. The cancer had already devoured much of his liver before they discovered it. He suffered for six months and then died in a fog of morphine. She shed the necessary tears, but knew them to be tears of relief.

Soon, she would whisper to herself, an hourly mantra. *Soon*.

And then two nights ago came Rima's call that Hasan had had a stroke.

Samira sank to her knees on the cold marble floor, the heavy receiver pressed to her forehead, gasping for breath that wouldn't come. She knew she must say something, any word of reassurance or comfort, but she was doubled over in a pain she had never imagined. This was it. This was the hell that she had created for herself, punishment for so many years of deception. Punishment for indulging in her desire when she should have cut it out of her heart with a sharp knife. For loving a man who was not hers. For loving a man and making him totally hers.

He was dying. She knew it. He would die and she would be left with nothing.

I'll be right there, she had whispered, replacing the receiver with a shaking hand.

And she went. She held her worried friend in her arms, and stood by Hasan's bedside with his children and grandchildren looking on. All she could do was briefly grasp his hand, the way an old family friend might. A breath of a touch. A good-bye pressed against comatose fingers.

This wasn't the plan.

He died in the night. She felt the moment of his passing as certainly as if an earthquake had shaken the building.

What she couldn't do, after so many years of pretending, was to go and comfort Rima.

He swore he'd die in my arms. He promised me.

Oh, Hasan. You promised.

Having loved and suffered alone for all these years, never confiding in a single soul besides Hasan, she could not face her grief alone.

She had not cried at all until a stranger came to listen.

❖ ❖ ❖ ❖ ❖

She dabs at her cheeks; the Kleenex, overwhelmed, leaves linty remnants on her crushed-velvet skin.

Her amber eyes glisten in afternoon light that inches apologetically from the lonely flat. *And now . . . I have nothing.*

Through the tears she stares at the ring she can finally wear on her left ring finger. *Except . . .*

I lean forward, desperate for any sort of redemption.

Sometimes, I think that despite the pain, God has given me a beautiful gift. Our entire lives, Hasan and I never argued. He never looked on me in anger or disgust. His gaze never held anything but love, his touch never grew careless, his words never surged up from anywhere but his heart.

Perhaps if we were to have been together like we dreamed . . . perhaps we would have tired . . .

She sighs a quivering sigh.

Still . . . I would have liked to know what it was to awaken in his arms. . . .

I stand on my balcony for a long time that night, watching the tide of souls slide like lapping waves over guilty currents.

What a wrenching rivalry: The heart that seeks surfacings. The city that glides along on rivers fed by sweet sweat slinking from arched spines.

✦ ✦ ✦ ✦ ✦

The firm rapping on the front door turns out to belong to Dr. Afkar.

I forgot you're not a morning person. Ma'lesh . . .

I usher her in, insisting that I was up, asking her what she'll drink. She points out the imprint of the sheet running along my cheek, and tells me she hasn't come for a visit.

I've already had my morning coffee, she says.

Indeed, the unmistakable scent of 'Abd al-Ma'bud's Turkish coffee has entered with her like a sultry specter, veiled in cigarette smoke.

I know you're leaving soon, and I wanted to be sure to give you these. She thrusts a shopping bag at me, and I peer into it.

Books . . . I say, starting to pull one out.

Not just any books. She crouches by the bag, pulling the books out one by one. *Poetry. The Arabs have been spilling their souls into poetry for fifteen hundred years.*

I brush my fingers over their bindings. The Diwan of al-Khansaa . . .

The great poetess of the seventh century, she rasps.

The Diwan of Jamil Buthayna . . . The Diwan of Majnun Layla . . .

Men who loved so fiercely that they became named for their women, she says, her eyes dancing.

Ahmad Shawqi, Nazik al-Malaika, Nizar Qabbani, Fadwa Tuqan.

Men and women of more recent generations: Egyptian, Iraqi, Syrian, Palestinian . . . Shaping our poetry anew, breathing into it the same soul.

I don't know what to say.

Her eyes grow serious. *They say the men in Guantánamo wrote poetry with pebbles on Sytrofoam cups until at last they were given pen and paper. The power of their words is so feared that their verses in Arabic are deemed "classified."* Her eyes lock with mine, then she reaches to pat my cheek. *Study. You don't know Arabic until you can read these. Come back soon, and tell me what you think.*

She kisses each of my cheeks briskly, then turns and heads rapidly for the door. *There's something else in there that you'll need to survive getting reacclimated back home.*

And then the door clicks firmly into place, and she is gone.

I stare after her for a while. Then, still clutching my poetry collections, I peer into the bag.

A small brass *kanaka* and a kilo of Turkish coffee return my swimming gaze.

✦ ✦ ✦ ✦ ✦

I accept an invitation to Huda's for a last tea.

She is still wearing black, and it makes her look pale. She had refused to take it off, even for the week-old party for the baby that had taken place the previous evening. Mama Selwa's absence had plaited thick strands of pain in among the ululations and the singing.

We sit on the balcony as the day wanes. The baby lies sleeping, tightly swaddled on her mother's chest. Visible is a shock of dark hair that Huda has smoothed with oil.

I cannot stop looking at them both, trying to adjust my images of Huda to include mother. The adjustment is not long in coming as I watch her hands alternate in stroking the tiny back.

The call to sundown prayer begins. The loudspeaker for the neighborhood storefront mosque is perched on the balcony next to Huda's, so the volume is intense. The baby stirs; her nose wrinkles, and sparse eyebrows undulate. Almost as quickly, a deeper level of sleep pulls her back into its clutches, a hidden hand smoothing her features.

We don't attempt to talk, sitting instead in silence as the *adan* pours out into the dusk. The muezzin's voice is rich and soulful; it rises and falls like waves breaking on smooth white sand, retreating, then welling up again to brush at the shore.

I rub at the hair standing up on my arms, and Huda tells me that the voice belongs to Ahmad from the corner bakery. The imam is an old man with a stutter, and when he discovered Ahmad had such a beautiful voice, he insisted that he do the *adan* from that day on. Ahmad is a sweet-faced boy of about sixteen, who always wears the same green button-down shirt.

I stand and lean against the thick cement railing to watch

as men and a few women from about the neighborhood start walking toward the tiny mosque. Some greet each other with warm handshakes and kisses on both cheeks; others merely nod, murmuring greetings of peace. All pause at the doorway to remove their shoes before entering. I watch as Karim the grocer/cassette tape hawker walks up arm and arm with one of the employees of Za'bullah's Sweets. They are talking animatedly, Karim laughing so hard he starts brushing at tears. Their voices only quiet when they pass beneath the elaborate calligraphy above the mosque door.

Ehab had slipped out of the apartment only moments ago, and he looks up and waves at us before walking in.

Huda waves back, her features peaceful.

I gaze at her. *Are you ever angry? About your life?*

She blinks at me, sipping. *My life?* Her eyes drift to a cluster of teenage boys strolling down the middle of the street, laughing raucously.

I wait in silence.

*My great-grandmother, Nayna, she was married when she was twelve years old, to a man who already had a wife, and who loved to be with other women. You know how he died? His—*she pauses to blush and clear her throat, then nearly whispers the word—*genitals swelled up and finally exploded. But Nayna, she lived on and on. She lived to count forty-six children of grandchildren, and a few grandchildren of grandchildren. . . .*

Despite him.

Ehab is nothing like that, you know. He's a very good man, and very good to me. He wants me to be happy, and he loves me. This is a gift.

She pats her baby tenderly.

Even so, Mama Selwa said to me once that "he" didn't matter. She never explained this to me before she died.

My mother has seen so much pain, finding a safe place for me was all she could think about. Safe meant marriage. It's the only solid ground she knows. Ehab is almost . . . almost beside the point. A device to anchor me in the line of women that stretches back to my grandmother's grandmother and hers and hers . . .

And so . . . my daughter's bones are woven with weft a thousand women strong. And knowing what I know, I can make it easier for her. And perhaps she will be the best of any of us.

When she looks at me, I can almost hear the currents' rush. I watch her face, somewhat assured by her deep-flowing grace.

In the building across the way, lights are being switched on and curtains drawn. We sit in the shelter of the balcony, low voices intersecting, river reeds swept together by a passing wave, released as gently as they are gathered.

Darkness descends on Hasan Murad Street like a soft quilt pulled over a child who shifts, resisting sleep.

* * * * *

As I zip my backpack I become slowly aware of a familiar thwacking that carves out an underlying rhythm for the surge of street sounds outside my balcony door. I turn the knob and peer out across the way to the girl with her rug beater. I watch the dust from the carpet float off the balcony, caught in an updraft, only to melt into the warm morning air.

She takes a backward glance before entering, casting a wave and a lopsided smile in my direction. Both fall upon me like tender benedictions.

The beauty of having rented a furnished flat is that, even though we are all packed, there are no mournful cardboard boxes and gaping, empty rooms. The apartment does not seem any different for our impending absence. Nothing appears out of the ordinary except the pile of luggage in the entryway.

Meg changed her return flight so we can go back together as far as New York. We sit on the balcony off the dining room, drinking a last cup of Nescafé, and watching Qasr al-ʿAyni Street roil along.

The cassette player at Mustafa's juice bar is cranked all the way up; today the Gypsy Kings have been replaced with Warda, whose throaty croonings vie with the yelping of car horns. A young couple, fingers tightly interlaced, pause in their strolling, look the small shop over, then step into the din and out of sight.

The felafel seller steps into view, taking advantage of a lull to lean against his door frame and smoke a contemplative cigarette. He picks at a stain on his apron, gives up and takes to watching the passersby.

Some of the men from the coffee shop across the street have pulled a small television set out onto the sidewalk. They gather around it in a tight knot, yanking at the antennas now and again. From the way they are cheering, it can only be a soccer game. An elderly woman in a long gelabiyya stumbles over the bright orange extension cord that links the TV to the outlet inside the café. She doesn't fall, but she turns on the group of grown men with a hail of invectives.

A little girl with scraggly braids dumps a bucket of soapy water into the street. She pushes a tendril of clinging hair from her eyes, then wipes her slim hands on her dress before disappearing into the photo shop she's mopping. The empty bucket thumps against her thigh.

Meg holds her coffee mug at a distance from her lips, and I watch the steam of it snaking up to brush past her forehead. Her eyes flit left and right, not remaining too long on any one scene. She breathes deeply, then becomes aware of my gaze.

What are you thinking? I ask.

She gazes out again across the terrain of souls. *There aren't enough words to wrap around it all*, she says softly.

The elevator awaits us with an air of contrition, hoping, perhaps, that by functioning on this day, the sweat of the stairwell on so many other days will be expunged from our memories.

As its iron grillwork clangs heavily shut, we huddle within, exchanging uncertain glances over the tumble of baggage, expecting the elevator to groan and shudder.

But it is somehow more stable under the weight we bear.

AUTHOR'S NOTE

The discriminatory plight of women in Islamic states . . . whether in the sphere of civil law or in the realm of social, political and cultural justice, has its roots in the patriarchal and male-dominated culture prevailing in these societies, not in Islam. This culture does not tolerate freedom and democracy, just as it does not believe in the equal rights of men and women, and the liberation of women from male domination (fathers, husbands, brothers . . .), because it would threaten the historical and traditional position of the rulers and guardians of that culture.

SHIRIN EBADI,
2003 Nobel Peace Prize Winner
Nobel Lecture, Oslo, Norway

It is useful—perhaps imperative—to approach the word *Islam* today with an awareness that the concept of Islam spans many different conceptual levels. There is *source* Islam, the contents of the Qur'an and Prophetic sayings. There is *scholarly* Islam, the elaboration of the religion that is found in the written output of a fourteen-hundred-year-old intellectual legacy. There is *political* Islam, wherein the religion is manipulated for the purposes of gaining or railing against political power. And then there is the Islam that one might call *cultural*—that which exists in the cultural practices and habits of persons who are Muslim by birth. Needless to say, the cultural practices of Egyptian Muslims differ radically from those of Russian or Chinese or Nigerian Muslims. Although this book deals with women who are culturally Muslim, at no point does it posit their practices as typical of all Muslims, or even all Egyptians.

Crucially, it is not the intention of this book to posit these practices as sanctioned by or existent in source Islam. This is not my novel about Islam. This is a novel inspired by women functioning within the boundaries of tradition and culture.

Today's Muslims are increasingly taking pains to rail against the abuses that occur in the name of Islam. In particular, Muslim women scholars are working to defend women against oppression that is rooted in patriarchal traditions and not in religion. In Egypt, the Association of Legal Aid for Women (CEWLA) lobbies against female genital mutilation, honor killing, and all violence against women. Organizations such as Karamah, Muslim Women Lawyers for Human Rights, in Washington, D.C., skillfully wield Muslim sources in articulating a defense of women's rights. Their task is huge, their field stretching from the United States to Nigeria to Malaysia and many points in between.

In Egypt, despite *fatwas* (Islamic juridical decisions) declaring it forbidden, female genital cutting is practiced on both Muslim and Christian girls. (Tellingly, it is not practiced in such countries as Iran, Iraq, or Saudi Arabia.) All Egyptian women are subject to the law—of French origin—allowing men to kill their wives for adultery and receive only negligible punishment. Yet Islamic law requires four eyewitnesses *to penetration* in order to convict in an accusation of adultery, and, even then, the husband cannot kill his wife.

The Islamic intellectual tradition has produced constellations of scholars. Mohammad Akram Nadwi's recent work of forty volumes details the lives of over eight thousand women who, as respected teachers of men and women, participated in learning and transmitting knowledge of religious law. The bulk of these flourished from the seventh to the fifteenth century C.E. That Muslim women—in the United States no less than abroad—are generally the last to discover this fact is one of the more astonishing aspects of modern Islam. Inviting Muslim women back to owning their human rights begins with encouraging education. Global women's literacy, and the economic justice that makes it possible, should be worldwide moral imperatives. To paraphrase Ebadi, those who know their rights will be less likely to cede them to forces patriarchal, traditional, or otherwise.

In the meantime, *all* women negotiate a mixture of tradition and patriarchal culture. Some women emerge from their experiences more gracefully than others. This book is my ode to that grace.

GLOSSARY

adan The call to prayer.

al-hamdu lillah "Thank God."

al-salaamu ʿalaykum "Peace be upon you. Greeting."

ʿam "Uncle." Often used in reference to older, lower-class men.

anisa "Miss."

ʿarq al-sus Drink made from licorice.

basboussa Eastern pastry.

bey "Sir, Mr." A term of respect often given to the upper class.

bowwab Doorman.

fatiha Opening chapter of the Qur'an—used in many ceremonies and social situations to demonstrate good intentions or seal contracts. The first phase of a wedding process, similar to a betrothal, is when the two families or fathers read the *fatiha* together.

felucca Wooden sailboat.

foule Bean dish known to be filling and cheap.

gelabiyya Flowing robe.

habibi "My darling, my love."

habibti "My darling," to a female.

hakim Local healer.

hamati "My mother-in-law."

hanim "Madame."

higab Literally, "barrier." The headscarf worn by some Muslim women.

infitah Economic policies of Sadat aimed toward "opening" the country to capitalism and foreign investment.

imam Prayer leader.

in sha allah "God willing."

khimar   Longer, drapier version of the *higab* that provides more coverage.

kufi   Muslim skullcap.

kusha   Large chairs, often decorated with flowers, sat on by a bride and groom during their wedding celebration.

mabrouk   "Congratulations."

mahr   Dowry paid to the wife by the husband upon marriage; the money is hers alone and is by law untouchable by the husband.

ma'lesh   "Never mind. Sorry. Don't worry about it."

millime   Smallest currency denomination.

muakhr   Agreed upon sum that a wife receives at divorce. Should no divorce occur, the money is never collected.

naksa   *Debacle.* A term often used to refer to the loss of the 1967 six-day war.

oud   Lute.

sahleb   Warm, sweet milky drink usually consumed in winter, often topped by raisins and nuts.

shaykh   Term used both for an official Muslim cleric and a neighborhood holy man.

shebka   Engagement gift given to a bride.

shisha   Water pipe.

sitt   Lady.

sitt-hanim   Term of address usually from a lower-class person to an upper-class woman.

sitti   "My lady."

surah   Chapter of the Qur'an.

tahara   Circumcision (literally, purification); also, *khitan.*

um   Mother. Mothers are often referred to as *Um* plus the name of their firstborn son.

wallahi   "By God." A way of swearing for emphasis.

ya rabb   "O Lord."

zeffa   Wedding procession, accompanied by a group of musicians.

DISCUSSION QUESTIONS FOR
The View from Garden City

1. Afkar and Samira live periods of lies. Compare and contrast the lie that Afkar lives for the sake of her family with the lie that Samira lives for hers.

2. Huda and Yusriyya both enter into marriages with certain goals—Huda, because she imagines it will bring peace to her home again, and Yusriyya, because she believes it is a means to an end to help her family. Discuss their sacrifices.

3. Cutting is a major theme of the book, from female genital cutting to abortion, from Karima's pain of losing Wagdy ("a portion of her soul sliced from her") to the metaphorical desire of Samira to cut her love for Hasan out of her heart (pages 194 and 314). Explore the intimate relationship between love and pain that inhabits the characters' experiences.

4. At the novel's beginning, Karima marvels at the narrator's cool ability to leave her mother behind to strike out on her own (page 25). Discuss Karima's relationship with her children. Have certain cultures been socialized to tame a mother's love into more convenient structures, while others allow it free rein? Reflect on your own partings from your mother.

5. Discuss Karima's relationship with her husband. What power does she hold?

6. It is Sulayman who rescues his daughter from clitoridectomy (page 164). Explore what might have propelled him to do so. Is it contradictory that he would also ask his wife to have an abortion (page 189)? Why could he do so little to keep Huda from marrying a man she did not want?

7. Patriarchal culture is defined as culture that perpetuates power

structures and traditions that serve male interests. What are some ways in which women become agents of patriarchal culture? What are some Western examples of this phenomenon?

8. Author Stephen R. Covey advised a man who came to him contemplating divorce because he wasn't in love with his wife anymore: "Love her," he said, explaining to the man that most of love was a conscious decision coupled with effort, not a passive "falling." Huda's father tells her essentially the same thing in their private discussion about marriage (page 65). Discuss your own conceptions of love and marriage, and whether these observations hold any truth for you.

9. The narrator deliberately remains anonymous and attempts to observe without influencing, yet also attempts to absorb Cairo's lessons. At the same time, she presumes to speak in the voice of the women about whom she writes, inhabiting them omnisciently. Explore this dichotomy.

10. Samira teaches Yusriyya to read. How significant is this in constructing notions of women's empowerment in developing nations? What do you think is the role of Western women in empowering women globally? What do you think women from developing nations imagine the role of Western women to be, if any? Is there such a thing as sisterhood—nationally, internationally?

11. Compare and contrast the fathers in the book. Discuss what it means for them to be fathers of daughters.

12. Afkar's father is a gentle, sensitive man, immersed in a centuries-old literary tradition, inclined to music. Discuss his uncharacteristic rage at the story's beginning (page 95). Explore the traditional frameworks in which he is trapped.

13. Much of the so-called "chaste" love poetry of medieval Arabia is said to have emerged out of the marginalization of the desert Arabs. The lack of political voice and submission to an authori-

tarian government found its expression in poetry characterized by doomed, death-craving lovers pining after each other to the point of madness. What elements of powerlessness and disenfranchisement are manifested in the characters of Garden City? How might the stories have differed in a different framework?

14. Words and language are a constant theme—after all, the narrator is there to learn a language not her own. Discuss the relationship between learning the language of another culture and cultural understanding.

15. Afkar accuses the great poets of having lied to her, while at the book's end, she insists that one does not know Arabic until one can read the great poets (pages 121 and 318). Investigate what propels humans to express themselves in verse and meter; in ink; in language.

16. Early in their relationship, Hasan searches in vain for language to encompass his emotions toward Samira (page 293). For her part, Samira little by little falls silent, unable to express herself with anyone but Hasan. Discuss the implications of these silences.

17. "My second son left me to live and work abroad, because he cannot make enough here to live better than a beggar," says Karima (page 191). Does reflecting on America's immigrant population as sons and daughters of pining mothers cause the issue to shift any in your consciousness?

18. "Is this it, then; is this what it looks like?" Samira asks herself in the Muqattam flat (page 305). What do you think she means?

19. Karima gives the narrator a look as if to say, "Do you think, perhaps, that you are more your own than I?" (page 195). What does this mean? What does it take for a woman to have self-possession? Give an example of your own life where you've sacrificed, compromised, given yourself away—what was the cause? Did you emerge strengthened or diminished?